THE DATING PACT

A SINGLE DADS' CLUB NOVEL

SOPHIE ANDREWS

CONTENT NOTE

The Dating Pact is a friends to lovers romance between a widower and his best friend. Don't let these two softies fool you, they're into some *stuff* and do a bit of kink experimenting.

Please note that these BFFs take part in recreational and safe marijuana use on the page and have discussions about grief and endometrial cancer and treatments.

For all the boys who made me into the woman I am, especially Alex, John, Dan, and Greg, the best friends a young girl could ask for. Pretty cool to see idiots with floppy hair transform into really great men and dads.

ONE
JUDE

We were always the first to arrive, so it shouldn't have bothered me. But today, it did.

I needed…

Well, hell, I didn't know what I needed.

A stiff drink and possibly to sleep for five years straight, though I had to settle for talking with my friends. We were all single dads and met once a month at Imagination Station and Play Center, but with school out for summer and everyone's mostly adaptable schedules, I'd called an audible and we'd arranged to meet again today, for the second time this month.

They couldn't deny me on my birthday.

Sebastian tucked himself into the corner, as per usual, with his Switch as Amelia scampered off to the fake grocery store. Imagination was supposed to be "educational," with play centers meant to teach kids about the real world. That was what the website stated, at least. But really, it gave parents time to relax while the kids ran themselves ragged pretending to be a veterinarian or firefighter.

I had started coming here after my wife died because I didn't know what to do with myself or the kids. It had been hard enough to get out of bed most days, and bringing them here had been an easy out for me. Then I'd met Dylan when he brought his kids around. Liam's son Finn literally ran into my legs the first day they'd arrived. And our little ragtag group of single dads was formed.

Although the other two weren't very single anymore.

Not since Dylan went and got engaged to his girlfriend a few weeks ago, and Liam fell ass over kettle for his son's nanny.

I was the odd man out.

"Hey. Where is everybody?"

I whipped my head around to Nate. "What're you doing here?"

"Got the bat signal," he said, studying the place with a furrowed brow as if he didn't know what to think about it. "Are those two kids trying to run each other over?"

I glanced to the far corner with the kid-sized car track and nodded as two boys took another run at each other. "Yep."

He blinked a few times like he didn't get it then helped himself to a seat next to me on the bench in front of the doctor's office.

Nate was one of my oldest friends, buddies since high school. He'd known me when I was still bright-eyed and bushy-tailed. Now I was...not so much.

He snagged one of my homemade peanut butter cookies when I held up the container, and he lifted it to me in salute. "My favorite."

Baking was another habit I'd picked up after Mira's death, and I'd come to excel at it. Not only did it calm me, but I could actually enjoy the fruits of my labor. Plus, the kids loved doing it with me.

"Seriously," I started, between bites of a cookie. "What're you doing here?"

"You texted the whole group. If you only wanted this to be a dad thing, you shoulda paid attention. 'Sides..." He brushed crumbs off his T-shirt and grinned at me. "You think I forgot it's your birthday?"

When he pulled a flask from his pocket, I smacked my hand over his. "What're you doing? You can't bring that in here!"

"Why not?" He swiveled his head, obviously checking for someone to catch him bringing alcohol into a children's play center.

"It's probably against code or something."

"Probably?" he repeated with a laugh and slid the flask back into his pocket. "Fine. But how are we celebrating today?"

I folded my arms over my stomach. "We're not."

He accepted my answer with a quiet nod and snagged another cookie as Dylan appeared to our right, following his two kids before bending to speak to them for a moment. Then Tucker sped off toward the climbing tree in the middle, while Scarlett skipped to the grocery store, waving at Amelia.

Nate raised his fist when Dylan made his way over to us. "What up?"

"What the hell are you doing here?" Dylan gruffed, knocking his knuckles against Nate's.

"Is that any way to talk to your future brother-in-law?"

Dylan rolled his eyes. Genevieve, the lovely lady who'd stolen Dylan's heart, also happened to be Nate's younger sister.

"If we're brothers, do I get to beat the crap outta you?" Dylan asked, pointedly rubbing at the side of his face. Last year, when things had gone a bit sideways between Dylan and Evie, Nate had coldcocked him. But the ship had righted, and now we were one big happy family.

"I'd like to see you try," Nate taunted. He wasn't as tall, but he did have a few pounds on Dylan. I didn't know who'd win in a fight.

Probably neither of them. It would be Liam, who showed

up carrying Finn. "If I have to talk to you about biting again, we're leaving. Do you understand?"

"Okay!" Finn kicked a few times, and Liam set him on the floor. The three-year-old sprinted off, stumbling after a few steps. Liam heaved a sigh and greeted us with a raised hand.

"Cookie?" I asked, and he nabbed three before taking a seat on the bench, all four of us squeezed together.

"Wasn't made for four grown men," Nate noted.

Dylan elbowed him. "So why don't you get up and leave it to the rest of us?"

Nate shouldered him, and Liam shot out his arm. "Don't make me parent you two." Then he lifted his eyes to me. "And, hey, happy birthday."

I nodded my thanks, and we all fell into a comfortable silence for a while.

Nate broke it. "What do you do here? Just, like, watch them play?"

I huffed a laugh. "Yep."

Liam stretched out his arm, dividing the room into thirds. "We play zone defense. We each take a section, make sure there's no bloodshed."

"Like that." Dylan jutted his chin in the direction of a woman kneeling next to a crying girl, patting her knee with a tissue. "Ropes course gets 'em every time."

Nate hummed. "This is terrible, guys."

The rest of us laughed.

"Wait till you have a kid," I said. "You'll change your tune."

He shook his head. "Never happening."

"He couldn't anyway," Dylan said, surveilling his area. "His balls never dropped."

Nate scoffed. "Least my dick is bigger than yours."

Dylan smirked. "Big enough to satisfy your sister."

"Oh, fuck off with that," Nate hissed in a whisper so no children would hear him cursing.

Dylan ignored him and looked at me expectantly. When I didn't say anything, Liam leaned forward, asking, "You needed to get out of the house or what?"

I tugged on my beard. "Or what."

They all waited for me to elaborate. Which, normally, I didn't have a problem with. But this? *This* was difficult.

"I had a long conversation with my mom last night," I started and rubbed the heels of my palms against my eyes. "She said she wanted to set me up with someone." I yanked at my hair. I'd left it down today, the long strands past my shoulders. "I don't... I never told you guys about Lulu's birthday," I said, using my daughter's nickname.

"Her birthday?" Liam asked. "Back in December?"

I nodded. Six months ago, my daughter had turned five, and as usual, I'd invited my parents and sister over to celebrate, along with Mira's family, including her parents, George and Youmna. We were all still close, and I'd never imagine my life without my in-laws. "She wished..." I took a breath. "When she blew out her candles, she wished for a mommy."

Next to me, Nate stretched his arm along the back of the bench, offering me comfort. Dylan curled his hand around the bill of his baseball hat, his elbows on his knees, mumbling, "Sorry, man."

"We were all stunned," I went on, "but then Youmna talked to me later. Brought up the fact that the kids need someone. Apparently, *I* need someone."

"Do you?" Liam asked.

"No." I shrugged. "I don't know."

Mira and I had been together since high school. She'd been mine since she'd smiled at me in that first biology class freshman year, and I'd been hers since that day sophomore year when she'd finally let me kiss her outside of school. Fifteen years. We'd had each other for fifteen years.

I'd expected at least another fifty.

I cleared my throat. "She told me Mira wouldn't want to

see me like this. She made me promise I'd try to find someone." I squeezed my eyes shut when they went unfocused in front of me. "So I did, but…"

I'd been on a handful of dates in the last year or two. Although the word "date" was a stretch. I'd either make the date and bail last minute or go and invent an excuse to leave a few minutes in. It wasn't like I didn't want companionship, because I did, but allowing myself to go out with another woman who wasn't Mira felt wrong. Unfaithful. I couldn't do it.

"So what happened?" Nate asked, bringing me back to the present.

"Last night, my mom reminded me of my promise to Youmna. Said she knows someone she wants to set me up with. I told her I'd think about it. But then this morning, Amelia brought up the mommy thing again, and…" I dropped my hands into my lap. Everything felt heavy today. "A part of me feels like, yeah, that little girl deserves and needs a mommy, and another part of me feels indignant, like, am I not enough?"

"You've been doing it on your own for four years," Nate said, as if I needed a reminder. "You have every right to be indignant, but you also have every right to… Move on isn't the right term, but I'm not sure what is."

"It's okay to admit you want someone in your life," Liam filled in.

"I don't, though." I stumbled only a little over the words.

Dylan eyed me. "What do you want?"

"Mira," I answered immediately, and all three of them turned away from me, giving me a few moments to get myself together. I rubbed my hand over my mouth, forming my thoughts into words. "I miss her. I miss what I had with her." Once my friends focused back on me again, I gestured toward Dylan and Liam. "I guess I'm jealous of what you have. What I *had*."

Nate patted my shoulder. "You could have that again, if you wanted."

"Could I?" Because I seriously doubted it. "Mira was it for me. You only get one love of your life."

"Says who?" Nate removed his arm from behind me to help himself to more cookies.

Liam, ever the academic, offered an introspective nugget. "I think you can love a lot of people in different ways. No one way is better or worse than the other. And I don't think you should feel bad about wanting love in your life again."

Dylan nodded in agreement.

"Setting philosophy aside, I don't know if I'm ready to put myself out there again. Not to mention, what it would do to Amelia and Sebastian." Answering my friends' unasked questions, I said, "Amelia's so desperate for a mom, she would be disappointed if I started dating and it didn't work out. And Seb..." I waved in my son's direction. "You guys know how much he's struggled. He hates whenever Amelia brings up having a mom. He doesn't want to talk about anyone who isn't Mira, and I don't want to hurt him."

Nate held up his hand, half a cookie clutched in his fingers. "I don't know anything about being a parent, but letting your kids drive how you make choices doesn't seem like a great strategy to me."

"Well, you did say you don't know anything about parenting," I snipped.

Dylan slanted his head toward Nate. "He's right, though."

Nate grinned. "I'm right."

Dylan shot him a glare before telling me, "You gotta make yourself happy to make your kids happy."

I hated that advice. Because if my kids weren't happy, *I* wasn't happy. That was what made this all so hard. My kids weren't happy without their mom. I wasn't happy without her either.

But I'd been trying to make the best of it.

Which hadn't been easy.

Nate flicked a careless hand in the air. "I say you should put yourself out there to have some sex, man. You don't need to get married again, but you could, at least…" He craned his neck around then whispered, "Bust a nut."

Liam rolled his eyes while Dylan winced, like he didn't want to admit it. "He does have a point, though."

Nate pumped his fist up and down. "Look at me. Two for two."

Dylan leaned forward, catching my eyes. "It is possible to keep feelings out of it, if that's what you want."

"Oh, is it?" Nate mocked because Dylan and Evie's whole relationship had begun with a supposedly no-strings-attached fling.

He palmed Nate's face. "Before Gen, that's what I did. Not saying you have to do that, but you could. If you wanted to. Lots of people are up for hooking up without commitment."

"That's what you want?" Liam asked, frowning skeptically.

"I couldn't do, like, one-night stands. I think I would need to know a woman for a bit. Or not. I don't know."

Liam tilted his head side to side. "It's not like you have to make a decision one way or the other. The point of dating is to see if you like the other person, right? No one's saying you have to do anything or continue down any road. You could always try it and see what happens."

Nate moved his hands up and down like weight scales. "Get laid or live like a monk. Get laid or live like a monk. Hmm?"

Liam ignored him. "Whatever you decide, we're with you."

Dylan nodded, and Nate smacked my back. "Right. So, you coming to the bar for a drink tonight?"

I shook my head. "Already have plans."

"Hey, Finn," Liam called, "watch what you're doing."

Dylan whistled through his teeth, waving down Amelia and Scarlett. "Girls. Share."

Nate shoved another cookie into his mouth.

I took the time to slide my cell phone from my back pocket and opened my text thread with Brooke. I texted her.

> We're still on for tonight, right?

BROOKE

> Of course!

TWO
BROOKE

Having the guests bring presents unwrapped was really the way to go. Not only did it cut down on the partygoers being bored to tears, but it actually gave everyone a chance to see all the presents. Besides, there were better things to do than watch the bride-to-be unwrap each one. Like playing games and drinking the fancy cocktail I'd put together.

"This is the best shower!" Sabrina threw her arms around me, half drunk. So, okay, *maybe* the punch was a *little* strong. "You're the best sister."

I rubbed her back. "No, you're the best."

Kim butted in, wrapping her arms around both of us. "No, I'm the best."

I laughed, squeezing each of my sisters in turn. I was the oldest at thirty-five and had dutifully and joyfully planned showers for both of them. We had an even four years between each of us, so at thirty-one, Kimmy had already had a bridal and a baby shower. Sabrina was the baby at twenty-seven, engaged to the guy she met on Tinder.

A fairy tale that started with a one-night stand who never left.

My fairy tale had never materialized. And it was fine.

I was fine.

Truly.

And I wasn't jealous at all.

Not really.

Only, like, the tiniest bit.

Barely noticeable.

I swallowed the lump in my throat and plastered a smile on my face as I released my sisters. This was Sabrina's day, and I wanted it to be perfect for her. She and Everett were happy, and she worked so hard. She deserved this.

If sometimes I imagined myself married with a houseful of kids instead of going home to my little condo and Dorothy, well, I kept that to myself. Because I was happy.

I had great friends. I had a great life, and that was all I could ask for. *Life.*

After letting go of my sisters, I snagged a cup of punch then took a seat at an empty table. No matter how much I enjoyed planning these parties, the extroverting was sometimes a bit hard, and I could feel my adrenaline crashing. Sipping my drink, I thought ahead to the bath bomb and new romance book I'd bought. Nothing like some good self-care to settle down.

I'd learned that lesson the hard way through my endometrial cancer treatment. What self-care really meant.

I could only pretend I was fine for so long. Now, I was better at drawing my boundaries and asking for what I needed. But I had to get through the next hour before I could go home and relax.

Slipping off my heels under the table, I settled my feet on another chair and released a sigh that was part foot pain, part memory pain.

By this point, I assumed I'd have all this—marriage and babies—too, but life had thrown me a few curve balls. First with the diagnosis and the grueling treatment that not only stole my fertility but also my fiancé. He couldn't handle it. Couldn't handle the loss of his chance at biological children or the care that I had required. I still hadn't fully recovered from the heartbreak.

Over any of it.

No matter how often my family told me I was better off without him, it was difficult to get it into my head. Because he'd made me feel like I had nothing to offer anyone anymore, and if he didn't want me, who would?

I watched Kim take baby Hayes from our mother and cuddle him to her chest as she bounced him. Hayes was the first grandchild for my parents, a perfect little gift for all of us to spoil rotten. At six months old, he owned more clothes than I think my sisters and I possessed combined. He had more toys than he could play with, let alone even understand. The other day, my dad had bought him a remote-control car, saying he needed to learn how to drive at some point.

Laughing into my drink at the memory, I kept my gaze on Kim as she walked Hayes over to the corner, lowering an inconspicuous flap on her dress to feed him. I absently dragged my hands over my chest and the sides of my breasts. Those, technically, were still functioning, though I'd never have the chance to use them like my sister. I was in menopause induced by my hysterectomy and managed by an inventory of so much medication that I owned one of those plastic S-M-T-W-T-F-S containers like an eighty-year-old grandma.

Sometimes that was what I felt like.

Shifting my attention from Kim to Sabrina, I smiled as she performed a little butt wiggle of excitement. Though she was the youngest and most excitable, she was the smartest out of the three of us. A future doctor—more specifically, an oncologist treating gynecologic cancers—inspired, she said, by me and my journey. So, if there was a bright side to come out of my medical history, it would be that a few years from now, women would have an amazing doctor treating them.

In a few weeks, she'd get married, enjoy a quick honeymoon, and then start her residency in Philadelphia. I was so incredibly proud of her.

"Whatcha staring at?"

Startled, I blinked over to my mom, wiping at where I'd spilled the punch down my chin. She bit back a smile and handed me a napkin. "Sorry, sweetie."

"It's okay." I cleaned myself off and removed my feet from the chair so my mother could sit. She shifted it closer to my own chair and leaned her head on her hand, her elbow on the table, creating a little bubble for only us.

"I wanted to come over and check on you."

"I'm fine."

She smiled tenderly. "I know you are. But how are you really?"

There was no use lying, so I merely lifted a shoulder.

She sat up, taking my hand in hers. "I know I told you before, but you've done a beautiful job with this shower."

"Thank you."

"You're so creative and…" Her trembling lips gave way to a laugh she tried to hide. "Type A."

My mother and Sabrina were a lot alike, easily amused. Kimberly and our father were similar, both of them easygoing. Me? I was the stereotypical first-born daughter, and I *got shit done.* I liked being in control and feeling a sense of accomplishment at the end of the day. Which was why the last few years had been a big learning curve, a retooling of how I wanted to live my life and still be in control without spiraling out about things I had absolutely no control over.

"So, you wanna talk about it?" my mother asked, always so in touch with her feelings.

"There's nothing to talk about." I offered her a close-lipped smile.

My mother sent me a flat look.

My next smile was all teeth, and she laughed. "Try again."

I added jazz hands.

She clapped. "Perfection. Exactly the energy you're giving off right now."

"I don't know, Mom," I said, giving in. "I'm daydreaming, I guess."

She spun in her chair, assessing the party for a few moments before facing me again. "It's been a while... You thinking about dating again?"

"Possibly."

"It's possibly scary," she guessed, and I nodded.

There had been a time in my life when I'd thought I needed to hit every milestone in my career to be happy. If I attained the next raise or promotion or job, I'd be satisfied, but I hadn't been. It took a life-altering diagnosis to finally push me to leave the nine-to-five corporate marketing world and jump into what I'd always been interested in, working for myself as a farm co-op owner. The fear of failing was real, and it had taken a long time for me to believe in myself and know that I could succeed. That was what held me back now.

The fear of putting myself out there again and failing, of having my heart broken. *Again*.

I truly didn't know if my heart or body could withstand it.

"But maybe you could find something even better than what you've imagined," Mom said, drawing my attention back to her. "Maybe there's someone out there who's been waiting for you to finally take the leap past maybe and say yes."

I gave in to a real smile. "You missed your calling as a motivational speaker."

"One of these days, I'll write everything down for my memoir." She slung her arm around me, hugging me to her, and I inhaled her familiar scent, finding comfort and love and strength.

"Thanks, Mom."

She kissed my cheek, leaning away enough to smile at me, her hands on either side of my head. "You've always been my favorite. You know that?"

I rolled my eyes at her common refrain. Each of us girls was her favorite, depending on the day or even the hour. "You're such a liar."

She grinned. "That's gonna be the title of my memoir."

"Do I get a commission?"

"Of course." She pulled me up with her when she stood. "Now, come on. Let's go play a game." I stepped into my heels and slipped my arm around my mother's waist as she whispered, "How much alcohol's in the punch? Because your sister looks like she might pass out in a few minutes."

"Eh?" I waved my hand. "She'll be fine."

My mother laughed and towed me to the wall where I'd set up a few games, including the very popular Pin the Bow Tie on the Groom with Everett's face on a poster of a groom in a tux sans bow tie. I'd included a few actual ties to wrap around players' eyes as they took their turns, but with the side effects of the punch, the guests didn't really even need to be blindfolded.

My mother had the same thought. "We should rework the rules. Take a shot of the punch, spin around ten times, and then try to do it."

My cousin volunteered to be the first to adopt the new rules, and my mother happily offered to help. She handed her a cup with a bit of the punch and then counted as she spun Nina around and around. Snort-laughing, Nina stumbled toward Everett, pinning the bow tie outside of his head.

We all giggled delightedly, and, really, I didn't need anything else in my life.

I was happy.

Sincerely.

So much so that I wasn't even going to answer when my

cell phone buzzed in the pocket of my sundress. But since it wasn't my turn yet, I pulled it out, genuinely smiling at the text message.

JUDE

We're still on for tonight, right?

I texted him back immediately.

Of course!

Meet you at 7 at your place?

JUDE

See you then.

THREE
JUDE

I didn't remember exactly when I'd met Brooke, but it was a few years ago, when she started appearing at the farmers market, selling veggies from her co-op. Mira had actually met her first, striking up a friendship, but it was only after my wife had died that Brooke and I grew close.

She'd found me one day, crying in my car—couldn't recall why or when, though obviously, it was not a good day for me —and without asking, she hopped into my passenger seat and sat with me for a while in silence, handing me tissues, lending me strength simply by being there. Once I'd settled, she'd informed me about how one of her coping strategies during her cancer treatment was marijuana. Then she'd aimed her charmingly crooked Drew Barrymore smile at me and asked, "Wanna get high?"

We'd been meeting regularly since then, talking about everything and nothing. Mira, my kids, Brooke's journey with cancer and her terrible ex, our families, our childhoods, our hopes and dreams—we talked about it all as we shared a joint or two. And then we ate our faces off.

It was a pretty great little friendship we had.

Since it was my birthday, my in-laws insisted they take the

kids so I could enjoy myself, and I easily agreed. It was important that Sebastian and Amelia remained close to Mira's family and they grew up knowing their Syrian side. I wanted to make sure they were fluent in Arabic and could cook all of Mira's favorite foods, because I knew she would want that if she were still here.

So, after Imagination, I dropped the kids off with Youmna and George and returned home to do all kinds of boring stuff like flipping the laundry and emptying the dishwasher. But I did it without the kids arguing and *Fortnight* or *Peppa Pig* blaring.

It was in quiet moments like this I talked out loud to Mira. I would tell her about my day, about how I didn't know what the hell I was doing, but I was doing it, right?

Right, *albi*?

She'd first called me that nickname when we were kids. Junior year, I'd earned my license and promised George I would drive below the speed limit and never dream of touching my cell phone with his daughter in the car. I'd cruised at an even twenty-five miles per hour to a drive-thru, where we'd ordered milkshakes and fries. I'd parked in a random Staples parking lot, and we'd listened to Dave Matthews while we ate. She had a bit of chocolate on her lip, and after I kissed it off, she had called me *albi*.

"What's that mean?" I'd asked.

"My heart," she'd responded with a shy smile, and my own heart had exited my chest cavity, finding a new home in Mira's.

I couldn't help what came out of my idiot sixteen-year-old mouth next. I'd blurted, "I love you."

She had merely laughed and flung her arms around my neck, whispering, "I love you too, *albi*."

Then I'd buried my face in my heart's neck and inhaled her familiar rosewater scent. I'd learned it was a perfume she borrowed from her mother, one Youmna had brought from

Syria. But ever since I'd had my first whiff, I'd been addicted.

Sometimes I still smelled it.

Even four years after my heart had left me, I occasionally caught a bit of rosewater in the air, and my chest cavity ached.

Every single time.

Finished with housework, I stepped outside to the back porch, opening up a new bag of chips and homemade hummus, courtesy of Youmna. The kids and I had gone out to breakfast before Imagination, but my mother-in-law never let me in her house without feeding me. So, I really wasn't hungry after her late lunch, although I didn't know what else to do with myself.

A common conundrum these last few years.

I played on my phone for a while, scrolling social media, counting down the minutes until Brooke showed up.

Which, apparently, was not that long since I accidentally fell asleep on the lounger.

I woke with a start when my chair was jostled. "Huh? What?"

"You know how easily I could've murdered you?" Brooke stared down at me, smiling. "You didn't answer your front door, so I came back around here and your gate was unlocked. If I was a murderer, you'd be a goner right now."

I swiped my palm down my face and blinked the sleep from my eyes, taking in my friend standing over me, wielding...an imaginary weapon aimed at my throat.

"Knife?" I asked.

"Pickax," she said, and I budged, making room for her to sit next to me.

"Seems a bit gory for you."

"You know I don't mind getting my hands dirty."

I checked out her hands. While she had no dirt on them today, it wasn't unusual for Brooke to have soil under her fingernails, smudges of it on her skin or clothes. She had come from a corporate background, but no one would guess from how she dressed now. Usually in boots, worn jeans, and some type of plaid or denim shirt. She never wore nail polish or much makeup, at least that I could tell, and usually had her long milk-chocolate hair tied back away from her face.

"Lucky for me, you don't actually want me dead," I said, crossing my ankles.

She made herself comfy next to me. "That's what you think." When I elbowed her, she laughed. "No. I could never lose you. Who else would smoke with me and watch *Emily in Paris*?"

I hit her with a serious glower. "I watch it for the fashion."

She tossed her head back and laughed up at the sky. I'd never met anyone who laughed more than Brooke. I wasn't even all that funny, but I always made her giggle, and each time she did, it healed my broken heart a little bit more.

"Truly. Was never a more fashion-forward guy than you."

I tugged on my T-shirt that had a stain—what it was, I didn't know—right below the collar. "Takes a lot to look like this."

She nodded, teasing me. "Lots of baking and Wawa."

I shrugged. "Not everyone can pull it off."

"That's for sure." She patted my stomach, which had become rounder with every passing year, and smiled at me. "I bought you something."

"You didn't have to do that," I said, but she shrugged my words away and put her hands in mine as she stood up, hoisting me with her.

"Got it in the car."

"Is it The Gobbler?" I asked, my hope in my favorite seasonal Wawa hoagie strong, even though it was the middle of June.

She huffed in amusement. "I wish."

I pocketed my cell phone, wallet, and keys then locked up

before we sauntered to her beat-up pickup. I hopped into the passenger seat as Brooke twisted around to grab something from the back.

It was a birthday cake.

But not any cake.

It was a cake with David Beckham's face on it, and I lost it. I bent over, heaving with laughter, holding my stomach as my eyes watered. Next to me, Brooke cackled, obviously proud of herself.

"I had to do it."

"Oh my god," I finally got out, "I can't believe it. I can't believe you."

"I know how much you missed it."

For my tenth birthday party, my parents had rented out a park with a soccer field because, at the time, I'd been obsessed with soccer. Posters of David Beckham had covered my walls, and they'd bought me a cake with his face on it, little plastic soccer balls decorating the sides. Unfortunately for me, I'd ended up coming down with some kind of stomach bug and puked in a trash can before I even had one bite of that cake. I'd relayed that core memory to Brooke a few months ago, and having this cake in front of me now was truly one of the best gifts I could've received.

Normally, we made a pit stop for snacks, but today, Brooke drove us right to our spot, her farm.

Pennsylvania had a good amount of farmland, but a lot of it was owned by corporations or non-farmers, who leased out the property. Brooke had been lucky enough to score herself a small plot of land on the outskirts of West Chester, buying it outright. Big enough to support her burgeoning farming endeavor, it boasted a small garage and a tiny old farmhouse she used as an office and distribution center for her co-op. Perfect for her needs. And ours.

I plopped down in one of the blue Adirondack chairs close to the giant oak tree with the tire swing I'd fixed two years ago, as Brooke jogged to the farmhouse, returning with the jeweled container she kept her supplies in. She had received her medical marijuana card long ago and bought everything from the dispensary. She'd tried to explain it all to me at some point, describing how she used a weaker strain with lower THC and higher CBD. Whatever that meant, I didn't know, but she rolled up the weed like the professional she was before handing it to me and holding up her neon-pink lighter.

I stuck the joint between my lips and leaned over, allowing her to light the end. I inhaled, closing my eyes as the burn made its way down my throat and lungs. The first time I'd ever smoked was with Brooke, and I'd hacked up my intestines for approximately an hour. But now, I was used to it.

Used to the way it felt—for a moment like I couldn't breathe, and then how my body became heavy. I helped myself to a second drag, blowing plumes of smoke into the air then passing it back to Brooke. She stuck the joint in the side of her mouth like some cool James Dean character in an old movie as she fiddled with her cell phone for a few moments, cuing up her playlist that was always a strange mix of genres and songs, from the Beatles to Doja Cat with Stevie Wonder and Hozier thrown in too. Because why not?

We were high and making up our own words anyway.

"So, how was today?" she asked after a while, accepting the last of the joint. She stubbed it out and tossed it into the little trash bag next to the cooler of drinks she'd brought with her.

I helped myself to a root beer. She somehow always found A-Treat in the old-school bottles, and I couldn't pass that up. I popped the top, flipping it back into the cooler. "All right."

She raised her brow, clearly wanting an explanation for my vague answer. "Yeah?"

I ignored her, and knowing that she'd been planning her

sister's wedding shower for weeks, I asked, "How was the party?"

"Really good."

"Yeah?"

She nodded, and we both stared at each other for a beat before chirping, "Yeah, yeah, yeah," at each other like a couple of knuckleheads.

Once we calmed down from our laughing fit, we enjoyed the setting sun and the warm breeze that rustled the leaves as Weezer's "My Best Friend" played out of the little speaker on the closed fire pit. It was times like these I wished I could press pause and live in them a little longer. Being here with Brooke, doing nothing, and somehow everything was perfect. Or, at least, as close to perfect as I could get anymore.

A different kind of perfect than what I used to have.

I took a breath and said, "I think I might start dating," at the same time, she said, "I think I'm ready to be in a relationship again."

Both of our eyes widened at our matching ideas, and Brooke stuck her finger in the air. "Let me get some forks. We need cake for this!"

I would've eaten my David Beckham cake with my hands, but I tipped my head. "Yeah, all right. Forks are good."

FOUR
BROOKE

With utensils in hand, I fell back down into my seat, and Jude removed the plastic cover from the cake I'd special-ordered last month. As soon as he told me that birthday story, I'd been waiting for his big day to roll around, and it was totally worth it. Jude's smiles came easy, but he didn't let his hair down very often. Metaphorically, of course, since his lion's mane locks were currently down and waving around his shoulders. He could've passed for a Viking with the beard and barrel chest. Only thing missing was some blue paint.

With the platter between us, resting half on his knees and half on mine, we dug into the marble cake with buttercream frosting. Jude had a major sweet tooth and would settle for nothing less than the sweetest of icings.

"So, you first," I said, pointing at him with my fork.

He shoveled a giant piece of chocolate into his mouth, mumbling around it, and I shook my head with a roll of my eyes. Although, really, I'd seen worse. We both had.

That was what I loved about Jude. I had no reason to impress him. We let it all hang out with each other. I teased him about his "dad bod," while his frequent joke for when something unlucky happened to me was, "What a kick in the ovaries, huh? Oh, wait. You don't have any!" He'd sometimes disappear from my presence for twenty minutes with a short, "Gotta drop the kids off at the pool," and I'd definitely let out a squeaker in front of him on multiple occasions. Nothing would surprise either one of us anymore.

He swallowed his bite of cake and licked a dollop of icing from the corner of his mouth. "You know how my family's been," he started because, yes, I did know. He'd told me about how Amelia had been asking for a mommy more and more lately, and how his mom and mother-in-law occasionally dropped hints about how he needed to get out. And to his credit, he had tried. Like, five times. But still, he *had* tried. He inhaled a breath that made his shoulders rise and fall. "I guess... I don't know. I guess I feel like I owe it to them to start dating."

I squinted at him. "You don't owe it to yourself?"

He scooped up a glob of icing, wagging his head side to side, though he stayed silent for a minute. So, I did too. Jude was a talker, often empathetic and perceptive, but sometimes he needed a few moments to form his thoughts.

"I hung out with the boys today," he said eventually. The boys being his best friends, whom I'd met in passing a few times.

"What'd they have to say about it?"

"They were all for it. Said I had to be happy for the kids to be happy."

I licked the tines of my fork. "Good point."

"But I am happy," he said, and I eyed him. "Mostly."

"What might make you more than mostly happy?"

He didn't answer, and I suspected it was because what would make him more than mostly happy was having Mira back.

"What's making you consider dating again?" I asked, and

he forked another piece of cake into his mouth, his gaze off in the distance somewhere.

"Sex," he finally answered, and I choked on crumbs that went down the wrong pipe, earning a few chuckles as he smacked my back.

"I didn't expect that," I muttered, opening a bottle of water.

"What? You think I'm some kind of asexual worm being?"

"More like Ken." I jutted my chin to his crotch. "Nothing but smooth plastic down there."

"Least I have working parts," he mumbled around another piece of cake.

I punched his arm, laughing. "My vagina still works. Just…not very well."

Sex since my cancer treatment had not been often or very good. It was basically dry as a desert down there, and the few times I'd attempted it, it had not gone well. He shouldered me, letting me know he was kidding, of course, and I playfully knocked my fork against his, batting him away from Beckham's face. I helped myself to his forehead.

"So, what?" I started, speaking with my mouth full. "You want to date to have sex?"

"Essentially." He shrugged. "I don't want to get married. I know I won't be finding my soul mate, but the guys talking about me being happy made me think…"

"Sex will make you happy?"

"Couldn't hurt."

The math made sense. Jude was a tactile guy, always hugging and high-fiving, patting shoulders and rubbing backs. I'd imagine he missed having that physical intimacy with someone.

He waved his fork in my direction. "Your turn."

"Not too complicated. I want to be married. I want kids." Even if those kids didn't come from my belly, I still wanted a family. "I want the white picket fence, but I can't get that if I stay holed up alone with Dorothy."

"Holed up with Dorothy? Why do you say it like that? Dorothy's great."

Dorothy was *not* great. She was moody and violent, especially toward men. Not Jude, though. Because everyone loved Jude. Even my grumpy cat.

I'd adopted her during my cancer treatment, before Tom had left me, and I assumed that was why she distrusted men. She was as scarred from that relationship as I was. Maybe she was onto something with her hatred of people with the XY chromosomes.

"If I don't put myself out there, I'll never find the one," I said.

Jude thought about that for a moment. "And you think you'll find *the one*?"

I settled back against my chair, swinging my feet up onto the stones of the fire pit. "I hope so." Then I brushed loose strands of hair behind my ears. "And you think you'll be happy with sex?"

"I'm not sure." He popped the lid over the cake we didn't finish and sipped on his root beer. "It's scary to think about going out on a date, but I wouldn't be able to pick someone out of a lineup to get naked with, you know?"

"Yeah. I get that."

"But I'm also not interested in a relationship either. I don't want my kids knowing what I'm doing."

I slanted my head back. "Why not?"

He stroked his palm over his beard a few times. "First of all, it feels like I'm cheating on Mira, which—" he held up his hand before I could interrupt "—I know, is not true, but that's how I feel. She's the only woman I've ever been with or loved, and it's impossible to ignore that. I know I'll never find someone like her again, but also… I'm lonely."

He met my eyes, and my heart broke for him. For his family. For everything that they'd all lost.

He went on. "It might be nice to meet someone to…have fun with again. Nothing serious. I wouldn't want to get Amelia's hopes up, and I know Sebastian would lose it if I ever brought anyone home."

I started to speak again, but he stopped me with a shake of his head. "I know. I know. I went over all of this with the guys, and I've been thinking a lot today, and…" He lifted his arms, fisting and unfisting his hands, shoving them in my direction. "You think my right forearm is getting bigger than my left?"

I didn't understand the question at first, but when it clicked, I burst out in laughter. He chuckled quietly next to me, folding his arms over his stomach.

"That your workout anymore? Your dick and your right hand?"

"Pretty much," he said, still smiling.

After seconds of quiet, I mused, "It's been over a decade since I dated."

"Almost twenty years for me," he said with a dramatic and slow blink, as if he couldn't believe it himself. "I don't even know where to start."

"Tell me about it." I squinted at him in thought. "What if we do it together?"

"Do what together?"

"Dating." The idea became clearer, and I gestured between us. "What if we help each other? We don't have to go through it alone."

"What? You want to, like, tag team?"

"Yeah, I guess. Soldiers in arms on the battlefield of dating."

He snorted a laugh.

"We could give each other advice or whatever," I said,

excited now. "I'll help you get laid, and you'll help me find a husband."

He considered me for a long time, eventually giving in with a nod. "Not the worst idea I've ever heard."

I slugged him in the shoulder, and he chuckled before holding out his hand. "A dating guide."

Shaking his hand, I corrected, "A dating pact."

He agreed, repeating, "Dating pact."

We went quiet for a while, the sky a rainbow of color in the setting sun, and I turned to admire Jude's profile. His high cheekbones above his light-brown beard, his straight nose, and golden hair highlighted by the dying light. He looked like a painting, and without thinking, I opened the camera app on my phone to snap a photo.

"What are you doing?"

I flipped my phone screen so he could view the picture. "For your dating profile."

"Dating profile?"

"We're doing the online dating thing, right?"

He jerked his head back. "Why?"

"How else are we going to do this? The old-fashioned way? Meet someone organically at a bar or grocery store?"

He frowned. "You're right. Online dating it is."

"Get your phone out," I told him. "We can set up our profiles, make sure we look good."

He pulled his out, tapping on it a few times. "Which one are we doing?"

I Googled *Best dating apps* and scooted my chair right up against his, so we could discuss our game plan while we finished off the last of the cake. After a few minutes of research, we decided on the first one listed, mostly because I didn't have the patience to read past the second suggestion of the article, and Jude went back to eating the cake.

Priorities.

With the sun sinking below the horizon, I started up the

fire pit, and between bites of David Beckham's face and sips of now-warm soda, Jude and I created our dating profiles.

He ordered me to use one of the photos from the shower as my profile picture, and I instructed him to leave voice notes for his answers because he had the right amount of gravel in his voice, especially when he got all drowsy from smoking.

"Husky in voice and body," he joked, and I cracked up, ordering him to make that his tagline.

"Nobody wants a fat guy," he said, and I rolled my eyes.

"How do you know? I like your dad bod."

He patted his stomach. "There was a time I used to be able to eat an entire pizza and still have a six-pack."

"You had a six-pack?"

"In high school. I wasn't too coordinated for sports, but I joined the track-and-field team."

"Really? I can't imagine it."

"Mira was a runner, and I never wanted to miss her in those tiny shorts." He squeezed his thumb and fingers together, raising his hand in the air, like his once-upon-a-time body was something to celebrate. "I was a specimen."

Pre-cancer, I'd been heavily concerned about my appearance, but now, I knew we were all simply floating through life in meat sacks. The important thing was if our meat sacks could keep us going long enough to get wrinkly and dried out. Like expensive salami.

Leaning my head on Jude's shoulder, I yawned. "You're still a specimen. I don't even mind that you're XY."

I felt his hot breath waft over me, his mouth against the top of my head, his beard tangling with my hair. "Thanks. I guess."

"You know what I could eat?" I asked, and I felt more than heard his curious hum. "Some meats and cheeses. Maybe some jam."

"If I wasn't in the candy business, I'd want to be in the meat and cheese business. Open a store and call it—"

"Oh my gouda!" I guessed.

He laughed and said, "Oh my cheeses!"

I pushed off him breathlessly. "Brie brighter."

"Havarti smarty."

"Speakcheesey." I couldn't stop giggling.

He couldn't either. "Pecker's Romano."

"What?" I couldn't breathe, laughing so hard. "That...that doesn't make sense."

"Pecker like pecorino," he explained while pointing to his junk.

I bent over to gulp in air until Jude patted my back. I eventually sat up and tucked my hair behind my ears, glancing over to him. He had his eyes closed and legs extended, his head resting against the back of the chair, his smile happy and content.

Which made my heart happy and content.

FIVE
JUDE

Another beautiful day, another shouting match between my children.

"Get out of the way!"

"I want to play!"

"Move!"

"Ouch!"

I cupped my hands around my mouth, yelling to them, "Hey, stop pushing! Seb, let her play with you. Lulu, you can't stand in front of your brother while he's swinging. You'll get hit."

They ignored me, going back to arguing, but this time quieter. I probably should have marched over to them and broken it up, but kids were like wolves. Sometimes you had to let them fight it out. Figure it out on their own.

It had been a week since my birthday, summer was in full swing, and I was already counting down the days until the kids were back in school. Amelia was headed to kindergarten in the fall. Crazy to think about how fast it all went. And yet, not at all.

It was true what they said. The days are long, but the years are short. Sometimes it felt like yesterday when we'd brought Amelia home in her soft pink muslin blanket. I could still remember how Mira had sat on the couch with Sebastian at her side, both of them staring at the baby in her arms, both of them so in love with the tiny bundle of joy.

I should've taken a photo, captured Sebastian's grin and Mira's watery eyes. I didn't take enough photos.

I regretted that.

I regretted not having more physical reminders of Mira around the house. It wasn't enough, especially for Amelia, who had barely learned to walk before her mother left us.

There wasn't enough time, not for any of us. But I'd never give up what I'd had, what we'd all had. Because while it wasn't perfect, it was beautiful. Every new day with Mira had been better than the last. She'd made me a better person. A better husband. A better father.

And since she'd died, it'd been a daily struggle. Getting out of bed eventually became easier, but the second-guessing never did. Neither did the pain of the yawning hole in my heart

At a shriek, I glanced up from my phone, finding Sebastian chasing Amelia, though for fun. I grinned when he gently tackled her, and she giggled, kicking her feet. Seb rolled over, allowing her up, only so he could chase her again. See? Sometimes they loved each other.

I filmed a video of them running around the yard and texted it to my family's group thread because *now* I took photos and videos. After responding to my mother's message about making sure they had on sunscreen and Youmna's series of emojis, I opened the dating app to scroll through the profiles of the women I'd matched with.

I had noticed Natalie's message last night. A simple **Hey! How are you?**

It should've been easy. All I had to say was **I'm good. How are you?**

And yet...

I scratched at my beard, feeling not for the first or even fifteenth time since creating a profile for this app that I was betraying Mira. She was more than my first and only love. She was also the first and only woman I'd ever dated. Hell, she was the first and only woman I'd ever had sex with.

I knew nothing except Mira.

I wasn't sure how to do the whole dating thing, but I was tired of keeping warm with only my memories. Even in my loneliest moments, when I fell down the rabbit hole of Mira's shy smile, the dip of her waist, her little outie belly button, the heat and smell of her skin, it was impossible to ignore how my body responded. While my heart wasn't necessarily ready for sex, my dick sure as hell was.

And I couldn't avoid the clawing need building inside me.

My mind drifted back to Brooke's words as we'd helped each other create our profiles. "It doesn't have to be forever, Jude. It can be for right now. And if it's not right, you can always say no. You can always stop." When I'd started to protest, she had held up her hand. "If your goal is to have fun, then that's what it should be."

She was so earnest, as always. Only wanting the best for me.

In the middle of my meditation on my past and what my future might look like, my kids raced up, hungry for lunch. Amelia was currently obsessed with Cinnamon Toast Crunch and ate it for almost every meal, but Sebastian was satisfied with microwavable pizza. As the kids argued over what to watch on the iPad, I helped myself to a premade bagged salad because, apparently, I needed to eat vegetables.

"Hey," I said, tapping my hand on the table. "As soon as you're finished eating, you're plugging that back in and doing something that doesn't melt your brains."

They both nodded and proceeded to eat *very* slowly.

I stuffed my mouth with the flavorless green stuff, letting my gaze wander over the brown cabinets and old wallpaper.

This house was supposed to be a starter home for us. Mira and I had barely begun to look for a bigger place, talking about what our dream house might look like, when she'd passed. She had wanted open cabinetry and a bigger kitchen. I wanted a finished basement with a sectional. We both wanted a bedroom big enough for a king-sized bed. As much as we both loved to cuddle, neither one of us liked to be squeezed together while we slept. And, of course, we wanted room for the kids to grow. We'd even talked about having a third.

On occasion, I'd considered selling this small Cape Cod with gray siding and a kitchen straight out of some '90s family sitcom, but I didn't know what was worse, living with the ghost of my wife in the walls or starting somewhere new with no evidence of her at all.

Neither choice seemed like the right one.

After I cleaned up lunch, Amelia settled with a coloring book, while Sebastian flopped on the couch to play a video game, leaving me some time to work. I passed through the living room and tapped on the corner of the big photo in the hall out of habit. It was the last picture of all four of us. From the day Mira died.

It was four years ago, an early spring day. While I'd played all kinds of sports growing up, I wasn't really good at any one of them and did it more for the social aspect than any real hope of being an all-star. Mira, though, she was an athlete and participated in multiple track events. Secured a full-ride scholarship to college and everything. She was fast, despite being relatively shorter than the women she competed against. She made up for her smaller strides with pure power. Her relay team even won a national title.

We hadn't attended the same university, but I'd gone to as many events as possible. It had been my absolute pleasure to follow her anywhere and everywhere, including through her training for the Olympic trials. Unfortunately, she didn't make the team and was crushed, but I had been so goddamn proud of her. I could never be anything less.

We'd ended up marrying after that, with Nate as my best man and bought this house. Sebastian had arrived after our second anniversary, and Amelia four years after that. We had been happy.

Mira had continued to run for fun, mostly charity 5Ks. *That day*, the kids and I had waited at the finish line with a sign Sebastian had made, and I'd asked someone to take our picture. Mira, grinning and flushed, held fourteen-month-old Amelia in her arms while Sebastian showed off his sign to the camera. I stood in the back, my arms around them all, a cheesy smile on my face.

Later at home, Mira had complained of a headache, but it hadn't been anything out of the ordinary. She'd popped a few pills, showered, and relaxed with the kids, but when the headache didn't go away, I'd told her to go upstairs and lie down while I ordered dinner. It was tradition to order Chinese from our favorite spot after every race.

As I'd sorted through the bags, I asked Sebastian to wake up his mom.

I'll never forget the way he ran into the kitchen, pure terror in his eyes, crying because he couldn't wake Mira up. When I'd checked on her, she'd remained unresponsive, and I'd immediately called 9-1-1. I'd known it was hopeless, but I'd refused to believe it was true. That my beautiful and vibrant thirty-year-old wife was gone. Stolen from us by a brain aneurysm.

My world had collapsed in an instant. We'd had so much life ahead of us, so many dreams, and they were all shattered. I hadn't known how to go about picking up the pieces of my life, let alone for a confused and frightened five-year-old and a toddler who would never remember her mother.

With the help of Mira's and my family and *a lot* of therapy, I'd managed. But it was difficult. I cried in private and attempted to carry on for the kids as normal, though I wasn't sure what normal even meant anymore. Sebastian had slept in my bed countless nights, afraid something would happen again. Sleep continued to be an issue for him. And poor little Lulu, she only wanted a family, a whole family, not one led by a heartbroken single dad.

With a sigh, I powered on my laptop and got to work, paying bills and finishing up last month's accounting for Gray's Candy Shop. My grandfather had opened the corner store in the fifties, and it had been in our family ever since. I loved the store, loved what it provided for all of us and the community, but I didn't spend a whole lot of time in the actual shop. When I'd graduated from college with a double major in business and finance, I'd come back home with plans to expand, which I'd done, by building an online store that delivered out of state, becoming a recurrent participant in the farmers market, and establishing a school fundraising program. I could accomplish all that behind-the-scenes stuff at home, which was great because I could align my schedule around my kids' needs.

Though recently, I'd been wondering if I'd been scheduling myself too much around the kids.

Hence this ridiculous plan to start dating again.

I closed my laptop and stretched my back, checking the time. It was almost four, and Brooke should be finishing up her work for the day. She was an early riser, to get out on her farm with the sun. I didn't know how she did it. Plus, she almost never touched her phone while she worked, which was why I was surprised when my cell phone beeped with a text message alert from her.

BROOKE

Got a date for tomorrow!

That was fast.

I assumed she was getting all kinds of hits from men liking her profile picture. I'd told her to use the photo from her sister's shower because she'd been wearing a dark red dress the color of licorice with sleeves that fluttered around her shoulders and a little bow that tied at her waist. She was girl-next-door pretty. The kind of beauty that soothed instead of intimidated. She had that endearing crooked smile with lines outside of her mouth and at the corners of her eyes to prove how often she graced the world with it. Then, of course, there was her charm. She was energetic and ambitious and one of the most thoughtful people I'd ever met. The total package. Any guy would be lucky to have her.

So, it was a shame what her ex had done to her. Not only had he left her at the worst possible time, he'd made her think she was somehow less because of her infertility. I knew how long it had taken her to recover. As long as I'd been mourning Mira.

It was part of the reason why we were such good friends; we'd both gone through really traumatic events at about the same time. And I hoped she found all she desired from this silly experiment of ours.

BROOKE

Kim can't because Henry's going out with a buddy, so she's home alone with the baby, and Sabrina has some last-minute school stuff she's got to deal with.

BROOKE

So it's on you, my friend.

BROOKE

Also

BROOKE

You're a dude, and I need a dude's opinion on the best first-impression outfit.

I'm pretty sure anything but your overalls will do.

She sent me a bunch of shocked-face emojis.

BROOKE

I thought you liked my overalls.

I do, but dudes won't.

BROOKE

Fair point. See you at 6 tomorrow!

Suddenly feeling anxious, I paced the room, flipping my cell phone over and over in my palm, needing to move, rid myself of the unusual tightness in my chest. I completed three laps before thumbing to the dating app, scrolling to Natalie's message. **Hey! How are you?**

If Brooke could do it, I could too.

I rubbed the tips of my fingers together, as if that would spark something, then typed out a reply. **I'm good. How are you doing?**

She replied immediately. **I'm good! Happy it's finally**

Friday tomorrow. Do you have any fun plans for the weekend?

Fun plans? My weekends were usually playing referee for my kids, eating junk food, and falling asleep during some movie Seb or Lulu put on.

Not much going on here, I responded. **What about you?**

I completed another lap. This wasn't so bad. Having a regular conversation. No big deal.

I was thinking about going to a winery with some friends.

I tapped out a reply before I'd even really thought about it. **That's cool. I'm not really a wine guy. I like beer.**

I froze and choked out a huff, lifting my attention to the window in front of me, my eyes unseeing as the words of my message hit me. "That's cool?" I repeated, frowning at the wall. "I like beer?"

Had I always been so awkward?

"Dad!" Amelia called, and I shoved my cell phone into my pocket.

I'd have to get back to that mess later.

Or not at all.

SIX
JUDE

knocked on Brooke's door and leaned against the jamb, waiting. When she didn't answer right away, I pulled out my phone to text her that I was here and then opened the stupid app again. My conversation with Natalie had fizzled out, so I tried one with a girl named Michaela. After she'd asked me why I was on the app, I told her it was to find something casual, thinking it was best to be honest. So when she responded with the question **What do you want?** I answered **Sex.**

I supposed that was *not* the right thing to say because she'd never responded.

Brooke finally opened the door in a flurry. "Hey! Hi, sorry. I was naked and doing my hair, so I had to put clothes on and—"

"Settle down, honeybee. It's all right."

She took a breath, her shoulders rising high. She puffed up her cheeks and blew it out, visibly relaxing. Then she smiled at me. "Hi."

"Hi."

She gestured for me to head inside her condo, the familiar smell of lavender enveloping me.

Brooke had worked her way up from a rented little plot of land, a few square feet where she grew a handful of vegetables for herself while she was still at her nine-to-five, to owning her own farm, managing three employees, and cultivating I didn't know how many crops throughout the year, as well as maintaining colonies of bees.

It was a literal and figurative statement, my nickname for her. She was busy as a bee.

She offered me a can of her favorite sparkling water. "Where are the kids tonight?"

"Staying at my parents' house. They're having a camp-out in the living room with a movie marathon, so we'll see how my dad does with a sleeping bag on the floor."

"Even my back hurts thinking about it," she said, directing me to follow her to her bedroom. I'd been to her home many times, but there were only a handful that I'd actually stepped foot in her bedroom.

Once when she'd needed help putting together furniture. Another time while she was away, I'd been charged with taking care of Dorothy, and that little heathen somehow got herself trapped in the bathroom. The last time was when Brooke had had a stomach bug, and I'd popped over to bring her some groceries.

I had never, in all our years of friendship, entered her bedroom to hang out.

I didn't know how I felt about that.

But...I didn't hate it.

"So what's your future husband's name?" I asked, flopping on the bed, gathering Dorothy in my arms. She lifted her paw as if to swat at me, but I dragged my hand over her head, and she purred before nuzzling my palm. Brooke shook her head in amusement at us then disappeared into her walk-in closet. "Cole."

"And what's Cole like?"

"I don't know. That's what the date's for."

I huffed and cracked open the strawberry mango water. For a person who analyzed every decision, she was certainly jumping into dating headfirst.

"What do you think of this?" She ducked out of the closet, holding up a shiny gold top. She wore a lot of yellows and golds and always looked good in them.

"I like it," I told her, moving back against the headboard and crossing my legs at the ankles. Dorothy splayed out in my lap.

"You don't think it's too dressy?"

Like I knew. I pointed at my Macho Man T-shirt in answer, and she tilted her head back, laughing as she pivoted back to her closet. She reappeared after a few moments with a dress in her hand. "How about this?"

"I don't know. I guess it's nice, but it's hard to tell on the hanger."

She conceded the point with a dip of her chin and disappeared again. The next time she walked out of the closet, she wore the dress, a plain black top with thick straps and a skirt covered in pink and purple flowers.

She twirled around. "What do you think?"

"I like it. The bottom's really shiny."

She gripped the side of the skirt, examining it. "Is that a bad thing?"

"No."

"You hesitated. Why'd you hesitate?"

I scrubbed my hand through my beard. "I don't know. I guess…it feels dressy? Where are you going?"

"We're meeting for drinks."

"What else you got?"

She spun back around, kicking off a fashion show.

She changed into another dress, this one with tiny straps and buttons along the front. It floated around her legs when she strutted across the length of her room.

"Reminds me of the beach."

"That's where I got it." She flashed me a smile, proud of my good observation. Then she held her breasts, lifting them up and letting them drop. "But I can't wear a regular bra with it. Choices are strapless or braless. What do you think?"

I swallowed down the sudden lump in my throat, and when it didn't go away, I chugged the water, allowing myself time to formulate a response.

She wrinkled her nose. "What?"

"You want my opinion on your boobs?"

"Yeah." She shrugged like it was no big deal.

But now that she'd pointed out the fact that she had boobs, I couldn't stop ogling them. At her hard and pointed nipples beneath the flimsy material. What the hell was it made out of? Gauze? Tissues?

She planted her hands on her waist and turned to check herself out in the mirror, shifting side to side, and I blinked away, determined *not* to think of her boobs or imagine them in any way. "I don't know about the bra, but I don't like the dress." When she whipped back around to me, I backtracked. "I mean, I like the dress. You look great in it, but maybe not the vibe you're going for?"

She seemed appeased, flouncing back into her closet, and I slapped my hand to my chest, feeling a ball of...something there.

I was still thumping on it when she walked back out, this time in a white button-up top that showed absolutely no boob but with a tight blue skirt that displayed a lot of leg.

Brooke was average height, but she stepped into high heels, and suddenly, her legs were a mile long. She sashayed in front of me, and I didn't know why I was there. This was so stupid. Me lying here in her goddamn bed as she showed off all that golden skin.

What was the point?

"What do you think?" She plucked at the skirt, proving exactly how tight it was. Barely any wiggle room.

"I don't know," I said, and her brow rose.

She faced her mirror again. "Might be too business?"

"Too business? What business are you going to do with your ass out like that?"

Her jaw dropped, and I honestly didn't know what I felt worse about. Me checking out her ass or that I was being a dick about it.

Then she burst out with a big guffaw, and the shame dissipated. "I guess my butt has gotten bigger since the last time I wore this."

I had the urge to point out her butt was fine, but I didn't want to inadvertently confess this fashion show had generated some new and awkward feelings about my friend. I crossed my arms as she disappeared into her closet for another round.

"How's it going on your end?" she asked, out of sight. "Any connections on the app yet?"

"Not a one." I could hear the clang of hangers and the rustle of fabric.

"What?" She stuck her head out, the angle revealing more of herself than I thought she intended, in only a beige bra with lacy sides.

For fuck's sake.

"How is that possible?" she asked, and I shook my head, shifting my attention to her closet only once I knew she was safely back inside.

"How is what possible?"

"How are you not finding someone?"

"I don't know. I screw it up when I start talking to them. I get all…" I trailed off as she sauntered out in the gold tank top she'd shown me earlier and dark jeans that sat high on her waist and flared out at the bottom like some cute disco chick.

"Get all what?" she prodded, circling to the mirror, brushing her hands over her hips and thighs. I wasn't exactly a fashion plate, but the color of her top brought out the gold and honey strands of her dark hair that she'd curled in waves around her shoulders. It also highlighted the column of her throat—since when I found a throat attractive, I had no idea—and the peek of her cleavage. She tucked the bottom of the tank top into the waistband of the jeans, right behind the button, and turned to me with her arms out. "What do you think?"

What did I think? She was gorgeous.

And I didn't know if I was allowed to think that. If I even *should* think that.

I shook my drink can to see if it had any water left inside. It didn't. Which was unfortunate because my mouth was as dry as the Sahara. So instead of answering verbally, I held my thumb up, and she grinned, twisting away from me once more. She fingered a few pieces of jewelry hanging on a tree-like thing on her dresser. "So, tell me what's going on? Why don't you have a date yet?"

"I don't know," I grumped, and she glanced over her shoulder at me.

I didn't like how her brows drew down, like she could tell that I wasn't being honest.

That I had a hard time keeping my gaze off her ass in those jeans.

She slid a few bracelets on her wrist. "Are you getting matched?"

"Yeah."

She rolled her hand in the air, motioning for more.

"I'm not so great at talking."

"Since when?" She poked the tiny bee earrings I'd given her into her earlobes. We didn't often give each other gifts, but when I'd spotted those at a craft market last year, I'd bought them immediately.

I sighed, suddenly not quite comfortable talking about this with her. "I'm bad at messaging with them. It's awkward."

After draping a long necklace with a turquoise pendant around her neck, she returned to her closet to fetch a pair of tan sandals with thick soles. Fully outfitted, she posed with her hand on her hip. "How do I look?"

Hot.

She looked hot.

She didn't need the makeup, but the smoky eyes and glossy lipstick plus the clothes… Damn, she was a bombshell.

I cleared my throat. "Great."

Satisfied, she sat next to me on her bed, holding her palm up. "Lemme see."

"What?"

"The messages. Lemme see what they say."

I opened up the app then handed my phone over before scooting Dorothy off my lap. She stuck her tail up, obviously miffed at being pushed aside.

Brooke scrolled for a few seconds, and I definitely did not let my eyes dip down to the dark arrow of her cleavage. Didn't think twice about how her thigh touched mine. Or how she smelled so good.

Nope.

None of the above.

"Oh my god," she snickered. "It's like you've never flirted before."

I dropped my head back, glowering up at the ceiling. "That's what I'm trying to tell you."

"That you've never flirted?"

"I was a fifteen-year-old kid the last time I flirted."

She breathed deeply and audibly through her nose then moved even closer to me, her shoulder, hip, and leg right up against mine. She held out my cell phone so we could both see it. "What about her? Melissa?"

We had matched but had yet to start a conversation, so Brooke began typing. "Pretend like you're talking to them in person. Whatever you'd say to their face, write it here."

She tilted the screen so I could read her first message to my next match. **Hey, Melissa! Love your profile picture. Looks like Italy, is that right?**

That did sound like something I would say. When Melissa didn't respond right away, Brooke tossed my phone onto my stomach and petted Dorothy's back. "Be your honest and fun self. They'll be falling all over themselves to get to you."

Right. "Until they ask me what I want, and I tell them the truth."

"The key is to let them know what you want without coming right out and saying it," she explained while she picked up a purse, stuffing a few things from the top of her dresser inside it.

"I have no idea how to do that," I said, and she motioned for me to follow her out of her bedroom before flicking off the light.

"You gotta get them to read between the lines. You want sex without commitment, right? So compliment their looks, especially things that make a person think about sex. Tell her she's got great lips, kissable mouth, or something like that."

I swiped my thumb over my own mouth, letting Brooke's advice sink in, ignoring how kissable she looked.

"Ask subtle questions about what she likes. If she's a cuddler or if she minds PDA."

I didn't know if those prompts were general or specifically designed, because I was a cuddler and I enjoyed some PDA. More likely, it was because she knew me and wanted whomever I hooked up with to be a fit for me. As opposed to some random girl I wouldn't get along with.

Which made me grateful I'd made this pact with Brooke.

She had my back.

"Then once you've eased her in, hit her with the *Do you kiss on the first date?* And *Have you ever had a one-night stand?*" At the front door, she spun around to face me. "No sending nudes unless they ask for them."

I scowled. "Is that really a thing people do?"

She nodded with faux solemnity. "Yeah, that's really a thing people do."

"Why? Dicks are ugly."

She smiled impishly. "Beauty's in the eye of the beholder, no?"

"If you say so."

She gripped my bicep, squeezing. "I have faith in you, young padawan."

"You know," I started, pointedly dragging my gaze down her body. "This gold is reminding me of Princess Leia. You wearing the buns and bikini next Halloween?"

"Nobody wants to see these thirty-five-year-old tits stuffed into a tiny bikini."

Since we were apparently crossing all the lines tonight, I told her the truth. "You'd be surprised."

Then as if to prove a point, she bent over, shimmying a bit while fiddling with her bra, before standing upright once again and turning to the side. "How do they look?"

Tempting, I didn't say. Grabbable, I thought. "High and tight."

"Perfect." She opened her door, waving for me to go ahead of her.

"What time is Cooper coming?" I asked as she locked up.

"Cole," she corrected, "and he's not."

The condominium had three floors, and although we could have taken the steps, we waited for the elevator instead. It was faster.

"Why isn't he picking you up?"

She tossed me a confused frown as we stepped into the elevator. "Because we're meeting there."

"He should be picking you up. It's the gentlemanly thing to do."

She elbowed my side. "You're so sweet and old-fashioned. I love that about you."

I shoved my hands into the pockets of my shorts. "It's not old-fashioned to pick up a date. It's good manners."

"It is, but I don't want a stranger to know where I live. Plus, I don't want to be stuck there if it goes sideways."

I'd never thought of that before. First, because I didn't go on dates, and second, because the only other woman in my life I spoke to regularly was my sister Phoebe, a lesbian who'd been with the same woman for years. I'd never had to imagine all the ways a date might go sideways for a woman out with a man.

"You sure you don't want to bring a sweater or something?" I asked, suddenly very aware of what this Carter was going to be seeing when he met Brooke. A beautiful woman with a low-cut top and a bra that did magnificent things for her thirty-five-year-old tits.

Men were dogs.

I should've told her to go with the white button-up.

"No, I'm good." She smiled cheerfully, stepping off the elevator. "You know I run hot."

I did. I knew besides generally being warm all the time, she experienced occasional hot flashes. Even with all the medication she was on to keep her menopause symptoms in check.

I walked her to her car and opened the door for her. "I guess I'll talk to you later."

She sat down behind the wheel, tipping her head back to meet my gaze. "Thanks for coming over and helping me."

"Of course. Any time."

After shutting the door, I waited until she buckled up, reversed out of her parking spot, and hooked a left onto the street to get into my own car, realizing that I'd never wished her good luck.

I probably should have.

And yet...

I was kind of glad I hadn't.
Fucking Caleb.

SEVEN
BROOKE

'd planned on giving Cole the benefit of the doubt. Really, I had.

When he'd arrived to the bar on a bicycle, I'd thought, *Okay, that's cool.* He's big into being active or saving on carbon emissions. So was I.

But he'd kept his cell phone next to him, checking it constantly. So much so that I'd asked if everything was okay. He had merely nodded and said, "Tell me more about this farm thing."

I explained how I'd always had a green thumb and loved to garden, but it hadn't been until I joined a community garden that I learned I could actually do it on a larger scale. Yet I could tell Cole only half listened, and I rolled my eyes as I picked up my own phone, for a little entertainment, at least.

To my shock, I had over a dozen texts.

JUDE

I know you're on a date but Melissa messaged back!

JUDE

She studied abroad in college. She's a little young.

JUDE

A lot young.

JUDE

Like 25 years young.

JUDE

But that's fine, right?

JUDE

Liam and Kennedy have a bunch of years between them.

JUDE

Me and Melissa have been talking for the past half hour.

JUDE

Mostly about random stuff, music and food.

JUDE

She said she likes my long hair. What do I say back to that?

JUDE

I told her I liked her hair too. I liked the red.

JUDE

She said it's not real but thought it matched her personality better because she's a little wild.

JUDE

A LITTLE WILD

JUDE

BROOKE. WHAT DOES THAT EVEN MEAN?

JUDE

I know you're probably planning your wedding or something but I could really use some advice here.

JUDE

I asked her what her definition of wild is and she said she likes adventure, inside and outside.

JUDE

INSIDE. IS THAT INNUENDO?

JUDE

It was innuendo.

JUDE

Because now she came right out and said it. She likes adventures in bed.

JUDE

Fuck me. What am I doing?

I bit back a laugh, imagining Jude sweating as he texted this girl. This twenty-five-year-old girl. I bet she didn't even have to wear a push-up bra.

Although I didn't know why that bothered me so much.

Probably because I never appreciated my twenty-five-year-old boobs enough back when I had them.

But also...

Jude had been talking to her all night, wheeling and dealing in innuendo, while I'd been here with Cole as he sucked down three drinks. I was still on my first.

I texted Jude back.

Sounds like it's going great over there.

JUDE

There you are! Finally! It's going terrible.

JUDE

I did what you said, asked her if she kissed on the first date, and SHE ASKED WHERE

JUDE

I thought she meant on the date.

JUDE

So I said oh I don't know the park or restaurant BUT SHE MEANT WHERE ON THE BODY

I covered my laugh with my hand, though I didn't need to since Cole had turned away from me, typing on his phone. I didn't feel bad at all about replying to Jude.

Wow. She's bold. I admire that.

JUDE

So do I.

JUDE

But I have no idea what to do with it.

What do you mean, you don't know what to do with it? This is perfect for you. You want sex, and she seems to be offering it up quite easily.

JUDE

So what do I say? Hey, want to have sex?

Essentially, yes, but I wouldn't use those exact words.

JUDE

What words would you use?

Want to get together?

He didn't answer, and I swallowed the last of my drink before leaning forward a bit to slide the glass to the bartender, and that was when I spotted Cole's phone screen. He was on the dating app.

The exact one I'd met him on.

"All right, Cole, this has been…" I let out a derisive laugh and shook my head. "I've got to go."

He spun on his stool toward me. "Really?"

"Yes, really."

He downed the last of his drink and stood. "You mind giving me a ride? I got a DUI and can't drive right now."

I outright laughed in his face. "Yes, I absolutely do mind. You can hop right on your bike and peddle to wherever you're going."

He scoffed and sat down, muttering, "Not even that pretty."

I waved to the bartender. "Drink's on his tab."

She winked at me, clearly having heard our exchange. "Got it."

"Bitch," Cole called out to my back, but I ignored it, even as my shoulders hiked up and my jaw clenched. My skin grew hot, scalding hot, and I scurried down to my car, pumping the AC. Whether it was a hot flash or residual anger from my date, I didn't know. Either way, I needed to cool down.

Calm down.

I dialed Jude's number, and he immediately picked up. "Hey, why—"

"Since you don't have the kids, can you meet me at Giant and then go to the farm?"

"Oh god," he said, low and rough. "The date was that bad?"

"Yep." I popped the P.

"All right. I'll meet you, but you aren't buying any baked goods. I already made brownies tonight."

Jude was a fantastic baker, and I pumped my fist. I'd had a shitty date, but it wasn't going to be a shitty night. Twenty minutes later, Jude and I ambled through the store, grabbing random things off the shelves.

"You're saving me twice in one night," I noted as we stopped in front of the chips.

He dropped a big bag of salt and vinegar into the cart. "I wouldn't call grocery shopping and picking out clothes saving you."

"It may not be to you, but it is to me. Thank you."

He tossed his arm around my shoulders. "I'm sorry Carson was such an asshole."

"Cole. But, yeah, he was an asshole. I can't believe he didn't even wait until after our date to find his next one."

"It's his loss. Not yours."

I nuzzled my thanks against his chest before stepping out of his embrace as we turned the corner, heading for the other end of the store. I needed ice cream to go with the brownies. "So, Melissa…" I started, and when he shot me a frightened bunny look, I waved him off. "Oh, come on. It can't be that bad."

"It's not bad. It's…intimidating. She's a decade younger than me, but she's… She's just… She…" He tunneled his fingers through his hair, and I patted his back.

"You're short-circuiting."

His full-body shake-off started at his head and rippled down like a dog, and I rolled my lips over my teeth to keep from laughing.

"You good?"

He nodded.

"Good." I stayed quiet as we moved through the store, heading to the ice cream aisle. As I decided on a flavor, he finally explained, "I thought it would be a while until I found someone okay with only hooking up, so she took me by surprise. And even though we've only been talking tonight, she seems pretty awesome, which is throwing me for a loop. Like, it can't be this easy, can it?"

I opened the freezer door, standing in the cool air for a few seconds. I wanted to tell him that, yes, it could be that easy. People did it all the time. According to the stories I'd heard, his friend Dylan used to do it. There was a whole culture around finding sex through apps, so I didn't know why something twisted in my gut.

Something like jealousy.

This wasn't a competition to see who succeeded first in meeting our goals, but I had to admit, it niggled me a bit that I'd secured a date first, which ended up a bust, while he essentially floundered his way into what seemed to be the perfect situation for him.

And that made me such a jerk, to be jealous of my friend. We made this pact to help each other.

So, help him, I would.

I placed the rocky road ice cream into the cart then steered it to the next aisle for a can of whipped cream. Jude tossed in some string cheese.

"Anything else you want?" I asked, and he shook his head. "Are you sure?" I nodded toward the pharmacy corner. "Because while we're here, you can stock up."

His forehead scrunched in confusion until I reached for the condoms. Then his eyes widened. I read from the box. "Helps extend pleasure and performance. Mmm, sounds good, don't you think?"

He craned his neck around, like he usually did when ensuring no kids heard whatever they weren't supposed to. But his kids weren't here, and I threw the box of Trojans into the cart while Jude dragged his palm down his face, muttering something indecipherable.

"Don't you want to be prepared?" I bent to study the bottles on the shelf. "You should get some lube too. Do you have a preference?"

He blinked at me. "Do I look like someone who has a preference of lube?"

"Personal appearance has nothing to do with sexual proclivity."

"Sexual proc…" He trailed off, slack-jawed for a few long moments before breaking into a reluctant chuckle. "Remind me to bring you in for the sex talk with my kids."

I shrugged. I had no problem teaching the birds and the bees. Not that I was a professional educator or anything, but it didn't embarrass me to talk about it. Before my cancer, I'd had a healthy sex life, which was part of Tom's problem. He couldn't adapt to the sudden and steep drop-off of my sex drive when I'd first started feeling sick. Sex hadn't been fun or even felt good at that point, and we hadn't known what it was. He kept telling me it would pass.

"Here." I handed him the blue box with the lube inside. "A lot of people think water-based is best because it's natural, but oil or silicone lasts longer. Harder to get out of sheets, though."

"And you know because…?"

"Experience."

His cheeks turned pink.

"Don't be embarrassed."

"I'm not, but I'm not used to needing any…" He gestured to the shelves.

"Well, you're gonna need to get used to it," I said, wheeling the cart to the self-checkout, where we bagged our handful of items and headed back out to our cars to drive to the farm.

Jude arrived ahead of me with his brownies in hand. He helped me out of my car, insisting on carrying the bags into the little farmhouse I'd converted into my office. I kept some utensils, plates, and cookware in the kitchen. There was also a tiny bathroom and the comfiest couch I could find. Working on the farm was physically difficult, with long days under the sun, so I made sure the office doubled as a place to cool down and rest when I or any of my workers needed it.

I pulled down two bowls from the cabinet as Jude opened the brownies and ice cream. We made our sundaes and settled on the couch by mutual silent agreement. I moaned when I swallowed my first bite. "This is exactly what I needed."

Out of the corner of my eye, I noticed Jude staring at me, and I shifted over so I could put my bare feet on the couch. "You're gonna get sick of me from hanging out so often lately."

He shook his head. "Never."

I plugged in my phone, hitting my playlist, and we ate in silence as Jason Mraz sang, my toes tapping against Jude's thigh. "What are you thinking about?" I asked after a while. "You have that arrow."

"What arrow?"

I motioned to my own forehead, demonstrating how his forehead crinkled. "Your wrinkles point down in an arrow."

He smacked his forehead. "Thank you so much for pointing it out."

"I've got cream for that."

"You've got a cream for everything, don't you?"

"What's that supposed to mean?" When he didn't answer, I left him to think while I cleaned out our bowls in the kitchen sink. Returning, I stood in front of him, my hands on my hips, as he fiddled with the supplies in my smoke box. "Seriously, what's wrong?"

He removed a tiny sheaf of paper and sprinkled some leaves into it, though his movements were clumsy. I sat right next to him, leaning over to help. "Fold it up carefully," I instructed, wetting my fingertips to help with the grip. I rolled the joint then I held it out to him. "Lick it."

He met my gaze and didn't drop it as his tongue poked up, sliding along the edge of the paper. I ignored how the back of my neck felt like it was on fire and ran my thumb over the length of our homemade cigarette, making sure it stayed together.

"Here." I handed it to him then reached across his lap to snatch the lighter from the box on the side table, and I swore he sucked in a gasp when my chest brushed him. But that couldn't be right.

He didn't see me like that. As a woman. With breasts.

Or did he?

We lit up and passed it back and forth while I detangled the new and strange thoughts infiltrating my brain about me and Jude and *Jude and me*.

We were friends. That was it.

And because we were friends, I tried again, "What's wrong?"

He shrugged, rubbing his knuckle across his lower lip.

I hadn't ever noticed how plump his lips were.

Dark pink and round.

No man had a right to lips like his.

Women paid money for that.

With marijuana relaxing my inhibitions, I scratched his beard, thinking he should trim it, if only to give those lips their due.

"I'm anxious, thinking about having sex again," he said, his lips forming words that made me blink. Once and then twice.

I was supposed to be giving him advice about this.

"Why?" I forced myself away from him. "You think it's changed or something since the last time you did it?"

He scrubbed his hand over the top of his head, strands of his hair falling out of the loose bun above the nape of his neck. "No, but, like... I don't know." He sighed. "I don't know what to do."

I cocked my head to the side. "Mechanics-wise? 'Cause it's pretty simple. Unless you've got bad aim or—"

"Dear god," he muttered, leaning over to set his elbows on his knees and cover his face with his hands.

I started giggling. "Are you dealing with a rocket in your

pants or something? Your dick's so unwieldy you can't control it, shoving it into whatever hole you—"

"Brooke," he snapped without any heat in his voice. Rather, he fought a grin.

"Hm?"

"I'm trying to be vulnerable here, and you're laughing at me."

"You're right. You're right." I sat up primly. "This is serious business." When he sent me a playful glare, I asked, "Should I draw you a diagram?"

He started to stand up. "I'm never talking about this again with you."

I laughed and wrapped my hands around his forearm, yanking him back down to the couch. "I'll be cool." With a deep, theatrical breath, I showed Jude I could indeed be serious about this topic. "Talk to me."

He crossed his arms, concentrating on the wall across from us. "I don't know how to start it…any of this, but I mean the physical part. I don't know how to initiate it."

I didn't know exactly where the idea came from, but I blamed the next words out of my mouth on being high. "Practice on me."

EIGHT
JUDE

couldn't have heard her correctly, and I tucked a hank of hair behind my ear. "You want me to *what*?"

"Practice on me," she repeated, though she kept her gaze down this time, focused on tossing away the butt of the joint.

"Practice what on you?"

She circled her hands like she didn't know what to do with them now that they were empty. "Your moves. Practice them on me."

I looked around, bemused, stunned…curious. "You're serious?"

"Yeah, I mean…" She shrugged. "If you're so anxious about it. Practice makes perfect."

This idea was ridiculous yet made sense. There was no one else I would be comfortable talking to about this.

Doing it with.

"Practice makes perfect," I agreed, trying and failing to bite back a smile. I felt delirious. "You're so high."

She grinned. "So are you."

I gestured between us. "Won't it be weird?"

"No. We're friends. Nothing's going to change that."

"Even when I put on the charm?"

She laughed in my face, and I shot her a scowl, which only made her laugh harder, falling into my side. I hooked my arm around her neck, pulling her into a headlock, and she flailed.

"Is your move to make your girl pass out?" she panted in between giggles.

When I eventually let her go, she smiled at me, flushed and so pretty that I swore she shone. "Okay. Okay." She held out her hands, palms down, as if calming excited children or feral rodents. Basically the same thing. "Pretend I'm…what's her name?"

"Melissa."

"Pretend I'm Melissa and we're alone and you're feeling randy."

"Randy?"

"I hate the word horny."

"But is it worse than randy?"

She pursed her lips, thinking quite seriously. After a moment, she wrinkled her nose. "Add it to the list. Don't use horny or randy."

I wrote an imaginary list in the air. "Got it."

She crooked a smile my way. "So, I'm Melissa. How would you let me know you want to move things along?"

I swallowed, dragging my gaze over my friend. My buddy, whom I shouldn't have been attracted to. In that glossy gold top, displaying the rounded tops of her breasts, and dark jeans molded to her thighs. Without thinking, I reached out to her shoulder and skimmed the tip of my index finger along the thick strap of her tank top.

Her skin was soft and tanned from the sun. I flattened my hand, wrapping my fingers around her arm, feeling her skin warm under my palm. Her chest rose and fell with each of her breaths, the pendant on the end of her long necklace swaying ever so slightly. I grasped it in my other hand, lifting it up to admire it.

"This is nice," I said, forcing my eyes up to hers, finding them sort of unfocused.

"Thank you." She blinked slowly, throat bobbing on a swallow. "That was good. *Really* good. Holding on to my shoulder to keep me close while touching the necklace. It's an excuse for your fingers to be close to my chest. Very, very nice."

I dipped my chin, remembering myself. We were pretending. "So, uh…" I cleared my throat. "What now?"

She eased closer to me. "I guess it depends. You have to look for signs."

"Like what?"

She placed her hand on my thigh, a few inches above my knee. An example of a sign. A green light.

I turned more toward her, bringing my left knee up on the couch, confessing, "I feel like a kid again. Trying to figure everything out."

"That's okay." She urged me on, leaning into me, both of her hands my legs. "What did you do when you were a kid? Might work now," she said with a half laugh, and I thought back.

Fought through the haze of this new and puzzling desire creeping into my chest.

I remembered what it was like, standing outside of school on that day Mira finally said yes to me. I told Brooke, "I asked to kiss her."

She nodded encouragingly. "That's good. You could do that."

So I did. "Can I kiss you?"

She nodded again, her gaze on my mouth, and I didn't know which way was up anymore. I had no idea what I was doing. But I kissed her.

I kissed Brooke.

She squeaked out a surprised sound, ripping her hands away from me, and I immediately apologized. "Sorry. I didn't..." I shook my head, trying to center myself, but I had trouble. Especially with how my hands had involuntarily curled around both of her shoulders. "I got... confused."

Her eyes widened slightly, her cheeks pink. "No, it's fine. It's... I was surprised. But I can do better."

I slanted my head back. "You can do better?"

She shifted onto her knees, nodding. "Kiss me."

"You want me to kiss you?" I repeated then wiped my palms down my face.

How high was she?

How high was *I*?

"I want you to kiss me," she said, and I could only blame my immediate reaction on the marijuana.

Because I kissed her again.

This time, she met me halfway, and I held her face in my hands. There was no surprise, no confusion. We were *kissing*.

She still tasted sweet like the chocolate of her brownie sundae when she opened her lips to me, allowing my tongue to find hers. I should have been reluctant or uncomfortable. This was the first woman I'd kissed in years, and yet all I felt was interest and awe and a need for more.

She smoothed her hands up either side of my ribs to my back, settling underneath my shoulder blades. The gentle weight of her palms urged me forward, and I followed. Or led.

I didn't understand the choreography of this new dance, yet I liked it. I knew that much.

And suddenly, we were horizontal, with more than enough room on this sofa that was entirely too comfortable, leaving me with no excuse to move from this position with my friend. With her hands searching under my T-shirt for my bare skin, I kissed down her throat, diligent about sucking on her skin hard enough to change her breath, but soft enough that I wouldn't leave a mark.

Then she wrapped her legs around my waist, and I settled my weight against her. In for a penny, in for a pound.

"Do you want to keep going?" she asked breathlessly and possibly a little hopeful.

I held myself up above her, my hands on either side of her head, studying her for an indication she wanted to stop.

There wasn't any.

And when her honey eyes drifted between my own, I was positive she searched my gaze for hesitation.

There wouldn't be any.

"Yes," I said, more sure of that answer than I had been of anything in a long time.

Her lips parted on an exhale that seemed gratified, and she wasted no time, pulling my T-shirt up, forcing me back to my knees so I could help her remove it. Her attention floated over me, and I refused to cover up and be nervous, allowing her to look her fill of me, at the hair that covered my chest and my stomach that hadn't been flat in years. This was *me*.

She merely raised her gaze to mine and offered me a smile before shucking her own top. The bra she wore kept her breasts high and round, and I had to assume it wasn't very comfortable. So, I did the gentlemanly thing and found the clasp at her back to relieve her of it. She shrugged it off her shoulders and tossed it to the floor, appearing a bit shy now, awkwardly crossing her arms as if she had an itch on her neck that needed scratching. I peeled her fingers away from her throat and held her hands in mine. "You want to keep going?"

She licked her lips, and I'd bet all of my money she didn't know how sexy she was. "Yes."

Only then did I let my attention wander over her throat, down the long chain that hung between her breasts, like teardrops with small, dark-pink nipples.

"What would I do now?" I asked, altering our game a bit.

"Now you would touch her," she directed me quietly. "Let

her know how much you want her...with your hands and mouth."

I cupped Brooke's breasts, dragging my thumbs back and forth over her nipples until they tightened, but I didn't stop. I kept going, caressing the undersides, lifting and weighing them in my hands, rediscovering all the things I loved about a woman. The curves, the softness, and the perfect sighs that they made.

Well, that Brooke made.

I forced my gaze up to her face, her eyes wide like melted caramel, and I kissed her again, our tongues tangling. She wrapped her arms around me, pulling me back down on top of her, and I didn't hesitate to suck one of her nipples into my mouth. She inhaled sharply, arching her back, and I skimmed my hand down her side, her skin hot under my touch, until I reached the waistband of her jeans.

I curled my index finger around a belt loop, tugging gently in silent question. When she nodded, I opened the button, pulled down the zipper, and stripped them off her legs, leaving her in only skimpy black underwear. I sat back to admire her. Brooke wasn't skinny, but she was solid, muscular from all of her physical labor. Her hips flared wide, giving way to thick thighs, and I slid my hands around them.

She bit into her lower lip, hesitating a moment before telling me, "Some women like to be grabbed. Hard."

I understood and grabbed her. Hard. Yanked her toward me. "Like that?"

Her answering sound of approval was the only thing I wanted to hear for the rest of my life.

I skated my fingers up and down her thighs and palmed the naked globes of her ass, wondering if she always wore thongs underneath her clothes. Under those worn overalls I pretended to hate but actually loved. Especially when she wrapped a bandanna around her hair. Like some 1950s farmer pinup.

I pulled off the tiny scrap of material, tossing it somewhere behind me, all my focus on how Brooke—my friend— spread her legs, propping her feet on the couch, allowing me to see *everything*.

The way her skin flushed from her face to her chest.

The surgical scars I knew she didn't like to show.

The triangle of dark hair between her legs.

She was beautiful, but still, I teased her.

"All natural, huh?" When her brow furrowed, I dragged my fingers over the horizontal scar on her lower abdomen to the patch of hair. "Like a '70s porno."

"You watch a lot of '70s porn?"

"What can I say? I enjoy classic cinema."

She cackled, flinging her foot out to kick me, but I caught it and pushed it down and back, forcing her legs on either side of me. She reached her arms up above her, holding on to the arm of the couch, and waited, unmoving.

I did too.

Until she told me, "You can touch me. However you want."

Only then did I rake my hands from her shoulders to her hips, lightly scraping her nipples with my fingernails. She seemed to like it, so I did it again. And again. Until she closed her eyes and swiveled her hips. I bent, pushing her breasts together, licking and sucking on each one until she moaned, wiggling underneath me.

That was when I inched my fingers downward, but she stopped me by putting her hand over mine. "I don't get wet."

"What?"

"I don't get wet anymore."

"Okay," I said because I didn't know how else to respond.

"Other guys, they think they can lick their fingers or something and it'll be fine. They think they'll be the ones to fix me."

I shook my head, understanding now. "You don't need to be fixed."

Her face softened, the tension she'd been holding leaching from her body. Brooke was always so confident; I hadn't expected her to be worried about sex. And maybe she needed this too.

This practice…or whatever it was we were doing.

"What do you need?" I asked.

"Lube."

"For everything?"

She answered with a nod.

"All the time?"

"Yeah. Some guys get offended or something. Tom didn't—"

"You don't need to explain it to me," I snapped, not because I was angry with her, but because of every man who had ever let her down. Made her think she was less than the flawless creature she was.

And it all made sense.

The few stories she'd told me, using vague language about her asshole ex not being "satisfied" and how she never felt connected with other men she'd had sex with. Every single one of them was a selfish prick.

I remembered the other purchases from the store tonight and stood up to retrieve the bag from the counter in the kitchen. I placed it on the side table next to the couch after pulling out the lube, eyeing her as I opened the box.

She still hadn't moved, and the trust she placed in me made my heart thud hard against my rib cage.

Once I had the small blue bottle in hand, I popped the top and squirted some onto my index and middle fingers before kneeling on the couch between her legs. "It's cold," I warned her as I lowered my fingers, dragging them down the seam of her pussy, and she gasped. "Told you."

She batted at my shoulder, laughing, but when I found her

clit, her playful smile slipped, her fingers tightening on my arm. I circled my fingers around the tiny bud, and her breathing increased, her nipples pulled even tauter. I kept working her over, finding the rhythm she needed, as I squeezed her breast, lowering myself to her side, flicking at her nipple with my tongue.

She squirmed and let out a soft breath, a near hiss, wrapping her fingers around my forearm. Her fingernails bit into my skin, but I wasn't going anywhere, wasn't slowing down. Not when I could give her this release. Especially not when she deserved to be given everything she wanted.

"You close?" I asked, my voice a ghost of itself, my bottom lip catching on her peaked and wet nipple.

She nodded and whispered, "Keep going."

Like I'd ever stop.

I bent my head back down to her breast, earning more of her sounds, circling and circling my fingers. The lube made everything slick, the sound heating my already fast-flowing blood, and I didn't realize I'd been unconsciously bucking my hips against her leg until she threaded her arm between us to squeeze my erection over my shorts.

It had been years since anyone else had touched it, and I practically growled. My brain went fuzzy with white noise, and I tucked my face into Brooke's throat, breathing heavily when I felt her hand snake beneath my underwear. Then her fingers were there, wrapped around my hard cock.

"Not quite a rocket, but bigger than I would've guessed," she said against my ear, and I couldn't help but chuckle.

"Always a ballbuster. Even now."

And thank god for that.

I needed her to keep it light. Keep me here with her and not in my past.

I raised my head, our eyes meeting, and both of us stilled, acknowledging the importance of this moment. At least, that was what I assumed. She could've been mentally counting bushels of corn or something, and the idea of possibly wasting this opportunity made me refocus.

I kissed her as I pushed her hand away from me, but when she attempted to grip me again, I nipped at her lips. "After. You first." I held her wrist above her head so she couldn't try again, and her eyes sparkled with something I didn't understand. "What?"

"I like that." She tipped her head and arched her back, which pushed her breasts up toward me, and I left an open-mouthed kiss between them.

"Like what? This?" I tightened my grasp on her wrist, and she nodded, a secretive smile crawling across her face. "Are you…" I lifted myself up a bit to get a better look at her. "Are you into…stuff?"

"Stuff?" She laughed at me. "Sure. I'm into stuff."

I had no idea. Not that we talked *a lot* about sex, but it had come up a handful of times in our conversations, and never once had she mentioned what she liked. Then again, she would have had no reason to because we were buddies.

Pals.

Best friends.

Who, up until this very moment, didn't cross any lines.

Yet we were so far past any line, we couldn't see one anymore. Probably wouldn't even be able to find our way back if we wanted to.

"Are *you* into stuff?" she asked, rotating her hips under my hand since I'd momentarily lost track of what I was doing. I gently pressed my fingers inside her, feeling how tight she was, offering her a few experimental thrusts before I went back to her clit, rubbing in the way she needed.

"I don't know," I said, finally answering her question. "I've never…" I'd never had complaints about my sex life, although thinking about it, I guessed it was pretty vanilla. "I've never really tried anything."

Not that I was opposed to it, but it'd never come up before.

She only pressed a kiss against my lips, licking into my mouth like she wanted to soothe me, ease me back into the moment with her, and I was grateful. I moved my fingers faster, drawing a sharp intake of breath out of her, and I could tell she was close to orgasming from the way her kiss turned biting and then eventually mindless, merely her lips against mine, her panting breaths hot and fast.

And then I felt it, the rigid tensing of her limbs and release of it all with a sigh. She relaxed under me, crashing her head back to the cushion, her face, neck, and chest red. I let go of her wrist and dragged my palm down her arm and between her breasts as she blinked her eyes open to me. Her smile nothing short of beatific.

"All right, honeybee?"

"Very all right." She pushed up, reaching for the elastic of my athletic shorts, jerking it down to get to my boxer briefs, the outline of my erection visible through the light-gray cotton. She folded those down too, allowing my cock to jut out toward her. On my knees, I was slightly higher than her, and she tipped her head back. I swore it felt like an electrical shock when she leaned forward, licking the dot of moisture off the tip.

Still, I didn't look away. She didn't either.

She wrapped her hand tightly around my thick length, pulling, and I shook my head. "I won't last long."

"It's okay," she said and lay back down, widening her legs in invitation.

I turned around, intent on grabbing the box of condoms, but she stopped me with a quiet reminder. "I can't get pregnant."

I faced her again, brows raised. "You don't want to use one?"

"We can, but I can't get pregnant and haven't had sex in

over a year." I didn't need to tell her how long it'd been for me. She knew. "I'm okay with it if you're okay with it."

Again, the trust. It made my chest ache with how much she gave me, how much faith she put in me. And perhaps it was because we were such good friends. What we had was more than a fling or a one-night stand, and she knew I'd never hurt her. Like she'd never hurt me.

"Okay," I agreed and opened the bottle of lube again, squeezing some onto my fingers to spread along my shaft. I wiped my fingers off on my discarded T-shirt before settling over her. She brought her knees up to her sides, and I notched the shiny head of my cock at her entrance.

"Tell me if it hurts or you need more lube," I instructed, and she draped her arms over my shoulders.

"You tell me if you need to stop," she said, and I rested my forehead to hers, silently thanking her for being so under-standing and uncomplicated.

I kissed her once then pushed in, both of us gasping. There was no shattering earthquake or dark thunderstorm like I feared might overcome me the first time I had sex again. There was only heat and pleasure and the embrace of Brooke's arms around me.

Inch by inch, I entered her, until eventually, I was seated completely inside, and she wrapped her legs around my waist, holding me tight to her, one hand roaming over my back, the other combing through my hair.

"It's okay to let go," she whispered into my ear. "I've got you."

I closed my eyes to the sting behind them and gave in, grunting with each drive. It was exactly like I remembered yet not at all the same. The sensations—being so tightly wrapped up inside and outside—brought me quickly to the brink, faster than I would have liked. But I didn't have time to be embarrassed because Brooke was kissing me, my shoul-der, my cheek, my mouth, my throat, murmuring encouraging words about how good it felt and not to wait for her. To come.

"Come, Jude," she rasped. "Come for me." She tugged at my hair, forcing my eyes to hers. "Let go of everything and come for me."

And I did.

I flew off the mountaintop I'd been so afraid to climb. I came inside Brooke with a shudder and sank all of my weight on top of her to roll us onto our sides. I tucked my face into her neck, breathing in her lavender scent while she skimmed her fingernails up and down my spine, helping my heart rate to return to normal.

We stayed like that for a while until she needed to use the bathroom. She scooped up her clothes on the way, and I stood in the middle of the room, cataloging everything, hunting for physical evidence of my betrayal.

I found none.

I cleaned up with a few tissues and dressed, waiting for the shame to hit.

It didn't.

I slumped back down on the couch, where I'd had sex with a woman who was not my wife—where I'd *enjoyed* having sex with someone who wasn't my wife—and absently rubbed at my tattoo. At Brooke's suggestion, I'd had the word *albi* inked in Arabic on my left wrist a few years ago.

To honor my heart, my wife…

Joni Mitchell's witchy voice filled the room, singing a melancholy song about clouds and illusions and love, and I rested my elbows on my knees, letting my head fall between my shoulders. I had always assumed the guilt I'd become familiar with whenever the prospect of dating came up would triple when it came time for sex. But I didn't feel any guilt whatsoever.

And *that* made me feel sick to my stomach.

Brooke didn't make a sound when she entered the room

again, didn't say anything as she sat next to me and slid her arm around my shoulders, didn't offer anything besides what she always did: herself.

She towed me into her, and I finally succumbed to my tears. She wrapped her arms around me, hugging me, petting me, allowing me to dampen her skin and tank top as I cried against her shoulder. She had the right to be offended or upset I was acting like this after we'd just had sex; she probably needed some time to process as well. But as always, she gave her comfort to me instead. Gave me a moment to come to terms with what we'd done. What *I'd* done.

I didn't know how long we stayed like that, but when I eventually stopped crying, she pushed my hair back from my face, wiped her thumbs under my eyes, and smiled.

She *smiled*.

Then she turned off the lights, locked up, and we ambled outside together, my arm around her shoulders. At her car, I pulled her in for a hug and kissed her temple. She rubbed my back and tugged on my beard. I closed the door after her and waved as she backed away before getting into my own car.

It was almost as if nothing had happened tonight.

When, really, everything had happened.

Everything had changed.

NINE
BROOKE

'd had sex with Jude.

Jude, my pal.

My pal, Jude.

And I had no idea what to do with myself. Had no idea what or how to feel.

One minute, we were laughing and joking and getting high. The next, we were kissing and touching and getting naked.

I wasn't thinking. Not when he pushed me down to the couch—or I pulled him; I didn't know. Either way, I'd thrown all common sense out the window. I'd let myself be swept up in the weight of him, in the heat of his mouth, in the gentle way he'd touched me. Not only did I not stop my friend from giving me an orgasm, but I'd practically begged him to.

And now! *Now*, I knew what his hard cock looked like. I knew what it felt like. I knew—dear god—I knew how good it was.

I could only hope it was my imagination. Like, it had been so long since I'd had sex that I'd imagined how good it was. A feast after a famine.

Because I didn't think I could bear what it meant otherwise.

That everything I'd felt for this guy, the relationship we'd built over the last five or six years, had been irrevocably changed. I wouldn't be able to handle losing him.

"What were you thinking?" I snapped at myself as I yanked a makeup wipe out from the packet and scrubbed my face clean in the bathroom mirror. "You *weren't* thinking, you idiot."

I grumbled and threw the dirty wipe in the garbage.

This wasn't me. I didn't make decisions on a whim. I was thoughtful and deliberate about my choices. I didn't jump into bed with anyone.

Then again, this wasn't *anyone*. This was Jude.

My Jude.

My sweet and funny friend.

"Oh my god!" I shrieked as I stripped off my clothes, flicking the shower on. "He saw me naked!"

I could only assume that now that he knew what I looked like under my clothes, he'd think of it whenever we were together. Because I sure as shit wouldn't forget about the soft sandy-colored hair on his chest, his "dad bod," which I liked even though he didn't, and the thick length of him jutting out toward me.

"He's supposed to be having sex with other people. *Other* people," I moaned, thumping my forehead against the shower wall.

I was supposed to be helping him.

Which…maybe I did.

I spun under the showerhead, letting the hot water soothe me. It didn't fully drain my anxiety, but it did slow my spiraling thoughts.

Jude had such a hard time with the idea of being with other women because he still mourned Mira, so it might have been a good thing he got that first time over with me. Especially since he'd broken down after. If it was guilt or grief, I didn't know, but I was sure he wouldn't have wanted anyone else witnessing that. Jude prided himself on being "fine."

So fine, he lived in stasis. He'd admitted to me on more than one occasion that he struggled to balance being a grieving husband and a single father. He never wanted Sebastian and Amelia to know how hard it was for him, so he had locked himself down, pretended he could handle being the captain of the ship alone. But too much in any one direction, and he feared the boat would tip.

Tonight, the boat hadn't tipped. It had capsized.

I only hoped our friendship wouldn't drown in the wreckage.

I washed my face, ignoring the pictures flashing in my mind, the ones of us laughing while kissing, joking while we'd lain naked on the couch, the way his dark eyes had dilated when I told him to hold my wrist tighter.

I knew so much about Jude, and he knew a lot about me, yet tonight, we'd shared pieces of each other that would be impossible to forget.

How he'd kissed me like a starving man and I was his favorite food.

How he'd grunted quietly when he'd orgasmed as if he was afraid to be too loud.

How he'd clung to me when he'd cried like I was his lifeline.

I wouldn't be able to forget any of that.

Even as I convinced myself I had to.

I rinsed off my body, careful of the tender flesh between my legs. I should've known Jude would be nothing short of respectful during sex. He was a gentleman in every sense of the word. Not only had he made sure I orgasmed first, but he hadn't batted an eyelash at giving me what I needed to accomplish it.

The boyfriend bar was in hell for heterosexual men.

For me, though, the bar hadn't been raised; Jude had thrown it into another universe.

I shut off the water and stepped out of the shower to wrap myself up in a towel. I brushed my teeth, ridding myself of the last physical evidence of Jude.

I wouldn't be able to taste him on my lips anymore.

Smell him on my skin.

Only after I changed into my pajamas and snuggled under the covers did I check my phone, finding a text from Jude.

JUDE

Are you okay?

I'm good.

Are you okay?

JUDE

Yeah. I'm fine.

I huffed a laugh and reached my hand out to Dorothy, but instead of cuddling against me, she waddled to the other end of the bed.

She must've known what happened with Jude.

Some kind of cat intuition.

And she hated me for it. Jealous shrew.

I plopped my head back on my pillow and held my cell phone up to type.

Is it going to be weird between us now?

The answer was yes. Yes, it was going to be weird between us.

JUDE

I don't know.

I gave in to a pitiful whimper, slapping my hand to my forehead.

JUDE

I don't want it to be weird.

Me neither.

I had no other bright ideas, so…

What if we forget it happened and never mention it again?

It took a minute for him to respond. A minute that made my neck prickle with sweat.

JUDE

Does that ever work?

First time for everything.

JUDE

I'll see you tomorrow?

Yeah. Of course.

Tomorrow was Saturday, farmers market day. No going back now.

————

I packed up the green beans in a paper bag to hand over to a customer as I heard a sweet, elfin voice call out, "Brooke!"

I finished up the transaction and turned in time to bend, catching Amelia in a hug. "Hey, girlfriend. What's going on?"

"Can you do my hair?" She patted her head with one of her ever-present stuffed unicorns.

"Yes. Of course. But where's your dad?"

"Nana and Pop dropped us off," she said, pointing in the direction of Jude's stall. I barely saw the top of his head through the crowd, but Sebastian was easy enough to spot, slowly making his way to us. Probably because he was supposed to escort his little sister here.

I waved at him. "Hey, Seb. How are you?"

"All right," he mumbled, then shot Amelia a glare. "You can't run away from me like that."

The market covered two blocks, with tents set up in the cordoned-off street. Though small, it attracted a fair number of people looking for fresh produce or gourmet goods. We were all relatively safe here, but Amelia was only five and quite tiny for her age. I caught her gaze, reiterating her brother's point. "He's right. Don't go running off."

She stuck her tongue in the corner of her mouth and covered half her face, obviously embarrassed at her behavior, so I hugged her again then spun her around to comb my fingers through her hair. "How do you want me to do it?"

"Braid! Like Elsa."

"You got it."

I dug into the pocket of my overalls for an extra hair tie and tried to tame her wild curls as I spoke to Sebastian. "I heard you two had a movie night with your grandparents last night. How was that?"

Amelia pumped her unicorn up and down. "Awesome!"

Sebastian shrugged, craning his neck around, as if seeking an escape. He was ten going on twenty, and the older he got, the more he looked like his father. The same wide brow and nose, with the dark coloring of his mother. Little Amelia was a twin of Mira, from her pint-size stature to her eyes, though Sebastian's personality was closer to his mother's, quiet and considerate. Amelia, on the other hand, was born of pure sugar, sweet and full of energy, a pixie all of her own making.

I separated her hair into three sections, careful to keep her curls in as I wound them together. Admittedly, I was vain about my own hair. I'd always loved my hair, but I'd become especially attached to it after my cancer. It was the one thing that made me feel feminine anymore, and funnily enough, it was what Mira and I had bonded over when we'd met. She'd had a full head of long black curls, and we'd traded hair care secrets.

I wouldn't say Mira and I were best friends, but we were more than acquaintances. I still had her number in my cell phone, hesitant to delete it. But now, after last night? I wondered how long girl code lasted. If I should feel guilty. Because I didn't, and I imagined she'd be happy if Jude was happy.

Her sudden death had rocked her family and the wider community since the Grays were well-known from their candy business. All of us regular vendors at the market had rallied around Jude as much as we could. I had taken it upon myself to check in regularly, which had snowballed into the friendship we had now.

Or not.

I didn't know.

We still hadn't spoken to each other today. Usually, we took turns treating each other to Miss Diane's coffee. I had yet to find a place with a better brew than the tent at West Chester's Farmers Market.

I liked an iced French vanilla, while Jude was partial to the French roast, but really, a person couldn't go wrong with any order.

But I hadn't bothered picking it up this morning. Neither had Jude. And it sucked running my booth uncaffeinated all morning.

"Finished," I said, tapping Amelia on the shoulder.

She whirled around, whipping her plait over her shoulder, pointing at my own braid. "Twins!"

I smiled, hands on my hips, shimmying my shoulders

until Amelia laughed. I split my attention between the siblings. "Got big plans for today?"

Amelia hopped up and down. "Da-daddy said we'll build me a new Lego set tonight!"

"Ooh, that sounds fun." I tipped my head to Sebastian. "What about you?"

"I've got a baseball game."

"That's right. Your summer league started, right?" When he only nodded, I tried again. "Maybe I'll come to one of your games. I'd love to see you play."

He had no reaction one way or the other, so I offered him a smile and stood up, tossing a hand out to Nicole, a young girl I paid under the table to help me out at the market. "Be back in five." Then I took hold of Amelia's hand. It was time to face the music. "Come on. Let's go back to your dad."

Sebastian trailed behind me and Amelia as she chattered on about her unicorn, the one she swung beside her named Purse. Amelia was obsessed with unicorns. I'd met a handful of them: Big Unicorn, Small Unicorn, Purse, Sophia, Butter and Bread—twins, obviously—and Baby Unicorn. I'd given her Small Unicorn for her first birthday. A small—duh—white unicorn with pale-pink hair and tail. It was supposed to play music after winding it up, but I knew for a fact that it had long ago lost the ability after Jude had put it in the washer because Amelia had thrown up on it. He didn't realize it wouldn't work if it got wet. But she still loved it.

And I loved that.

We stopped at the Gray's Candy stall, and I helped myself to a stick of watermelon licorice as Jude finished up with a customer. When he finally turned to face me, tension bracketed his features. I chose to ignore it. "Found these two raga-muffins begging for brussels sprouts."

"No!" Amelia giggled. "Gross!"

I ruffled her hair, laughing, and Jude loosened up a bit too. Sebastian, on the other hand, heaved a sigh fit for a brooding teenager as opposed to a ten-year-old and threw himself on the folding chair behind Jude's table.

It was about closing time, and Jude glanced over his shoulder at his son. "Why don't you start packing up the boxes, and we can get out of here?"

Sebastian didn't respond, merely pulled his handheld gaming system from his pocket.

"Seb." When he didn't answer, Jude repeated, "Sebastian. Help me to start packing up, and we'll be able to get out of here faster."

Sebastian eventually followed his dad's direction but only after rolling his eyes and slipping off the chair like he'd been asked to clean up piles of elephant poop.

Jude puffed up his cheeks and blew out an audible breath, his eyes on mine, frustrated and a little tired. On the upside, him sharing his reaction with me meant we were back to normal.

No awkwardness at all.

Well, a little bit of awkwardness. I had seen him naked and had his cock inside me. So…

I bent down to Amelia, hugging her before I pointed to Jude. "Gonna help your daddy clean up?"

She nodded excitedly. "I'm a good helper!"

I tweaked her nose. "Of course you are. I'll see you later, okay?"

She skipped around the table to help as I stood, and he inclined his head toward me, a silent thank-you.

I smiled.

He smiled.

And yeah, we would be okay.

TEN
JUDE

A week after the so-called sex practice with Brooke, I made plans with Youmna and George to drop off the kids for the weekend. I didn't tell Brooke that I had time to hang out, and I didn't know if that made me a bigger asshole or coward, but I was saved from deciding when Nate texted to come to his bar. Walt's was hosting some kind of local fundraiser with the money being donated to a charity for Huntington's disease. So Liam, Dylan, and I made plans to head there for a few hours.

I pulled up outside of the modest single-story house Mira had grown up in with a manicured lawn and flower bed in the front. As I stepped out of the car, the front door swung open, and George ambled out. He was a tall and broad man, though he really needed to get his limp checked out.

Amelia, always excited to see her grandfather, danced in her car seat until I unbuckled her so she could sprint toward him. "Jiddo!"

"Lulu!" He crouched down to catch her, waving his hand at Sebastian, who approached much slower.

He and I hadn't been able to get on the same page lately. It felt like in the last few weeks, he'd lost that little boy air about him, and I struggled to adjust to having a preteen, while he couldn't seem to shake his moodiness, let alone the whole not listening to me thing.

It was possible I was being oversensitive because he didn't want to cuddle with me anymore.

And that was the real problem.

The only thing to excite him anymore was baseball, and he seemed to like Dylan more than me right now because Dylan was his coach. I was the guy making him clean up his bedroom.

"Hello, Bissi," George said, wrapping his arm around Sebastian, who didn't return the embrace.

George raised his brow to me in silent question, and I shrugged, not letting on to my suspicion that Sebastian objected to still being called *little kitten*.

Mira had given Seb that nickname when he was born, and the whole family had quickly adopted it. But I guessed he was too old for that too.

Once Sebastian entered the house, George adjusted Amelia to his hip, so he could pat my back. "How are you?"

"I'm good." I motioned to his leg. "I see you still haven't gone to the doctor."

He let a familiar sound rumble from the back of his throat. The one that stated he did not want to discuss it, so I grinned in good humor and walked inside, where photos decorated almost every inch of the walls, chronicling Youmna and George's journey from Damascus, Syria, to West Chester, Pennsylvania.

The décor hadn't changed in twenty years. There were still doilies on nearly every flat surface, vases holding fresh flowers in the windows, and a cabinet containing fine china I had been allowed to eat off exactly twice in my life.

Youmna sauntered out of the kitchen and greeted Sebastian with a kiss to his forehead, her hands curved around his cheeks, speaking in soft Arabic. He let her hug him for a moment before rushing off to where they'd redone one of the bedrooms for my kids when they slept over. Then my mother-in-law turned her attention to me, greeting me in the exact same way she had my son. Pulling me to her with her palms on my face and her lips on my forehead. "Habibi," she murmured, smiling, eyes roving over me in inspection. "You look good today."

"As opposed to every other day?"

She whacked my arm with a cluck of her tongue. "Yes. Come on. Come eat."

I dutifully followed her into the kitchen, while Amelia sat on her grandfather's lap, playing with some kind of wooden puzzle.

"I'm going to eat out," I told Youmna, hoping to stop her before she started cooking.

"Have a snack." Then she proceeded to place an array of small dishes in front of me on the table, stuffed grape leaves, tabbouleh, and spinach pies. I stopped her when I noticed her reaching for the loaf of bread.

"This is enough, Mama."

She reluctantly sat down across from me, silently urging me to eat before setting her chin in her palm. "Now tell me, how are things?"

I filled her in on Sebastian's attitude as of late and asked if she could sew the mouth that had come undone from one of Amelia's unicorns, which she happily agreed to. Then she slid her hand over my hair, down the side of my face to my beard. "When are you going to cut your hair? You are too handsome for so much of it."

I covered her hand with mine, nuzzling her palm. "I will. I'll cut it soon."

She nodded in satisfaction. "You are doing what you promised. Finding someone?"

I bit into one of the small savory pies to buy myself some

time. My mother-in-law, always patient, waited me out, smiling. As if she could tell something had changed.

I swallowed and cleared my throat. "I'm trying."

She couldn't have looked more pleased. "Who is she?"

"No one in particular," I said around the spinach pie lodged in my throat. "Just...trying to go on dates."

"You will find someone to help you and love the children."

I didn't want to confess that I wasn't interested in a wife, so I let her fantasize about my supposed *someone* while I tried not to recall the feel of Brooke's skin and the way her lips tasted. How she wrapped her hand around my cock and the way her breath caught when I entered her. The sounds she made when she came on my fingers.

I shook my head out of my reverie.

It had been happening more and more lately. The more days passed, the more my brain had demanded I remember.

At the most inopportune times. Like when I visited with my mother-in-law.

I finished the pie and wiped my hands on a napkin. "I won't be late tonight."

She waved me off. "If you are, they can sleep over."

I didn't like continually asking my parents and in-laws to take the kids, but these summer days felt like they went on forever. I thought they were as sick of me as I was of them sometimes.

"I have to work in the store tomorrow," I said, and Youmna tapped the table.

"Good. They will stay here tonight, and you can pick them up after you are done working tomorrow. Okay? Okay."

I laughed since that was all settled and stood up with a kiss to her cheek. I called out to Seb that I was leaving, which he barely responded to, and left with a hug to Amelia and a handshake for George.

I arrived at Walt's to find a big crowd. The Anchormen, a

band that sometimes played there, covered "Only the Good Die Young" by Billy Joel on the small stage in the corner, and I made my way through the throng of bodies to the bar. Nate, in the middle of pouring a beer at the taps, tipped his chin to me in greeting.

"Gimme a Blue Moon," I shouted to him, slapping some cash down before skating my gaze around until I found Dylan and Liam, Genevieve and Kennedy in tow. Nate slid me my beer and informed me he'd be over in a minute, so I wound my way to my friends, scooting in on the end of the booth.

"Am I old, or is it too loud in here?" I asked in a near shout.

"Old," Evie answered with a big smile, her side tucked up along Dylan's.

Liam, the oldest one out of all of us at thirty-eight, winced. "It is loud in here."

Which had Kennedy grinning. "Come on, it's for a good cause!"

"Too many damn people," Dylan grumbled, almost inaudibly.

"What's the deal anyway?" I asked, and Kennedy proceeded to explain the drummer in the band had opened a Huntington's disease charity, in honor of his brother who suffered from it. Kennedy knew all the inside information because her sister's boyfriend also played in the band and had been friends with the drummer since high school. I barely listened, too focused on my cell phone and the message from Melissa asking if I wanted to grab coffee.

Coffee didn't seem like a big deal. And yet I gaped at the screen as if she'd asked me if I wanted to go cliff-diving.

Because *What? Are you nuts?*

"Hey." Dylan pounded his fist on the table. "You lookin' at dick pics or something over there?"

I spluttered on a gulp of my beer. "Dick pics?"

"You look frightened. I assumed."

Evie leaned over, peeking at my screen. "What is that?"

"It's, uh…a dating app."

That had everyone's full attention.

"You took the plunge?" Liam asked, while the girls tossed each other confused glances. But before I could answer, Nate slid into the booth, enlightening everyone.

"Jude's finally going to get laid, if he hasn't already. So, where do we stand?"

"*We* stand nowhere." I set my cell phone on the table, so they could all view Melissa's latest message to me. "But *I* was asked to go out."

"What are you going to say?" Kennedy asked, and I shrugged.

"If you wanna have sex, you gotta say yes," Nate said, earning him an eye roll from his sister.

"Why are you even here and not behind the bar?"

"Because Tabitha's got it covered."

"You leaving her to fend off the wolves by herself?" Evie scoffed, referring to the dark-haired female bartender.

All of us turned to the bar, where Tabitha simultaneously took a payment, filled a drink order, and tossed a towel onto a spill. All without breaking a sweat.

Nate lounged against the back of the booth. "She's earning her paycheck."

Liam eyed Nate. "What's that mean?"

"She asked for a raise."

Evie sat up tall, interested. "What'd you say?"

"I'd think about it."

She threw a balled-up napkin at him. "Don't pretend you're not gonna say yes. She's been your manager for, what, five years?"

"Six," Nate said, his gaze toward the bar, presumably on Tabitha.

"And she's been here since you opened the bar," Evie

went on. "You wouldn't be able to keep yourself afloat without her."

"I know that." Nate frowned at his sister. "But I don't want *her* to know that. These are how negotiations go."

"I didn't know this was a Fortune 500 company. Excuse me."

"Listen, Little Miss Sassypants, I don't need any of your lip."

We all busted out in laughter, with Kennedy saying, "Okay, *Dad*."

Nate shuddered. "Please don't speak that into the universe."

"What? I think you'd be a great dad." She looked between all of us at the table for agreement. I would have if I didn't know all of Nate's hang-ups from his childhood about his own father.

Evie pointed to the bar, telling her brother off. "Go help her. And then go give her a big raise. She deserves it for all the shit she puts up with from you."

Nate slanted his head toward Dylan. "You gonna let her talk to me like that?"

Dylan merely slung his arm around her shoulders.

Nate huffed. "What happened to bros before hoes?"

"First of all, if you call your sister a ho, I'm gonna crack your jaw."

Nate grinned. "As if you could."

"And second of all, she's right. Tabitha deserves all the money she wants."

"Of course she does," Nate said easily. "But I have to make her sweat it out for a little bit. That's good business sense. Now..." He extended his arm along the back of the booth. "What's the plan with sweet Melissa?"

I palmed my phone, scrolling back through the messages with her. Sweet would not be the word I'd use to describe Melissa. "I don't have one yet."

"You want to see her?" Liam asked, and my mind flashed to Brooke and how we'd agreed to never talk about what happened last week.

So I dropped my head back to my shoulders and blew out a breath. "Yeah, I want to see her."

"Hey, man, it's only coffee," Dylan said. "If you're not feeling it, you could leave. No big deal."

All my friends nodded, including Evie and Kennedy.

Only coffee. I could totally do that.

"Yeah," I mumbled to myself, forcing my thumbs to type out the words. **I'd love to grab a coffee with you. Let me know when you're free.**

ELEVEN
BROOKE

The July Fourth holiday weekend came and went with the usual fanfare of fireworks and a busy morning at the farmers market, but my sister and I had a date at Gray's Candy Shop. The bell above the door tinkled when I opened it, and Sabrina audibly gasped at the scene in front of her. Truth be told, each time I entered Jude's family's store, I had to rein in my excitement. It was like something straight out of the 1950s. Probably because it hadn't changed since it first opened two generations ago, with its black-and-white checkered tile floor and blue walls.

"It smells amazing in here," Sabrina exclaimed after a deep breath. The scents of sugar, caramel, and vanilla lingered in the air. She spun in a circle, taking in the candy, the quirky style, the one-of-a-kind packaging. It was fun and brought in lots of people. Even now, customers milled about, laughing and filling up their bags, weighing them on the old-school scales hanging from the ceiling.

The quaint store was filled with rows of old-fashioned candy jars. Chocolates, each perfectly formed and drizzled with various toppings, took up one entire wall. Another held nostalgic candies like saltwater taffy, Pop Rocks, Bottle Caps, and hard candies grandmas always kept in misshapen home-made dishes in their living rooms.

Sabrina pointed to the chocolate-dipped strawberries. "Ooh. Everyone could get a little box of these. What do you think?"

"I'm not sure how long they'd last, or if they'd need to be refrigerated," I said, snagging a little plastic bag to fill with peach rings. While we were here to scout favors for her wedding, that didn't stop my gaze from coasting around the store for Jude. He didn't often work here, but I'd texted to see if he'd be in, and if not, could he meet us. He, of course, agreed.

My sister made a slow circuit of the store, stopping occasionally to inspect the treats. She held up a candy necklace, brows raised at me as she laughed. She used to love candy necklaces. I shrugged. "Why not?"

"No, I couldn't. People wouldn't like them."

"So what?" Jude's voice sounded behind us, and we both pivoted to find him leaning against the door to the back. "It's your wedding. You do what you want."

I agreed, aiming a peach ring in his direction. "Exactly. It's your wedding. If you want to give away candy necklaces and fireballs as your favors, you do that."

Jude smiled, and I stuffed the whole peach ring into my mouth, smiling back at him.

"How's it going?" he asked me.

I answered midchew. "It's going."

"Have you—"

Sabrina interrupted him. "Jude, I love this store!" She held on to his shoulders, her eyes wide. "Seriously, do you love your job or what?"

"Yeah. It's pretty great."

"I think I could live here."

"You're welcome to," he said, moving to stand next to me,

his arm brushing mine. "Not much furniture to speak of, though."

"I could lay my head down on a pillow of cotton candy. It's fine."

He grinned, glancing at me before telling her, "Go ahead and look around. Let me know if you have any questions about anything." After she flounced away, he headed behind the counter to find a pad of paper and a pen. "Remind me of the wedding date again."

"August fourth."

He jotted it down in his tiny block handwriting then rested his forearms on the counter, finally bringing his eyes up to mine. "How've you been?"

"All right. Busy." I spent summers harvesting and selling a lot of produce, not only with my co-op, but to some smaller grocers who featured local produce. My days were sunup to sundown. "How 'bout you?"

He stopped gnawing on the cap of his pen to answer a question from the worker who'd made a mistake on the iPad while ringing up a customer. He quickly fixed the error and tossed a smile to the middle-aged couple purchasing a few bags of candy before making his way back to me, the pen behind his ear. He drummed his fingers on the glass counter. "I, uh…have a date on Thursday."

My breath left me like I'd been punched in the gut, and I froze with a peach ring halfway to my mouth. I only forced myself to breathe and move when the arrow wrinkle appeared between Jude's brows. "Wow." I blinked. "That—good for you."

He didn't seem to believe me, so I tried again.

"That's really great. Is it with Melissa? Is it because of all my tips? I told you I'd get you laid."

As soon as the words were out of my mouth, I squeezed my eyes shut as if I could take them back. Erase the last three seconds.

I'd certainly gotten him laid. And we weren't supposed to be talking about it.

"Scratch that," I mumbled, opening one eye and then the other in time for him to snatch the peach ring out of my hand. He chewed it, lips pressed tightly together as if attempting not to laugh at me.

"You're the worst," I muttered, shoving another peach ring into my mouth.

A moment later, my sister bounded over to us. "I've decided. I'm going to get *His* and *Hers* stickers made and put baggies together of our favorite candy. The necklaces for me and Swedish Fish for him."

"Sounds good." Jude withdrew the pen from behind his ear. "How many pounds of the fish do you think you'll need?"

"I'm not sure. Enough for one hundred people to get a scoop."

He bit back another laugh, scribbling down a few numbers. "Got it. One hundred scoops. I'm assuming you'll want one hundred candy necklaces too? I'll order extra of both to make sure there're enough."

"Amazing. Thank you." Sabrina could barely keep still, radiating energy. "How much do you think it'll be?"

He shook his head. "Family discount."

"What's that mean?" my sister asked at the same time as I chided, "Jude, no."

He split his attention between us and shrugged before going back to writing on the pad of paper.

Sabrina quirked her brow at me then Jude. "Is he—are you giving me all of that for free?"

He kept his head down. "Yep."

"Jude." She pressed her hands to her heart. "That is so kind. Thank you."

"You don't have to do that," I told him, and he finally

stood up straight, tucking the paper away and the pen behind his ear.

He stepped out from behind the counter. "I want to."

Sabrina gasped, her *I have an idea* face on. "You have to come to the wedding!"

Before I could respond, she went on, "Come with Brooke."

He shook his head, waving the idea away. "No, I'm sure she'll have a date."

Sabrina flicked her hand. "No, she won't."

I snorted. "Thanks."

My sister appeared sheepish. For only a second. "I know you've started dating again, but it's next month. You're going to find someone to bring to my wedding by then?"

"Yes," I answered, dragging out the word petulantly.

Sabrina ignored me completely to speak solely to Jude. "You're coming. I can't wait. It's going to be amazing. And I want you there. Even if Brooke ends up with a date, you're still coming, okay? I'm putting you on the guest list as soon as I get home. Let me know if you want the chicken or vegetarian option for dinner." Then she threw her arms around him. "You're so great. I'm glad my sister has someone like you in her life. Someone to look after her."

He met my eyes over Sabrina's shoulder. "She doesn't need looking after."

"No, but she should have it anyway." My sister backed away, talking as if I couldn't hear her. "She hasn't had a man in her life in so long."

I rolled my eyes. Jude merely smiled, listening good-naturedly.

"And Tom was such a jackass. Did she ever tell you what he said to her?"

"Brina," I warned, but she kept right on going.

"She was laid up in bed after having just…well, I won't go into *that* detail, but suffice to say—"

"Sabrina," I hissed, tugging on her arm in an attempt to shut her up.

She didn't, and Jude ignored me now too, his brows drawn together, mouth in an angry tilt. "What happened?"

Sabrina lowered her voice. "She had an accident in the bathroom, and he refused to help her, claiming his weak stomach. That *he* would throw up if he needed to clean it up."

Jude's fingers curled into fists, and I ducked my chin, embarrassed.

"So she cleaned it and herself up on her own then crawled into bed. Imagine, she had no hair from chemo, her port still in, and was recovering from a life-changing surgery, but *he* couldn't handle it. Told her he wasn't strong enough. Can you believe that?"

I covered my heated face with my hand. I'd informed Jude about Tom. He'd known that my ex had left me at the worst possible time, but I hadn't gone into detail. Too humiliated. Too traumatized.

Jude shook his head, nostrils flaring, and I couldn't take it, that feeling of inadequacy. It had been years since Tom and I had broken up, when I'd thrown my engagement ring at him, but it still pained me to remember. To think I still might not be enough.

I began to turn away, but a warm hand wrapped around my wrist. Before I could protest, Jude had me enveloped in his arms, his mouth against my temple. "You didn't deserve it."

I nodded against his shoulder.

"He's a piece of shit, and you're amazing."

When I didn't respond, he took my head in his hands, his palms on my cheeks, forcing my eyes to his. "Honeybee, listen to me. You have nothing—*nothing*—to be ashamed of. You're one of the best people I know, and all those voices in your head? They're wrong. Everything he made you believe about yourself, it's bullshit. You're perfect. You were then, and you still are now. You hear me? You're perfect."

I sniffled, eyes stinging. Who'd have thought I'd be so emotional in the middle of a candy shop on a Sunday afternoon.

"He's not worth your tears." He kissed my forehead, only for Sabrina to clear her throat.

She held up her cell phone. "I'm gonna head outside and give Everett a call."

I supposed this was one way to get her to shut up. I leaned back into Jude's hug. "Thanks. For the candy and for what you said."

"It's my pleasure. All of it." He held me at arm's length, the glimmer in his amber eyes making me think he wasn't only referring to today, but I didn't have it in me to truly examine the innuendo and I stepped away from him.

"You're too generous."

"Not when it comes to you." He pressed his hand between my shoulder blades to escort me outside, where Sabrina played on her cell phone. He offered her a hug goodbye. "I'll let you know when the candy shipment's delivered." Then he hugged me again, saying, "I'll text you later."

His message finally arrived after I'd changed for bed.

> **JUDE**
>
> I hope your ex's dick gets gangrene and falls off.

> **JUDE**
>
> But in the interim, I would like to know his last name and address.

> Why?

> **JUDE**
>
> No reason.

> ??

JUDE

Me and the boys want to take a trip. Say hi
to him.

You're funny.

JUDE

I'm not kidding.

You gonna beat him up for me?

JUDE

I'd murder for you.

Be still my heart.

JUDE

Seriously. That guy needs to be dragged
through the street and strung up by his dick.

It was you who told me he wasn't worth it
today, wasn't it?

JUDE

Not worth your tears. But beating the shit out
of him would make me feel better.

I've moved on.

JUDE

You still think about it. You still cry. And that
makes me want to punch things.

You big teddy bear, you. Never change.

JUDE

You don't either, honeybee.

TWELVE
JUDE

I did not expect to be talking about sex on a Thursday afternoon at a coffee shop. But Melissa was exactly as forward in person as she was on the app. It wasn't like I was a prude. Rather, I didn't know how to talk to a virtual stranger about whether I minded being tied up.

I tipped my head to the side and scratched at my beard. "I've, uh, never really thought about it."

The corner of Melissa's glossy lips rose, along with her eyebrow like a cartoon villain with a devious idea. "You should think about it. You might love it."

I cleared my throat with a sip of my coffee, inconspicuously checking the time on my watch. We'd been here for half an hour. A new record for me being on a date, but I didn't know how much longer I could stand it.

The date or the woman.

So, as usual, I used my kids as an excuse. "Listen, Melissa, this has been great, but I gotta head out to pick up the kids."

I didn't. Sebastian was at one of his friend's houses, and they'd be going to baseball practice together later, while Amelia was at Gen and Dylan's house, spending the day with Scarlett.

Melissa pouted briefly, probably thinking it was cute or flirtatious.

It wasn't.

"Okay." She stood when I did. "It was so nice meeting you in person."

"Yeah." I accepted her hug with one arm.

"We should do it again."

I failed to come up with an excuse, so I merely grabbed my keys and headed out with a wave. "Mm-hmm. See ya later."

I hopped in my car and blew out a breath, accompanied by a full-body shake off.

And I immediately texted Brooke.

> Holy shit.

BROOKE

What? Your date?

BROOKE

Holy shit good?

> Holy shit bad.

> We talked about sex the whole time.

BROOKE

It could've been worse.

> How?

BROOKE

You could've been talking about murder and burying bodies the whole time.

> We've talked about murder and burying bodies before.

BROOKE

True.

BROOKE

What was so bad about the sex talk?

That's all we talked about. She basically sat down and was like "what's your favorite position?"

BROOKE

Quite an opener.

You're telling me.

BROOKE

What did you say?

I mostly let her rip. Smiled and nodded a lot.

She told me she's recently started getting into shibari.

I didn't know what that was so I asked.

It's when you get tied up.

She likes to do the tying.

BROOKE

Ok.

OK????

What do you mean ok?

I don't even know if she gets along with her family or if she had pets growing up but I know that she likes to tie people up.

BROOKE

I'm not sure what you want me to say here.

BROOKE

But isn't it better to know that up front? So you aren't surprised later?

> I guess.

> She also talked about masks.

BROOKE

Masks?

> Yeah. She has fantasies about people wearing masks.

> I didn't have the balls to ask her what kinds of masks. Was afraid to open that Pandora's box.

It took a minute for her to respond.

BROOKE

Want to smoke tonight?

> Yup.

Hours later, I stood next to Dylan at the chain link fence while Sebastian's baseball practice finished up.

"One more lap!" Dylan shouted with his hands cupped around his mouth then removed his hat to swipe his hand through his hair before placing it back on his head. "What's up with you? You seem all jittery."

"I had a date this afternoon."

He flicked his eyes toward me, his only reaction.

"It was...awkward."

He nodded, not requiring any more explanation.

"Thanks for taking Lulu today."

"Yeah. No problem." He glanced over his shoulder at his fiancée, who sat with Scarlett and Amelia in the stands. "Gen had a girls' day with them. They loved it." Then he clapped a few times, calling his team's attention. "Nice work! Collect all your equipment, and I'll see you at the game on Thursday!"

The boys scattered, but I kept my gaze on Sebastian as he

laughed with his friend. Baseball was doing wonders for his confidence, but I didn't like how it pulled him away from me.

As if Dylan knew the path my thoughts had gone down, he elbowed me. "Seb's doing great. His motivation's improved, his skill, his attitude... He's a good dude."

I nodded. "It's hard, you know? It's been only me and the kids for so long. It's hard to have them leave the nest."

"Are they leaving the nest, or are you?"

For a grumpy son of bitch, he could be quite perceptive.

"Look at you being all philosophical," I said as Sebastian reached us.

"I have my moments." Dylan held out his fist to my son for a bump. "Nice work today."

"Thanks."

I ruffled Seb's hair. "You have fun today?"

"Yep."

"I'm gonna drop you two off at Nana and Pop's to sleep over."

"Again?" he whined. "We were there the other day."

Dylan deliberately turned away as I explained, "Yeah, but I'm going out for a bit, and Nana said she's got everything for fancy grilled cheese."

Fancy grilled cheese because it had lots of different cheeses in it, and the kids loved to pull it apart with all the ooey-gooey strings.

Sebastian didn't care. He rolled his eyes, grumbling something about me going out a lot, and I chose to ignore him. Once he stomped off, Dylan pivoted back around to me, brows drawn together in question. I shrugged. "Gotta pick my battles, right?" He nodded and walked with me over to the stands, where Amelia threw herself at me. "Daddy!"

Gen greeted me with a smile, holding up a small pink backpack so Scarlett could gather up all her toys and put them inside. "Thanks for taking Amelia today."

"It was fun. Whenever you need to, drop her off."

I tickled Amelia's side. "Say g'bye. We gotta go."

She hugged Gen, Dylan, and Scarlett each, thanking her aunt and uncle. Even though we weren't related by blood, all of our children called each of us aunt and uncle. At this point, I believed the more family my kids had, the better.

I ushered Amelia away, and Sebastian caught up to us with his bag, ignoring me as we all settled in my car.

Amelia chatted the whole ride, bouncing one of her unicorns along the window and her car seat, annoying her brother, until he finally yelled at her to knock it off, which led to an argument I chose to ignore. I rolled down my window, letting the warm summer air drown out their fighting.

Arriving at my parents' house, I dropped them off with a few words to my mother. She told me to take my time with my "errands," though her over-the-top wink let me know she guessed I wasn't heading to Target.

"Have fun," she practically sang, following me to the door, pushing me to go.

Little did she know, I'd already been on my mildly terrifying date.

Fifteen minutes later, I pulled up to Brooke's farm as Gunner was on his way out. He'd been Brooke's right-hand man for a while. An ex-convict who'd applied for a part-time position after he'd been released from serving time on felony drug trafficking charges when Brooke had first opened Fraserbrooke Farm. She'd once told me how she felt compelled to hire him because she couldn't believe a white woman like herself could buy and use marijuana without repercussions, while a brown kid whose home circumstances forced him to be the moneymaker at seventeen years old would be thrown into jail for years, perpetuating the cycle. Hiring Gunner was her small way of trying to right the world.

"Hey, man." Gunner greeted me with a dap. "Haven't seen you in a while."

"Been busy."

He aimed his thumb over his shoulder, toward the farmhouse. "That why she's been in a bad mood lately?"

I blinked. "She's in a bad mood?"

"Spittin' fire all afternoon," he said with a shake of his head. "See what you can do about that, huh?"

"I doubt I can."

Gunner sucked air through his teeth. "Yeah. Right." He wiped his forehead with his T-shirt sleeve then offered me a head nod. "Later, Gray."

I headed to the farmhouse, contemplating Brooke's supposed bad mood. She hadn't seemed like anything was wrong during our text exchange.

Unless…

I stepped through the door, mentally chiding myself for the ridiculous notion that she'd been in a bad mood *because* of our text exchange. Like she was jealous or something.

But that was dumb.

There was no way she was jealous. We were doing this whole dating thing together. If she was in a bad mood, it certainly wasn't because of me and my date.

Inside, Brooke stood at the kitchen counter, compiling a sandwich, layering turkey, lettuce, and tomato, her lips pursed as if chewing on the inside of them. She did that when she was annoyed.

"Hi," I said, and she jumped, whirling on me with a crimped brow before her features softened when she realized it was me.

"Hey."

So, okay, maybe she was in a bad mood.

"Gunner said you were, uh…"

She eyed me. Fire in her brown eyes.

I changed tack. "Hard day?"

She slapped a piece of bread on the top of her sandwich

and lifted it to her mouth, biting into it. "Not particularly. Just hangry."

I accepted her answer and helped myself to making my own sandwich then put everything back in the fridge. After nabbing a root beer, I followed her outside to take a seat around the closed fire pit.

Once we both finished eating our dinner, I broached the subject again. "Wanna talk about it?"

"Talk about what?"

"The reason you have pinchy mouth."

"Pinchy mouth?" she repeated, obviously trying not to do the pinchy mouth.

"You say I get a wrinkle between my eyebrows." I tapped her lips. "Well, you get pinchy mouth."

She swatted at my hand, jerking her head back, but I curled my hand around her neck so she couldn't get away. She froze, eyes wide, pinchy mouth gone.

In its place were soft and welcoming lips, pink and parted. The taste of them was still seared in my memory, and I forced myself to let go of her, giving both of us space.

"What's got your panties in a twist?"

She grimaced. "Don't say the word panties."

"Why not?"

"It's in the same category as randy and horny."

I leaned my elbow on my chair. "This list is getting to be quite long. What other words are on it?"

"Moist."

"What's wrong with moist? How else am I supposed to describe my brownies?"

She tugged the elastic out of her hair, shaking out the long tresses. "It's fine in the baking sense, but not in the sex sense."

"Okay, no moist panties. Got it."

She met my gaze, her usual good mood back in place, her smile perfectly crooked, eyes crinkling in the corners. "Be right back."

She made her way to the house, and by the time I'd polished off my root beer, she returned with a small joint, already lit. She passed it to me and sat back down. "So, Melissa…"

"Scares the shit out of me," I conceded, holding the smoke in my lungs.

She inspected me for a few seconds, but I didn't know what she was looking for, if anything at all. She eventually rolled her head along the back of her chair and accepted the joint when I passed it to her. "What exactly do you want out of this? You're going on dates to find someone to have sex with, right?" Her tone bordered on waspish, and again, I ignored the voice in the back of my head hinting that it was because of *me*. "This girl is basically throwing herself at you, but you're not into it?"

I swallowed thickly. "I don't know. I guess I'm not into her."

We each had one more puff before she stubbed it out, and I didn't think I was high enough to answer her when she asked, "Are you afraid of having sex with her or all the kinky stuff she brought up?"

I rubbed at my beard. I hadn't been afraid of sex with Brooke, so I couldn't place the niggling feeling whenever I tried to imagine doing it with Melissa or anyone else. I didn't want to analyze it at the moment, so I said, "The kinks, I guess."

She waited for me to go on, folding her hand across her stomach, over her tank top that clung to her body. I let my attention coast down to her legs, tanned and nearly naked with the minuscule cotton shorts she wore. I didn't have a problem picturing myself touching her there, kissing her, making myself at home between her thighs.

I wasn't scared of that at all.

"Do you want to try it?" she asked, hauling my focus back

up to her face, and it took me a moment to wrap my mind around our conversation.

"Try what? The shibari? The masks?"

"Yeah. All of it."

"I don't know. Might be uncomfortable with someone I don't know," I said, speaking the thought I hadn't realized I'd buried under all my hesitation. "Have you ever tried that stuff?"

"Have I tried shibari? No. But I've been handcuffed before."

I extended my legs out in front of me, pinpricks of sensation running along them. I kept my eyes on Brooke's, not letting them linger anywhere else but her gaze. So I didn't picture her wrists handcuffed to a bed with another guy over her. Instead, I tortured myself by asking, "What about masks?"

That had her tipping her head to the side, her finger idly tracing shapes on the arm of her Adirondack chair. Her tongue slipped out, wetting her lips, leading to a suggestive smile.

"What?" I asked, sitting forward.

"I read romance books."

"Oh. Okay." This was a new tidbit of information, and I didn't know how it had never come up in conversation before.

"So, no, I've never tried, but it's in some of my books."

"What's that mean?"

"I read dark romance, and sometimes some of the guys will wear a mask and..." She trailed off, her eyes focusing on a point over my shoulder. "It might be fun to be chased by a bad guy...and be caught...and..." Her cheeks blazed red, and she cleared her throat before she met my gaze again. "You know?"

I shook my head, images bombarding my brain. "No, I don't know."

But yeah, I could picture it. Brooke running. Adrenaline pumping. Me catching her. Wrapping my arms around her waist. Lifting her off the ground. My lips on her neck. My cock hard against her back as she begged me.

I willed my blood to stop rushing, for my dick to get the message to settle down.

But Brooke clearly didn't need to send her body the same messages because she kept right on going. "It's kinda hot, thinking about it being rough."

It was the marijuana. That was it. The reason I asked, "Rough? Like how?"

She crossed her legs, and my eyes went right to the point between them, where her gray cotton shorts were trapped. "I guess a little hair-pulling. Maybe a little choking."

"Choking?" I snapped my eyes up to where she placed her hand at her throat.

"Yeah, but not hard, only a little pressure. And some dirty talk."

"Dirty talk?" I croaked. "Like what?"

She laughed. "God, Jude, don't you know anything?"

"No." I rubbed my hands over my face. "I had sex with exactly one person before you, and wild for us was me bending her over the kitchen counter."

Neither one of us touched that part about *before you*, and she shrugged. "Oh. Well, that can be hot too."

Except now I was imagining bending Brooke over a kitchen counter. I shook my head, but the picture didn't go anywhere. "So, what else? What else do I need to know?"

"You need a manual?" she asked, amusement in her voice.

I held her gaze. "Yeah. That would be good."

And then we were kissing.

THIRTEEN
BROOKE

How we'd ended up here again, I couldn't be sure. Some mix of lowered inhibitions and heightened desire. Though I didn't know which one outweighed the other.

Because when Jude kissed me, all of my senses amplified. No traces of slower body function to be found, only a pounding heart and tingling skin. He gripped my face like he was afraid I'd leave. Kissed me like he wouldn't have another chance.

I dug my fingertips into his shoulders, having somehow ended up on his lap, my legs on either side of his waist, and sighed into his mouth.

He seemed to like that and tunneled his fingers into my hair, gripping the strands by my scalp, holding tight, pulling slightly. Perfectly.

I moaned, and I swore I felt an appreciative rumble from his chest before he tugged on my hair again.

Because this man could take direction.

"You like that?" he rasped, not merely to turn me on, but to truly know if I liked it.

I kissed my affirmative against his lips, and one of his hands snaked over my collarbone to my throat, spanning the width, pressing gently, his thumb and index finger under my jaw, holding me. He slanted his head back, eyes boring into mine. "And this?"

I nodded, my ability to speak gone.

He kept that hand around my throat, using it to direct me to the angle he wanted, nipping and biting at my lips, keeping me close.

Me.

This was the second time we were doing this now. Him talking about another woman but ending up here, like this, with me. He wasn't scared. He didn't hesitate. He was wholly himself.

I loved and hated it.

That we had this amazing foundation, allowing us to discuss all the things we hid from everyone else and still find what we needed in each other. Yet, we were here because we wanted two different things.

Even as he wrapped one arm around my waist and the other under my butt, lifting me up when he stood from the chair to lay me on the ground, I had to remind myself that he didn't want what I wanted.

Marriage.

Family.

He was doing this for fun, for release, to forget about his anxiety for a while.

Not to say I didn't thoroughly enjoy being his playmate in this moment, but I had to remember this wasn't the same for him as it was for me. No matter that he skimmed the tip of his nose up my neck, inhaling deeply. Or how he wrapped his hands around my breasts reverently, brushing his thumbs across my nipples as his eyes shone with something that looked a lot like adoration.

We were simply two friends taking part in…sex lessons?

That idea had a giggle bubbling up my throat, and Jude canted his head back, eyebrows raised in question.

I shook my head, not wanting to give away everything I'd been thinking.

"You all right, honeybee?" he asked, and I curled my lips over my teeth.

Didn't he know? Didn't he realize what he was doing to me?

Evidently not.

He made quick work of my shorts and underwear, leaving me in only my bra and tank top, but even that felt too suffocating, so I shucked them off as well. Naked as the day I was born and on display for the world to see, I lay back on the ground. Fortunately, my land was out of the way, and the driveway alone was one hundred yards deep. No one would be able to spy how Jude's hungry eyes roved over me, how his fingers gripped my thighs, pushing them open. There was nothing and no one to witness how he licked his lips and splayed out on his stomach on the ground between my legs.

He wrapped his hands around my hips, his palms hot while the blades of grass cooled my back. "What do you like for dirty talk?"

"I don't know." I met his gaze over the length of my body, and I probably should have felt awkward that I was naked while he remained completely clothed, but I didn't.

There was nothing awkward about it.

"I've only read it in books. No one has ever done it with me," I said, and I swore his nostrils flared, but he ducked his head too quickly for me to really tell, and then his mouth was on me. He dragged his tongue up my slit, teasing and light, and I reflexively jerked my hips up at the first contact. He merely pushed me back into position, holding me down, and I didn't hate it.

Not one bit.

He dragged the flat of his tongue up me again, this time finding my clit, flicking it over and over, and I dug my fingers into his hair, loosening the bun on the top of his head.

"Tell me how it feels," he directed, his hot breath wafting over me, and I easily complied.

"Warm and soft."

He hummed against me then dragged his tongue up in long, languorous strokes.

"It feels like when I watch you lick your fork or spoon while you're eating dessert," I said, and I'd never before heard the sound he made.

He pressed his face more fully against me, his beard scraping along my innermost thighs, his jaw working up and down as he lapped at my clit.

"It feels like I've been missing out," I admitted, curving my back. He dipped his tongue inside me, but I tightened my grip on his hair, whining, "No, please, no."

He tipped his head up, eyes hooded, cheeks ruddy. "What?"

"Doesn't feel good. Need my—"

I didn't get to finish my statement because he fastened his mouth to the bud of my sex, sucking, and I hissed out a breath. "Yes, like that."

He didn't move, didn't slow down, didn't speed up. Stayed exactly like that, flicking and sucking at the most sensitive part of me. Since I suffered with dryness, it always took me a while to orgasm, and I couldn't without stimulating my clit, but I didn't need to explain that to him. He'd already guessed.

Nor did he try to slide his fingers into me without lube. I briefly thought about reminding him of the condoms and little blue bottle we'd bought. They were still in the office, but I didn't want him leaving me to find them.

"Don't stop," I panted, circling my hips, holding his head

to me. He made a noise, as if telling me he wouldn't stop, and let go of my legs to reach his hands up to my breasts, squeezing them.

I could feel the edge of an orgasm become clearer and squirmed under him, so much that he pinched my nipples, silently ordering me to stay still. But he might as well have strummed a chord on an overstrung bow for how I arched off the ground, crying out to the heavens.

"Oh god," I whimpered. "Please, please don't stop."

He doubled down, plucking at my nipples and licking at my swollen flesh until I couldn't take it anymore. My climax erupted. I squeezed my eyes shut, heat spiraling from my belly and spilling out to my arms and legs as I bucked and shook. I went so hot all over, even the sticky July air chilled my sweat-dampened skin.

Jude levered over me, placing one hand on the ground next to me while he skimmed the other up and down my side. "Okay, honeybee?"

I nodded, noticing how his hair flopped to the side, a mess from my fingers. I gave in to a drunken giggle and wiped at his mouth and beard before tugging the elastic out of his hair so it curtained either side of his face.

"I'm okay," I told him, wrapping my hands around his neck, urging him toward me to kiss his lips. I wanted to make a joke, bring us back to the place of banter and ribbing each other, but I couldn't. Couldn't bear to let go of this feeling.

He stared at me, perhaps to make sure I was indeed okay, or in search of something else, an answer to what the hell we were doing.

I didn't dare ask, fearful of putting a name to the way my chest tightened and my heart thudded a little too fast behind my rib cage. Scared he didn't feel any of that too.

Afraid to cross the Rubicon and lose my friend. My best friend.

"Are *you* okay?" I asked, and he nodded before reaching

for my bra and shirt. He helped me sit up then retrieved my underwear and shorts.

Only once I dressed and we were both standing up did he answer. "Yeah. I'm okay."

"Are you sure?" I asked. "Because of…" *Because of what happened last time,* I didn't finish. *Because of how you cried. Because of how you miss your wife.*

He rubbed at his tattoo. The one he'd gotten for Mira the same night I'd had the monarch butterfly inked on my ankle, a reminder that I'd survived. I'd done something really fucking hard, and I'd come out the other end.

Jude's tattoo was a physical reminder of his beloved.

And I knew I could never have anything more than this with him.

Which was why it hurt so bad when he said, "There's no one else I'd do this with besides you."

I bit the inside of my cheek and rolled my head to the side, focusing on the horizon so he couldn't see how his words affected me. I cleared my throat, forcing a smile on my face and in my voice as I turned back to him. "Yeah. I'm a real saint. Helping you learn while I get some orgasms." I met his eyes. "Tough job but somebody's got to do it."

He licked his lips and blinked a few times, craning his neck, peering around. The sky had turned purple, the sun nearly gone to bed while we'd been fooling around on the ground. "I didn't mean it like—"

I stopped him with my hand up. "I know. I'm kidding." I closed the distance between us, trying on a bit of honesty. "Too bad you're only looking for sex. Because you're the whole package." I let out a derisive laugh. "You've set impossible standards for anyone I date."

He placed his hands on my hips, his gravelly voice like crystalized sugar. "Good. Make them all jump through hoops. They should want to if they think they deserve you."

I wrapped my arms around his shoulders. "Careful. You're gonna make this hard for me."

He grunted softly and tucked his face against my neck, leaving a quick kiss there before letting go. "I should go."

"See you at the market?"

"Yup." He waved and headed to his car.

And I plopped back on a chair and lit up.

FOURTEEN
JUDE

It had been days since I'd last seen Brooke at the farmers market, where we chatted as if everything was *fine*. As if I hadn't learned she liked an occasional hair-pull or hand around her throat. As if I hadn't stripped her naked and feasted on her like she was my last meal.

This was *Brooke*.

The woman I'd known for years.

Who had wiped my literal tears. Who'd helped me hold on to my sanity when I thought I'd lose it. Who'd kept me steady on days I felt like I'd be swept away. She had held my hand and walked with me through the highs and lows of the last few years. Didn't talk me off the ledge but sat with me on it.

Brooke.

My friend.

My very good friend.

My *best* friend.

More than Dylan, Liam, and Nate, I could be completely open and honest with her.

And yet I hadn't told her this secret. That I hadn't been able to stop thinking about her, about what we did.

How I enjoyed—no, more than enjoyed—I *loved* going down on her. I loved learning what she liked, what she needed to orgasm. I loved being the one to give it to her.

But I tried not to think about what it meant that I wanted more. That I had to force myself to leave because I'd doubted my own restraint, and I physically wouldn't have been able to sit there with the taste of her pussy on my lips and in my beard without wanting to make her come again.

I loved Mira. I would continue to love her. But the anxiety I'd always felt about living my life without her didn't exist when I was with Brooke, and I assumed that was what Youmna meant when she said I needed to find someone.

I needed someone who would understand my past and the journey I still charted. I didn't know if I would ever stop grieving Mira and the life we didn't get to live, but I no longer feared it.

I could map out a new path. At least, that was what my therapist told me. I didn't have to stop loving Mira to love someone else. Like my children. I didn't give up any piece of my heart for Sebastian when Amelia was born. Rather, my heart grew to accommodate both.

I could do that.

I could have love again.

If I wanted.

With my left arm behind my head, I scrolled through the pictures Youmna had texted me. She and George had taken the kids for their annual trip to visit family in Allentown, a week with relatives, time for my kids to play with cousins and practice their Arabic, hear stories of family in Syria, and teach them all the things Mira would have but that I couldn't possibly.

As much as I needed time away from the children some-times, I missed them when they weren't here, especially when they were gone for so long. I worried about Amelia and if she was being patient and sharing. I fretted about Sebastian and if he was sleeping. Most nights, he ended up in my bed or in his sister's, still afraid to sleep on his own after all these years, and he didn't do well sleeping in places he wasn't used to.

As if she knew, Brooke texted.

BROOKE
How you doing? How are the kids?

I'm good. They're having a great time.

BROOKE
Great. Nobody is homesick?

If they were, Youmna wouldn't tell me.

BROOKE
What about you? You homesick for them?

A little.

BROOKE
You need a distraction?

Is this a trick question?

BROOKE
No, why?

I thought it was an invitation to something.

BROOKE
Connect the dots for me here, buddy.

Like

sex

BROOKE
OOOOOOOOOO

BROOKE
No.

BROOKE

HAHA

Cool.

Make me feel like a pervert.

BROOKE

You want a tit pic? Would that make you feel better?

Don't be weird.

BROOKE

Me?! You're the one who brought it up.

BROOKE

But here. Here's a distraction.

I clicked on the link she sent me to a book with a grayscale cover of a man in face paint or a mask of some sort.

BROOKE

I want to hear what you think about it.

I didn't even read the summary, instead hit that yellow purchase button immediately and read it on my phone.

Despite the tiny words, which I had to enlarge to quadruple their size on my phone screen and the burning of my eyes from staying up late, I finished that bad boy motherfucking book in two days.

I can't believe you read books like this.

BROOKE

You didn't like it?

I don't know how I feel about it.

Emotionally or mentally.

Physically, I got a tingle.

BROOKE

HAHA

BROOKE

Yeah?

A little uncomfortable.

BROOKE

Come over later.

BROOKE

Bring a mask.

Well, shit.

I pulled up to the farm as the sun started to set, and when I didn't spot Brooke in the immediate fields, I headed into the farmhouse. The screen door slammed behind me, and I needed to fix that. Or, I mean, find someone else to fix it. No one in my family was particularly handy, and my father wasn't the type to take me into the garage to show me how to patch a tire or build a birdhouse.

"In here," I heard Brooke call out from her office in the living room, and I walked through the kitchen to find her on her laptop.

I leaned against the doorjamb, sticking my hands in my pockets. "Hey."

She smiled up at me from her place on the couch. The couch where we'd had sex. "How was your day?"

"Good. All your sister's candy came in. You want me to hold on to it or…?"

She picked up her cell phone, typing on it, presumably to ask Sabrina. "She said she'll come pick it up tomorrow."

"Okay." I ran my hand over my beard, catching Brooke's attention. She narrowed her brows. "You got a trim."

"Yeah." I scratched at the shorter bristles on my jaw. "Figured it was about time."

She shut her computer and stood, still studying me with her probing gaze. "Your hair too."

I'd had a few inches cut off this afternoon. "My mother and Youmna will be happy."

Brooke laughed and combed her fingers through the strands, skimmed her palms over my beard as if she liked it.

"What do you think?"

"You're always handsome, but I can see more of your face now, which is nice." She took the elastic band I'd habitually worn around my wrist and used it to tie her own hair back.

"You don't have enough hair ties of your own?"

"It's like stealing a boyfriend's sweatshirt. Sure you can use your own, but his is always better."

I didn't know why it made me so inordinately happy that my black elastic was wrapped around her ponytail, but I crossed my arms over my chest, as if I could cover up how my heart pounded.

"So, the book," she started with her crooked smile. "You liked it, huh?"

I let my gaze wander over her face and then down to her T-shirt and stained jeans. She must've been working in the dirt today. She always wore jeans when she tended the fields.

"Yeah. I bought book two." I skipped over how I'd texted Dylan and Liam about it. A few months ago, they had both admitted to occasionally reading romances with Evie and Kennedy, and I hadn't thought I'd ever want to do that. Yet here I was. A full-fledged dark romance reader.

"I knew down deep you were a sex fiend," she said, grinning. "Did you bring a mask?"

I pulled a light blue medical mask from my back pocket, holding it up between us, and she threw back her head, cackling in delight.

She smacked my shoulder. "You know that's not what I meant."

"I know." I tossed it on the table in the corner then yanked out the mask I'd found in the big tub of old Halloween costumes. One year, Mira and I had dressed as movie serial killers, her as Patrick Bateman, me as Ghostface.

"This what you wanted?" I showed Brooke the well-known mask from *Scream*, and she gasped, clasping her hands in front of her.

She nodded silently, teeth sawing into her bottom lip, her cheeks pink. There must have been some primal animal instinct still inside me because I swore I could smell her pheromones change. Feel her anticipation and excitement. Made my own skyrocket.

"I'll give you a head start." I slipped the mask on over my head, but she stayed in place in front of me, gaping wide-eyed. "Better run, honeybee. Might not like it when I catch you."

She backed away, her chest rising and falling with rapid breaths.

I stepped toward her. "Ten."

She shrieked in laughter.

"Nine."

"Oh my god!" She ducked around me as she ran out of the room, her footfalls heavy through the house.

"Eight," I shouted, and the screen door slammed.

Underneath the mask, I grinned. I liked this game.

After counting down, I made my way outside, my palms sweaty and tingling. I didn't run, but my heart raced. I wore jeans and boots, and I clomped along the dirt path to the field, pausing to listen to movement, waiting for her laugh. It would give her away anywhere.

"I'm coming for you, honeybee," I hollered, and I heard it, her giggle from behind the corn stalks.

Careful not to knock any down, I ducked between rows,

following the rustling. Once I stepped out of the corn, I started a jog, weaving around lettuce, potatoes, carrots, and parsnips. She was always trying to get me to eat parsnips, but I didn't even know what the hell they were.

Brooke glanced over her shoulder, running between the trellises with vines of tomatoes, cucumbers, and peppers, her smile bright in the dying sunshine, her ponytail flying all over the place.

"You think you can hide from me?" I asked as she darted toward the eggplants.

"No, but I can outrun you!" She hit a hard right and dodged my hand when I leaped for her, jumping over the squash. She squealed, narrowly avoiding me, and I pivoted, determined to catch her, my adrenaline pumping relentlessly. Like all my blood.

I didn't think it would be so hot. Not metaphorically, at least. Yet, here I was, my cock already hard, the idea of finally catching her making every step difficult. This was possibly the hottest thing I'd ever done with a woman in my life. Definitely the kinkiest.

Chasing her.

Chasing Brooke.

"Pretty little bee," I droned, slipping more and more into character with every stride, and Brooke stopped, spinning on me, beautifully flushed.

Her smile faded the tiniest bit. "That's actually really scary."

I cocked my head to the side, and the whites of her eyes expanded. Her reaction sent goose bumps up my arms, so down for this cat-and-mouse game.

"I'm going to catch you," I told her low and slow.

"And then what happens?"

For every step I took toward her, she took one back. "I'm going to take that elastic band out so I can wrap your hair around my hand."

She tripped, bringing us even closer together, almost at arm's length. "And then what?"

"I'll put you on your knees."

She inhaled sharply. She *liked* that idea.

"I'll stuff my cock into your pretty little mouth."

She licked her lips, and I gritted my teeth to keep from reaching for her and tearing off this mask to kiss her.

"Holy shit," she murmured, stunned.

If I didn't need to follow through with this fantasy, maybe I'd laugh. But she wanted this. Maybe even more than I did.

And fuck, did I *want* it.

She tried to run away again, but I shot my arm out, fisting the hem of her T-shirt, towing her to me.

"My honeybee," I grated, my skin on fire, blood in my ears, "always so busy. Let's see how you do when you can't go anywhere."

I laced my fingers with hers and pulled her over to the house, shoving her back against it. She didn't fight me, went quite willingly, in fact, staring up at me from where I pushed her to kneel on the ground.

As promised, I tugged the band out of her hair and wrapped the strands around my fist, forcing her head back as I unbuckled my belt and lowered my zipper with my other hand. Her breath was hot and heavy on me as I pushed my underwear down to grasp the base of my shaft, but she didn't budge, waiting for the next move in our game.

Using my grip on her hair, I urged her head forward at the same time I thrust my hips, doing exactly as I said I would, stuffing her pretty little mouth full. She wrapped her hands around the backs of my thighs, and I nodded, unable to verbalize what this did to me, seeing her like this, out of breath and on her knees in the dirt, sucking me off like her life depended on it.

She was sloppy, a bit overzealous, and probably a lot out of practice. But so was I, and the way she accidentally dragged her teeth over the head nearly had me doubling over with a mixture of pleasure and pain. Realizing what she'd done, she popped off me, but I shoved it right back in her mouth. "Don't stop until I tell you."

And she didn't. Not when she laved me with her tongue from root to tip, following with her hand, jacking me with her fist, driving me wild with her wet suction at the tip.

My muscles trembled with tension, trying to lock it down. But my orgasm barreled toward me like a runaway train, every swipe of her tongue sending me closer to careening off the rails. I locked my jaw, tightened my hold in her hair, and dropped my head back to my shoulders, hissing when her fingers wandered past my balls, tight and heavy with the need to come, and prodded at the sensitive ridge.

That was all it took.

I exploded without warning and slapped my hand on the worn siding of the farmhouse, grunting and cursing as I came inside Brooke's mouth. She didn't move, save for her throat, swallowing down every spurt of my orgasm on her tongue.

Exhaling a ragged breath, I ripped off the mask and let go of her hair, swiping my forearm over my forehead. "Shit, I'm so sorry."

Still on the ground, she blinked a few times, tenderly releasing my swiftly deflating cock from between her lips, still stroking it, teasing and light. "It's okay."

"I should've—"

"Jude. It's okay. I'm okay. I'm happy you came in my mouth." She let go of me, and I helped her up with my fingers curled around her elbows.

"You are?"

Even though she was streaked with dirt and damp with sweat, I didn't think she'd ever looked prettier. "Yeah, I'm happy," she said, smiling impishly. "I loved it. I think you loved it too."

"I did."

"That's all that matters."

I tucked myself back into my pants and hugged her close to me, laughing into her hair. "I can't believe we did that."

"Me either." Her lips brushed against my ear. "It's kinda weird, isn't it?"

I wrenched back from her. Was this the part where she told me we couldn't be friends anymore?

"Don't look at me like that." She traced her thumb along my forehead, my arrow wrinkle. "It's weird that it's not weird, right?"

I kept waiting for the anguish or grief to hit, and it never did. Maybe because what Brooke and I were doing was so outside of anything else I'd ever experienced, I couldn't compare it. The way I felt about her was unlike anyone else in my life. So, yes, it was weird. Because nothing about it felt weird or wrong. It felt exactly like what I needed.

"We've been through it all together," I said. "Why should this be any different?"

"It shouldn't. It won't." She stepped out of my arms and held her palm in the air for a high five.

I smacked my hand against hers, lacing our fingers together. "Having a Shark Week party next weekend. You should come."

"Shark Week party? Sounds awesome. What should I bring?"

"Yourself. Just bring yourself."

And truly, I could never lose this woman. It had been hard enough to mourn Mira, but if anything ever happened to break up this friendship, I'd lose the last bit of my sanity. Not to mention my heart.

FIFTEEN
JUDE

'd rigged up a television on the patio to play Shark Week shows, laid out a Slip 'N Slide across the yard, and filled up a plastic kiddie pool. I'd also bought some blue streamers and random shark decorations to stick on the back door. Sebastian used to be really into sharks when he was little, and the tradition had started as ordering pizza and a marathon of shark videos. Two years ago, we'd had a little picnic. Last year, a party. This year, a bit bigger. Why not?

Sebastian had invited a couple of friends over, and the four of them took turns throwing themselves down the slide, hopefully avoiding breaking anything. Amelia hung out in the kiddie pool with Scarlett and Tucker, playing with plastic fish.

I stationed myself at the grill, sipping an ice-cold beer, courtesy of Nate.

"It's hot as shit," he said, swiping the hem of his tank top with a cartoon shark on it over his forehead.

Dylan nodded in agreement, turning his hat backward as he repositioned his feet, propping one hand on his hip, allowing Evie to slip her arm through his. "What'd I tell you about that?"

"What?" he asked, bending his head to her, a ghost of a smile on his face, and I swore I'd never seen that guy smile more than since he'd started going out with her.

She tipped her head flirtatiously. "Don't play all innocent. You know."

Dylan playfully smacked her butt, and Nate winced, face strained like he wanted to say something about one of his best friends and his sister but didn't.

Making real progress.

"Rawr!"

We all whirled around at the screech. Finn sprinted into the yard with Kennedy jogging after him, a big bag hanging off her shoulder. "Be careful! You'll slip and—"

"Ah!"

We snickered as Kennedy picked up Finn, brushing him off, while Liam shook his head, bringing up the rear, a Tupperware of what appeared to be cupcakes in his hands. He set it on the table then crossed the yard to his family. Kennedy wrestled with Finn, swiping sunscreen over him as he kicked and shrieked to get down.

"Tucka! Tucka! Help!"

Tucker came to his rescue, water gun in hand, squirting at Kennedy. She set Finn down to run behind Liam, forcing him to take on the water. He lunged at both boys, eliciting screams of delight as they scampered off.

"How's everybody doing?" I asked when the pair approached, Liam's arm around Kennedy as she wiped water from his face and neck.

"Not bad." Liam accepted a beer from Nate.

Evie greeted Kennedy with a hug. "Do you want a margarita?"

"Yes. Definitely," Kennedy answered with a clap, the two women headed inside to my kitchen, and all at once, the four of us men started talking.

"Finn got tall."

"You and Kennedy seem to be doing good."

"How was the kids' trip with your in-laws?"

"What do you think girls talk about? Do you think they're in there, drinking margaritas and gossiping about us?"

Liam nodded at Dylan. "Yeah, it's like he grew three inches overnight. He's eating everything."

Then Liam looked at me, a goofy grin slashed across his face. "Kennedy and I are doing well. Really well."

In response to his question, I told him, "The kids had fun. Seb's been in a good mood since they came back home."

And the three of us turned to Nate. He answered his own question after glancing to the girls now sitting at my kitchen table with margaritas, laughing over something. "They're definitely talking about us."

We all nodded.

Dylan elbowed Nate. "Why don't you go in and join them? You love to stir up shit."

Nate accepted the words like a compliment and gestured to Liam with his beer. "Worked out well for O'Neil. And you, actually."

Nate had sort of set up Kennedy to be Liam's nanny, and if it weren't for Genevieve working at Nate's bar, Dylan never would have met her. Nate was really their fairy godfather.

Dylan ignored Nate's "You're welcome" for a sip of his beer, which only gave my old friend room to stir up shit with me.

"What's with the haircut?"

"It was time," I said and pointed to a platter, which he handed me.

"You working out too?"

I removed the burgers and hot dogs from the grill, pivoting to find all three of them studying me. I brushed past them. "I might've started using my old rowing machine."

Dylan hummed quietly, while Liam patted my back. "If it makes you feel good, go for it."

Nate's eyes twinkled with a knowing spark. "Did you get laid?"

I remained pointedly silent.

"Dude!"

"Shut up," I murmured, placing the platter down on the table and whistled for the kids to come eat.

"No wonder you're carrying yourself differently," he said in a hushed voice. "I told you, sex would help ease your stress."

The kids lined up with minimal jostling as they grabbed their food. Tucker attempted to steal three of Kennedy's cupcakes before Dylan intercepted him. The girls returned to the patio with drinks in hand and smiles on their faces, sitting at a table under the umbrella, while the kids spread out on towels and blankets on the grass.

The last thing on anyone's mind appeared to be sharks.

Especially when Brooke showed up at the gate, wearing that long, loose navy dress she'd tried on for me weeks ago. The one with tiny straps and buttons all down the front. The same one she'd said she could either wear a strapless bra with or none at all.

Goddamn it.

Amelia ran straight over to her, hopping around her legs as Brooke steadied the tray in her hands. "Oh, careful, sweetie. Don't want to drop these."

"What are they?" Amelia asked, walking backward.

"Shark bite shots. Special ones for the adults, and blue raspberry for the kids. See?"

Amelia squealed excitedly when Brooke showed them to her, the little cups filled with blue and red Jell-O, topped with gummy sharks and Swedish Fish.

"Daddy! Look!"

"I see." I accepted the tray from Brooke and placed my hand on her back, ushering her to the table in the shade. "I think you know everyone already."

"Yeah." Brooke waved at the group. "Hi."

Evie and Kennedy immediately pulled her into conversation, and I pivoted to my friends, gawking at me.

"What?"

Silence.

"*What?*"

Nate dipped his chin, shooting me a reproachful glare. "Did you *forget* to tell us you were fucking your farmer friend?"

I frantically waved my hands. "Say it louder. I don't think Sebastian heard you."

Dylan took the opportunity to slug Nate in the arm.

"I don't want anyone to know." I explained in a near whisper, and they leaned in, creating our cone of silence. "It's… not… It just happened."

"What do you mean, it just happened?" Liam asked, and I rolled my eyes.

"You, of all people, need a biology lesson?"

"No, but sex doesn't just happen. It takes a little bit of forethought."

"Yeah." Dylan huffed out a gruff laugh. "Since when are you so spontaneous?"

I pulled at my T-shirt, suddenly uncomfortable. "Since, I don't know… Since we got high and had sex."

Nate crossed his arms. "When? Where?"

"It started a few weeks ago."

"It started a few weeks ago!" he whisper-shouted. "And you didn't tell us?"

"It's none of your business."

"You're my business," Nate declared, index finger angrily aimed at the ground like he was claiming me as his land. "You're my best friend." Then he waved that finger across Dylan, Liam, and me. "You motherfuckers are all my business. You hurt, I hurt. You're happy, I'm happy."

Dylan actually nodded and tossed his arm around Nate. "That's really sweet, man."

"Yeah," Nate went on, still miffed, "and it doesn't feel so nice when something really great happens to you, and you keep us out of the loop."

"Nothing happened," I said, hands up. "There was nothing to tell."

Liam eyed me. "That really true?"

"You're cutting your hair and losing weight and wearing your good shorts for no reason?" Nate added, and I spared my light-blue dress shorts a glance. I didn't consciously do any of those things because of Brooke, but…

"It's not a big deal," I said, and my friends stared blandly at me, waiting for an explanation about my obvious lie. I sighed. "We were hanging out the night of my birthday, and we decided we were each going to start dating. We set up profiles together and sort of agreed to help each other."

"With sex?" Dylan guessed.

I scrubbed my fingers through my hair, wicking away the sweat at my temples. "She went on a date with a shit guy, and I was freaking out about this girl I was talking to. We got high, and one thing led to another and…"

"So it was only one time?" Liam asked around a sip of beer.

I shook my head.

"I can't believe you didn't tell us." Nate backhanded my bicep. "So, what? You're dating now?"

I shook my head again.

"Just fucking," Nate supplied.

"It's…" I trailed off, not knowing how to defend myself. If I even could. Brooke and I were not just fucking. We were not *just* anything. And the fact that I hadn't realized it—until this exact moment—made me ill.

We'd agreed to this stupid dating pact because she wanted to find her happily ever after, but by constantly asking for her attention, I had hindered her journey. I couldn't do that to her.

She was my friend.

My best friend.

She deserved the world.

"She wants to get married," I told my friends, and they filled in the rest.

"What are you gonna do?" Dylan asked, fist by his mouth, gaze narrowed on me. He'd been in my position. He had only wanted a fling too and found Genevieve.

But I didn't intend to find anybody, and I knew what I had to do. I slipped my cell phone out of my pocket, tapping on the app.

"What?" Nate peered over my shoulder. "What are you doing?"

"Finding a date."

"Didn't you…" Liam glanced over to the table with the girls then back to me. "Don't you like Brooke?"

I nodded. That was the exact problem. I liked her and couldn't continue to steal all of her time and energy. We needed a reset. Get back to our original goals.

Nate motioned to my cell phone as I scrolled. "You sure about this?"

"Emma," I said, clicking on the profile of a woman I'd matched with, "is a Libra who loves good conversation and Taylor Swift." I turned my screen to show the guys. "She's cute."

They didn't agree but didn't disagree either. All of them stared at me with various dubious expressions.

I typed out a quick message to her, not even thinking about how it sounded or second-guessing tone. **Hey. How's your day going?**

By the time Emma responded, the boys and I had finished our burgers and moved on to a discussion of who'd win in a fight: shark versus orca.

Hi! It's going great, she messaged. **I took my dog to the park this morning, and I'm about to grill up some dinner.**

You grill?

Yeah. I love to grill. My dad was big into BBQ, and I love some good smoked meats.

I sniffed a laugh. **I like a girl who knows her meats.**

LOL. That's me. What are you up to today?

"What's she saying?" Nate asked, leaning over for a peek at my phone.

I shrugged. "She seems cool."

I'm having a Shark Week party. I snapped pictures of the decorations and the Slip 'N Slide, sending them to her.

THAT'S BRILLIANT, she sent with a ton of laughing-face emojis.

Thank you. *Tips hat* My kids love it.

That's adorable. You're adorable, she messaged, and I grinned.

I didn't know if it was my newfound confidence or desperation, but I took a leap. **I know this is a little fast, but would you want to grab dinner tomorrow? Maybe find some good barbecue?**

You know what? It is a little fast, but there's something about you. So, sure. Let's get dinner.

I interrupted my friends in the middle of an argument over whether an octopus could kill a shark. "She said yes."

"Who?" Nate lurched back. "This new chick?"

"Emma. Yeah. We're going to—"

"What's going on over here?" Brooke popped up out of nowhere, looking like sunshine and smelling of lavender.

I didn't answer, my focus momentarily caught on the thin material of the dress, trying my best not to acknowledge her nipples. Since she, for sure, had gone braless today.

Goddamn it.

Nate, ever the shit-stirrer, answered for me. "Jude's making a date."

If I didn't know her so well, I wouldn't have seen it, how her face fell for half a second before she blinked and brightened. "Oh? That's great."

I slid my phone into my pocket like a traitor waiting for execution.

Nate, Liam, and Dylan studied Brooke, most likely waiting for a reaction. But she would never betray herself *or me* like that.

She cleared her throat and held up the tray of shots she'd made for the party. "I already handed out some to the kids. The sharks are on top of the plain Jell-O. The Swedish Fish have the alcohol in them."

I took one, which set off a chain for the guys to also snag one each for themselves. "Thanks for bringing these."

She smiled impassively down at the small cups. "So, when's your date?"

"Tomorrow night."

"Do you have a babysitter?"

"I haven't made arrangements yet."

She squinted up toward the sky and then over to me, her throat bobbing on a swallow. "I can stay with the kids."

I slanted my head back. "Really?"

"Yeah. Of course." She nodded, and out of the corner of my eye, I noticed Dylan shake his head, while Liam downed his beer. Nate blew out a noisy breath. She smiled a smile that wasn't fooling anybody. "What are friends for?"

But I had to do this. Rip the Band-Aid off. She needed her happily ever after, and I needed…

"Let's do these shots," I said, holding up my cup. The boys all saluted with theirs, and we sucked back the Jell-O, almost all of us coughing.

"Jesus," Nate wheezed. "How much alcohol did you put in here?"

"Too much?" She bit back a laugh. "I eyeballed it."

"By pouring the whole bottle in?" Dylan asked, smacking his lips.

Liam shrugged and snatched another one. "I like 'em." Then he tossed over his shoulder, "Angel, you're driving home tonight."

Kennedy waved in acknowledgment. "Got it."

Since I didn't have to drive anywhere, I reached for a second shot. Might as well take down the whole tray. I'd already stolen the light from Brooke's eyes today; I wasn't about to let anything she brought to the party go unfinished.

Who needed a liver anyway?

SIXTEEN
BROOKE

I knocked on Jude's front door at quarter to six, refusing to let myself fall into a pit of despair and jealousy. Yesterday, when he'd told me he'd arranged a date for tonight, it felt like my stomach plummeted out of my body.

Once again, he was headed out on a date. Charming and funny and kind Jude found yet another willing woman, while I couldn't even find a guy who was interested in me past a few conversations. Not that I'd been trying very hard. Not since my disaster of a date weeks ago and what happened after with Jude on the couch of my farmhouse.

So, yeah, I was a jealous shrew.

Jealous that he matched up a storm of women, while I had not had the same luck.

Not to mention, I was jealous of whoever this woman was, who so easily made Jude forget about what happened between us. Not once or twice, but three times!

Sex was a big deal for me, and I knew Jude planned on sowing his wild oats or whatever, but it had never occurred to me to go back to the app to find a match. That *he* would go back to the app.

So maybe, for a minute or two, I'd become disoriented by my delusion, believing what had happened between us meant something more for him too, but…

I slapped on a smile and volunteered myself to babysit. Because I was a mature adult and Jude's friend. And I could be happy for him.

"I get it! I get it!" Amelia shouted a moment before she swung the door wide open. "Hi!"

"Hey, girlfriend." I rubbed her back when she threw herself around my leg, hugging me tight, along with Small Unicorn. "Daddy said you're gonna stay with us tonight!"

"I am. You happy?"

She nodded, practically vibrating.

"Me too."

"Will you play Go Fish?"

I bent down to her level, telling her seriously, "I would love to play Go Fish with you."

"Yes!" She took off, sliding on the wood floor with her socks on. "I'mma get them!"

I closed the door behind me, poking my head around the wall to the dining room, finding it cluttered with backpacks, toys, papers, and shoes. Walking into the kitchen, I spotted Sebastian over the pass-through, lounged out on the couch in the living room as Amelia tossed pillows around, on the hunt for her Go Fish cards.

"Hey, Seb."

He briefly turned to me and waved before going back to his handheld gaming system.

"Found it!" Amelia raced toward me, smacking into my legs. "See? See? It's-it's-it's fish. All different fish! What's your favorite fish?"

"Hm. I don't know. No one has ever asked me before."

"Swordfish? Starfish? Seahorse?" she guessed rapid-fire.

"Yeah, maybe seahorse. What's—"

"Hey."

I spun around as Jude entered the kitchen, tugging at the collar of his short-sleeved black button-down. With his hair slicked back, his beard trimmed, and his sun-kissed tan, he looked… Well, he looked hot.

He held his arms out for my inspection and, as if to rub it in, asked, "What do you think?"

I deliberately dragged my gaze over his body. From the two buttons open at the top of his shirt, to the black shorts that fit his thighs perfectly, down to the dark-gray canvas shoes, and then back up. I gave him a thumbs-up.

The corners of his eyes crinkled as he squinted, like he didn't believe me.

I brushed my hand across the front of his shirt. "Fits you really well."

"Thank you." He tugged at his collar again then bent to pick up Amelia. He kissed her temple. "Be good for Brooke, okay?" He kept her in his arms, and the way he held her would've melted my ovaries if I'd had any. Crossing to the living room, he laid a hand on Seb's head. "I don't want you on this all night. Only a few more minutes, okay?"

He frowned. "Where're you going?"

"A meeting," Jude said without missing a beat.

"A meeting?" Obviously unconvinced, Seb tossed his game on the couch. "For work?"

I noticed Jude's shoulders tense and knew he wouldn't want to continue to lie to his son, so I butted in. "Hey, I was thinking about ordering pizza for dinner. That all right?"

Jude and his kids looked over at me. Seb and Amelia both agreed, while Jude reached into his pocket for his wallet as he headed back my way. He placed a credit card on the counter in front of me then set Amelia down too. "Get whatever you want," he told me then smiled down at Amelia. "But no soda past six o'clock for you."

She widened her eyes in my direction as she flipped Small Unicorn in the air, kicking her feet. "Sugar makes me crazy."

I popped my hand on my hip, brows raised in Jude's direction. "Wonder where she gets the sugar demand from?"

He glanced over both of his shoulders, searching for the culprit, before grinning back at me. "I shouldn't be too late."

I followed him to the door. "Any last-minute instructions?"

"Besides the sugar for her, no. He might give you a hard time about putting his Switch away, but other than that, give me a ring if you need anything."

"I won't."

He stepped out onto the stoop, holding the door open between us. "I appreciate you coming over."

I waved him off. "Have fun."

He nodded but didn't move. Merely stood there, staring at me.

"What?"

"You got sunburned a little bit." He touched the bridge of my nose. "Right here."

"You have no shade in your backyard," I said defensively since I *always* wore SPF. Didn't want to trade one type of cancer for another.

"I have an umbrella."

"*An* umbrella," I repeated. "Could use a gazebo or something out there."

He nodded, his eyes far off, considering. "Next house, I'll get you a gazebo."

I huffed. Who would he be with when he got this next house? Who would *I* be with?

"All right. Get going." I shoved him away. "Have fun."

"See you in a few hours."

I waited until he was seated in his car to head back inside his house, greeted by Amelia splayed out in front of the door, cards divided into two piles. "I counted your cards. We each have six. See? See? One, two, three, four, five, six," she tallied, showing me her Go Fish cards. "I go first. Do you have a crab?"

"Hold on." I gathered up the cards. "How 'bout we move this party to a table?"

She followed me to the dining room table, where I cleared off space for us to play. "Do you have a crab?"

"No."

"You hafta say 'No. Go fish!'"

I stifled a laugh at her serious reprimand. "No. Go fish."

After inadvertently showing me all of her cards as she picked a new one, I tried a card I knew she didn't have, earning a giggle. "No! Go Fish!"

I let her beat me quite soundly and stood to pop my head into the living room. "Seb, you want to come play Go Fish with us?"

He shook his head, eyes down on his controller.

"Okay. Well, how about in another fifteen minutes, we order pizza?"

"Yeah. Whatever."

Amelia and I finished another two games while she told me about something funny Scarlett, Dylan's daughter, had told her and how she wanted Santa to bring her a yo-yo for Christmas. I ordered pizza from a local place, and since Jude had left his card to use, I added some garlic knots and little mini cannoli for dessert.

"You got a few months to wait until Christmastime," I told her as we settled on the couch in the living room, admiring the blown-up picture of Jude, Mira, and the kids after her last race. I tried to imagine being in Jude's place, lifting the weight of his own grief along with the weight of his children's. It was exhausting.

But he was doing well, and I couldn't have been more proud, especially in following through with his desire to put himself out there. It took bravery. I knew because I was doing it too. Or, attempting it.

Once again, I pushed away the creeping jealousy in my veins as I thought about him with some woman, making her laugh, curling his warm hands around her waist, kissing her in the same way he kissed me, like spun sugar and pure sin. Giving me everything I could ask for, fulfilling every fantasy, and somehow still holding on tightly to what we were at the core: friends.

I couldn't stand it. Picturing him with someone else. So I tapped Seb's shoulder. "Why don't you pick a movie? Whatever you like."

His eyes lit up. "Even rated R?"

"I wouldn't go that far, my guy."

He sniffed a laugh and traded his game for the remote control, flipping through their streaming services.

"Ooh! Ooh!" Amelia danced around. "H-h-how 'bout *Ratatouille*?" She turned to me, her face so close to mine her eyes became one. "It's a rat cooking, and he-he is so funny. Pulls on the guy's hair and, like..." She acted out some scene from the movie, and I nodded to her brother.

"What do you say? *Ratatouille*?"

Amelia threw herself at him, hands folded. "Please, brother!"

He heaved a sigh, though he couldn't hide his smile. "Fine."

He put the movie on—it was actually quite cute—and we all ate our pizza in the living room with promises that they wouldn't tell their dad, then laughed together as Amelia reenacted her favorite parts. I worried Seb would give me a hard time, but the three of us had fun. I may have paid him off with a gigantic ice cream sundae, but still, a ten-year-old boy calling me "awesome" was *awesome*.

Bedtime was pretty easy, both of them self-sufficient enough to take a bath or shower by themselves, changing into pajamas and brushing their teeth. All these two needed was a bit of prodding and a few minutes on my cell phone, one of them on either side of me as I flipped through an Instagram account that featured videos of farm animals doing cute things, like baby goats hopping around or a cow lying on top of her favorite human to cuddle.

"That was the last one," I said, shutting off my phone.

"One more?" Amelia pleaded, big eyes blinking up at me.

It was already past 9:30, and I assumed Jude would be coming home soon. I couldn't be the babysitter who let the kids rule the roost.

"Next time," I told her. "You want me to tuck you in?"

She nodded, but when I asked the same of Seb, he said he was fine and walked to his bedroom. "I'll be right here," I told him, and he offered me a tight-lipped smile.

Couldn't lie. My heart did flip once or twice when he closed his door with a quiet, "Night, Brooke."

My heart flopped for the third time when I bent over Amelia in her purple bed, her arms reaching out to me. "Hug."

I happily obliged, cuddling her tiny frame to me, kissing the side of her head. "Goodnight, sweet girl."

She yawned against my ear. "Night night. I love you."

"I love you too," I whispered, giving in to my need for another embrace. When I let her go, she immediately rolled to her side, snuggling three of her unicorns under her arm.

I quietly cleaned up the kitchen for a bit, but it wasn't long before I heard the lock on the front door unlatch. A few moments later, Jude sidled up next to me at the sink. "Hey. How was your night? How were the kids?"

"Perfect angel babies." I opened the dishwasher to load it, giving me an out so I didn't have to meet his gaze. "How'd the date go?"

"Good. Fun. She's…"

I finished lining the dirty dishes on the bottom rack and stood up straight, raising my brows in his direction at his incomplete thought.

"She's more my speed."

I slanted my attention to a dish towel, nodding absently, trying to be adult about this. Remembering to relax my jaw.

"Hey. You all right?"

I cleared my throat. "Yeah. Fine."

"You seem it," he said, finely threaded amusement lacing his words.

I felt him move closer to me, the heat of him against my side, and I tried to be adult about that too. About how his familiarity meant nothing. We were friends and helped each other work through some intense and intimate things and…

And that was it.

I bent, closing the dishwasher door with more force than necessary. Smashing my thumb in the process.

"Oh shit," I hissed, backing up, right into Jude's chest. I waved my right hand in the air. "Fuck."

"What?" He spun me around. "What happened?"

I curled my fingers around my thumb, shoving it between my legs, as if hiding it would take away the pain. "Jammed my thumb in the door."

He tugged on my arm, urging me to release my tightly gripped fist. "Let me see." He uncurled my fingers, his breath hot on my hand as he held it close to his face, examining it, gently flipping it over. "It's not bleeding, but you pinched it good. You've already got some bruising under your fingernail."

I squeezed my eyes shut, feeling my heartbeat in it. "It's throbbing."

"You want some ice?"

"No, it's okay. I—"

Then his mouth was on my thumb, kissing it, his lips pressing into the skin on the inside, below my knuckle, once, twice, three times. I opened my lids to find him staring at me, his dark eyes hooded, nostrils flared.

"Better?" he murmured against my knuckle.

I nodded silently, the fire in his gaze burning away my ability to speak.

"How about this?" He dragged his tongue over my knuckle, and I felt the echo of it between my legs, my mind instantly back to the day he'd pushed me to the ground and licked me until I screamed out to the sky. And I didn't feel the painful throb in the tip of my thumb anymore, not when he drew it into his mouth, gentle suction eliciting a groan from the back of my throat.

He responded in kind, closing the few inches of space between us, backing me up against the counter, his thigh between mine. He sucked again, and my nipples hardened under my bra, hips rolling to find some kind of relief for the growing pressure in my core.

I whispered his name, and he released my thumb, only to take my mouth, his fingers roughly combing into my hair, stealing my breath right from my lungs. I curled my fingers into his shirt, holding on to him for dear life, mindlessly grinding against his thigh, unable to get what I needed.

"You showed up tonight in these little shorts and smelling sweet, like lavender and honey." His pebbled voice caressed my skin, leaving goose bumps in its wake. "It was hard for me to leave." His words curled in my belly, soothing the wretched, jealous parts of me.

"It was hard for me too," I admitted as he molded his palms to my face, his thumbs brushing over my cheeks.

"I'm sorry."

I held on to his forearms, leaning into him. "You don't need to apologize."

His eyes wrinkled in the corners, tension bracketing his features, but I cut off his argument with another kiss. This time, I led, sweeping my tongue into his mouth, licking against his, and it occurred to me, as he trapped my bottom lip between his, pulling slightly, that this was the first time we weren't high or playing a game.

This kiss was real.

Sober and sincere, shucked of all pretenses.

He nudged his thigh farther between mine, skimming his hands down to my waist, and I arched my back, my breasts against his chest, my skin tingling.

I panted, mouth open against his, catching my breath. "I need…"

"What? What do you need?"

"I—"

"Dad?"

We tore away from each other at the sound of Sebastian's voice. I pivoted to the sink, slapping my hand to my chest, hoping to calm my racing heart, as Jude adjusted himself a second before his son crept through the doorway of the kitchen.

"Hey, buddy," Jude said, his voice not quite steady. "Shouldn't you be in bed?"

"I heard…"

I chanced a glance over my shoulder to find Seb's eyes pinging between me and his dad.

Jude draped his arm around his son's shoulder, directing him away. "Sorry. Were we talking too loud?"

Sebastian mumbled something I couldn't make out, and when Jude tossed me a look, I nodded in understanding. I'd have to let myself out.

Once I heard the click of the bedroom door, I bent over the counter, shaking my head, laughing quietly.

Amazing how quickly kids could put out a fire.

I found my purse and made my way to the front door, pausing briefly to see if I could hear anything from Sebastian's room, and when I didn't, I sent a text to Jude, informing him that I'd put the leftover pizza in the fridge.

I received a reply about an hour later.

JUDE

Thanks for tonight.

My first instinct was to respond **Anytime!** But I refrained because I didn't want to offer my babysitting services anytime. Not if it meant he would be going out with someone else.

No. No, thank you.

SEVENTEEN
JUDE

'd been in Sebastian's bed for about forty-five minutes, my head laid on a pillow propped up against the headboard and my legs crossed at the ankles, thinking about Brooke and the barely audible moans that escaped her throat as I licked into her mouth. Too much and yet not enough.

My date with Emma had been great. She was a recent divorcée with one kid and wasn't looking to jump into anything serious. Perfect situation for me.

Except Brooke had strutted into my house with her cutoff denim shorts and loose Freddie Mercury T-shirt, worn so thoroughly I could tell her bra was purple. I'd had the urge to text Emma, call off the date, and tunnel my fingers into Brooke's hair. She'd smelled so good, and a few hours with my head in her lap while we watched a movie sounded like the perfect night.

But that was impossible. Not with the kids around.

I already knew Amelia was attached to Brooke, and I didn't want to put any more ideas in her head. And Sebastian? He was onto me.

So, it didn't surprise me when he sat up, the star lights

strung along the ceiling illuminating the room enough that we could see each other well. "Where did you go tonight?"

"I told you a meeting. I—"

His face scrunched. "Was it a date?"

I couldn't lie to him. After a harsh exhale and a scrub of my hair, I met his gaze, unflinching for a ten-year-old. "Yeah."

That wrinkled suspicious expression turned venomous, though he stayed silent.

"Listen," I started, unsure where I planned on going, but it didn't matter. He flipped over, giving me his back.

But since he didn't tell me to leave, I assumed he wanted me to stay. And I did.

I pulled my cell phone from my pocket, texting Brooke to thank her for coming over and nearly describing Seb's reaction, but I didn't know what to say about it. I didn't even know how I felt about it.

I understood why he was upset. He probably assumed I'd forget his mom or try to replace her. Yet, I wasn't getting married. I wasn't bringing anyone home, and it wasn't like I could discuss the nuances of adult sexual relationships.

For now, I had to leave it.

At least until tomorrow.

After Seb finally fell asleep, I snuck out of his room and padded upstairs to my bedroom. To the bedroom that still looked almost exactly the same since Mira had decided we would paint it beige with an "accent" navy wall behind the bed. What did I know? Nothing. My job was simply to nod and paint the damn wall *twice* because, originally, she'd wanted it a lighter blue and then didn't like the finished product. The argument had begun after I'd told her she could repaint it if she wanted, and it had ended with me storming out of the house after finally hollering I didn't give a shit what color it was. I'd only wanted to be done.

But she'd been a perfectionist. Never settled and *never*

backed down from a fight. She was sweet as pie and relentless when she thought she was right.

I sniffed a laugh at the memory, skimming my fingers over the blue wall as I sat on the bed to peel off my socks, shorts, and shirt, tossing them all in the corner. I didn't even bother taking off my underwear, only shoved them down far enough to curl my hand around my cock, squeezing it roughly and closing my eyes. Until recently, this was what I'd done, taken myself in hand to get myself off because I didn't have any other release, but since Brooke and I had started experimenting, I hadn't needed to.

Now, I thought of her giggling as she ran from me on her farm, the red of her cheeks as she sucked me off, the feel of her hair gripped in my fist. I remembered my mouth buried between her legs and how I'd hated to brush my teeth that night, ridding myself of the last vestiges of her flavor from my beard when I'd washed my face. I thought of the way her hips had bucked and rolled, how she'd stared at me with a drowsy smile. I recalled that first night on the couch, how she'd trusted me to give her everything she wanted. How she'd told me exactly what she needed and hadn't held back. How she'd understood what I needed and offered it being asked.

I came quickly and opened my eyes, standing up from the bed, but instead of trekking to the bathroom, I considered my bedroom. Wondered if it was time to change it. If it was time to finally move.

With a shake of my head that did nothing to clear it, I stalked to the bathroom and cleaned up before scrutinizing myself in the mirror. I didn't think I appeared a lot different. But I *felt* different. I had cut my hair and trimmed my beard, that was new, although the few freckles that always appeared under the summer sun weren't unusual. My eyes looked the same, maybe less tired. I had lost a few pounds, so that might've been the reason why my posture had changed.

And—I laughed.

Why was I lying to myself?

If I couldn't be honest with myself, I wouldn't be able to be honest with anyone else. At least, that was what my therapist always told me.

So, truth, *I was in love with my best friend.*

———

The silence on the drive to Sebastian's baseball practice was deafening. Even Amelia seemed to know something was off and kept herself busy, playing with the toys she'd brought in the car. I kept glancing at Seb in the rearview mirror, but he remained stoic, staring out of his window, brow furrowed.

When we arrived at the field, he jumped out without a word, so I took Lulu's hand and headed toward the playground at the other end of the park when I didn't see Dylan's kids in the stands. It must've been their mom's weekend.

I pushed her on the swings for a while then we stared at the clouds, trying to find shapes. When she got tired of that, she played the game where she pretended to be different animals, and I had to guess which ones. They were almost always unicorns or bunny rabbits.

After walking back to the field, we sat in the stands so I could watch the end of practice while Amelia played on my phone. Seb looked good, getting better and better. Certainly took after his mother in the athletic department.

The team finished up their drills, and when Dylan told them to run laps, I made my way down to him. "How'd it go today?"

"Good." He kept his attention on his players and crossed his arms, even as he angled toward me. "There was some talk today about the traveling team. One of the boys brought it up, and then none of them could shut up about it. Thought I'd give you a heads-up Seb seemed real interested."

"Yeah? What do you think about it?"

He didn't answer for a minute, removing his cap from his head to curve the brim more before putting it back on. "These traveling teams, they're intense."

"Did you do them?"

"Baseball was all I did. Took up all my time." He met my gaze then. "It's an expensive commitment, and the parents… It can get really political with tryouts. I think kids should have fun, you know? Playing sports is supposed to be fun. Not everybody is going pro, and even if you do…" He vaguely motioned to himself.

Dylan had been drafted into the MLB, but his career had stalled after only a few seasons because of injuries. He was eventually released from his contract, and now he coached nine- and ten-year-olds.

"I guess if he wants to try out, I'll cross that bridge with him about commitment when we get to it," I said, watching Seb laugh with his friends. "Maybe it'll score me some points."

"Why? What happened?"

"He asked if I went on a date last night, and I couldn't lie to him, so…" I shrugged. "He's pissed at me."

Dylan grunted. "I could tell something was off about him today."

"He hasn't talked to me all day."

"Sorry, man," Dylan said with a flick of his gaze to me before shouting to the team, "Round it up!"

They all gathered together with their hands in the middle of the circle and chanted their team name before breaking up.

When Dylan took his place back at my side, he asked, "He know about you and Brooke?"

I shook my head. "And I'm not sure what to tell him either. It's not like I know what Brooke and I are."

He smirked.

"What?"

He rubbed his palm over his mouth, his voice low. "You're a dumb motherfucker if you don't know it's written all over your face. Hers too."

I huffed because this grumpy son of a bitch hadn't known his head from his ass until Evie showed up. He certainly didn't know anything about Brooke and me. "Our faces are fine."

He stayed silent but nodded sarcastically, gesturing for me to follow him to help put away the equipment. Once we finished, he clapped my shoulder. "Lemme know if you want me to talk to Seb."

"Talk to Seb? Why would I need you to do that?"

He shrugged. "I figured it might be easier for me to talk to him about what's going on in his life."

I didn't know what offended me more, having my friend point out to me that he might be able to do a better job of communicating with my kid or that Seb would remain upset with me.

"Sometimes it's easier with someone on the outside, you know? You're his dad, but I'm his coach. His uncle."

He had a point, and my shoulders shrank at the idea that I might be out of my depth on this.

I motioned for Amelia and Sebastian to meet me by the fence as Dylan told me, "Hey, it'll be all right. You'll get through this."

I accepted his words with a nod and one-armed hug. "Thanks. I'll see you later."

"Later." He ruffled Amelia's hair and fist-bumped with Sebastian. "Bye, Lulu. Seb, nice work today."

They waved to their uncle in every sense of the word but biological, and we hopped back into my car. I might've been on my son's shit list, but I knew the surefire way to get off it. "Who's up for Red Robin's?"

Amelia shot her hand up, bouncing in her car seat, and I

looked to Sebastian. He couldn't hide his growing smile. My kids loved bottomless fries. Hell, who didn't?

EIGHTEEN
BROOKE

The forecast called for rain. Shoppers didn't hang around the stalls as usual this morning. They wanted to get in and get out before the storm, which didn't feel too far off between the dark sky and warm winds whipping the flaps of the tents back and forth.

Nicole, the college student who helped me out on weekends, played on her phone. We hadn't had a customer in about twenty minutes, and with the dwindling crowd, I doubted we'd be getting any more.

"Can you start packing up the extra crates? If the rain starts, I don't want us to be stuck breaking everything down."

She nodded and got to work, stacking the empty crates and folding up all the cardboard boxes to reuse next week. I packed up most of the unsold produce, save for a few of each in case anyone stopped by in the next half hour. I occasionally brought some to Jude since the guy needed more vitamins in his diet, and I popped a few zucchini and an eggplant into a basket for him.

"Nic, I'm going over to Jude's stall for a bit."

"Got it covered here." She smiled. "Tell your boyfriend I said hi."

"He's not my boyfriend."

"He's not?" She appeared genuinely shocked. "I thought… He's always… He brought you coffee this morning and…"

I laughed, waving her off. "We've been friends for a long time."

And having sex for the last few weeks, but to-may-to, to-mah-to.

I scooted down the street to find most of the vendors had the same idea as me. I waved to Bill, the cheese guy, as he packed up, and high-fived Alicia, Sara Ann and Tori's toddler. They sold homemade soaps and other personal hygiene products, totally organic and vegan.

"Your sign," I called, speeding up to catch Jude's self-standing sign that lost its fight with the wind.

He spun around, and we bumped right into each other when we reached for it at the same time.

"Hey, whoa." He set the sign up with one hand, wrapping the other around my bicep.

"Sorry. I didn't want it to get wrecked."

"It's fine, but are you okay? I stepped on your foot." He motioned to the folding chair behind his table. "Sit."

"I'm fine."

"Sit down," he ordered, and I bit back a smile, doing as I was told.

"I came over to give you some veggies."

He accepted my basket, deadpanning, "Great."

"Oh, come on. If you don't want to make the zucchini for dinner, you can make some bread with it."

"Why would I want to spoil perfectly delicious bread by mixing something green into it?"

"You've made banana and chocolate chip bread before," I pointed out, and he tossed his hand in the air.

"Yeah, because that's delicious."

"So is zucchini bread."

"You know what zucchini tastes like?" he asked, placing the basket down on his table so he could return to packing up. "Slimy."

"I'm sorry. What?"

"Zucchini tastes slimy."

"That's..." I snickered. "That's not a thing."

"Yes, it is." He smacked his lips. "How could you eat something with a texture that's so wet?"

I tipped my head to the side. "I don't know. You tell me."

He froze and slowly turned to me. "Brooke Abigail Fraser, did you just make a vagina joke?"

I bit my teeth into my lower lip to keep from grinning.

"Your vagina doesn't even work," he teased, and I shot out my foot to kick him.

"Hey! My vagina works great, thank you very much."

"You're right." He bent, his hands on the back of the chair behind me, lowering his face to mine. "I would know."

I swallowed, no longer finding this funny.

"And I think about it a lot," he confessed in his distractedly roughhewn voice. "About smoothing lube over my fingers before pushing them inside you and feeling that first clench."

I closed my eyes, unable to hold his gaze as he spoke my fantasy out loud, what I thought about when I pulled my vibrator out of my nightstand drawer.

"That first inch, that's when your breath hitches and your fingers curl."

"Jude," I whispered, my nipples hard beneath my bra. "Please don't."

"Don't what?" He tucked a few strands of hair behind my ear. "Tell you that I dreamed of your legs around my waist last night and woke up hard as a rock? Okay, I won't."

My responding laugh was more of a whimper, and I opened my eyes to push him away from me. "You can't say things like that to me."

He stood up straight. "Why not?"

"Because…" I coasted my gaze around the farmers market, searching for the right answer.

Because what we'd been doing wasn't only fun and games for me.

Because we were more than friends, but I didn't know what else to call us.

Because if he couldn't follow through, then he had to stop.

I licked my lips and tried on honesty. "Because I think—"

"Hey, Jude."

We both whirled around at the voice, and he immediately backed away from me. "Hey, Emma."

Emma? I didn't know an Emma.

Jude dragged his hand over his hair a few times, splitting his attention between this woman and me.

"Emma, this is my friend, Brooke. Brooke, this is Emma." When I stared indifferently at him, he filled in the blank. "We went out last weekend."

Oh. This was *her*. His date.

With short blond hair and a fuller figure, she seemed… fine. Pretty, unfortunately.

"Hi." She waved at me then smiled at Jude. "I had to come check everything out since you told me about it. Although, I don't think I beat the rain."

She held her hand palm up, and I squinted out of the tent to see a few drops hit the ground.

"Where are your kids today?" Emma asked, and Jude returned to packing.

"They're with my parents. I didn't want to bring them with the weather."

She lit up. "My son's with my ex this weekend too. Since we don't have them, you wouldn't want to grab lunch, would you?"

He paused, glancing at me, something settling over his dark eyes that I couldn't read before facing Emma once again.

"Yeah, sure. I've still got to pack up here, so do you want to meet somewhere?"

"You like Two Birds?"

He nodded. "Yeah. I could meet you there in about twenty minutes."

"Perfect." She waved at me, like she hadn't ruined everything. "It's nice meeting you."

"You too," I mumbled, thinking of the cute little café that served brunch, and how Jude and I had been there once, sharing stuffed French toast and an omelet. Because we liked to try each other's food.

I swallowed hard as Emma jogged away, a knot forming in my stomach. When I stood, Jude narrowed his eyes on me, and I hoped he couldn't see everything written on my face.

All of my hurt and anger. The clawing jealousy and devastating disappointment.

Jude and I were friends, only fooling around. What happened between us, it clearly meant nothing to him.

It was practice. That was all.

That was the friendly agreement we'd made. Get him back on the horse, and find me a husband. Well, he'd certainly found his stride. Only, I never expected it to feel like this. Like being torn in two.

Half of myself happy for him because he was getting what he wanted. The other half completely heartbroken.

I lowered my head, playing with my hair, giving myself time to clear my throat and eyes.

I had no claim over Jude. He should and would go out with whomever he liked. And I had to do the same, find someone who wanted the same things I did.

But I couldn't do that around Jude. I couldn't stand here while he made dates with other women. Waterboarding might've been better than this.

"I'll get going. Let you finish up," I said, unable to meet his eyes.

"Brooke, wait."

I didn't. I walked out of the tent, right into a downpour.

Good. He wouldn't chase after me. Not with the rain, and all of his candy and cardboard boxes getting soaked.

I hightailed it to my tent, where Nicole—angel baby—had nearly everything cleaned up. We had it all loaded in my truck in one trip, and in the safety of the cab, with the pounding rain on the roof, I pulled out my phone, opening the app. It didn't take me long to find the conversation thread I'd let fade.

So, I picked it right back up. And made a date with a man named Holland.

Hopefully he was a seven-foot-tall Dutch guy with a good personality and impressive oral skills.

Time to find my future husband.

NINETEEN
BROOKE

The date was going great. Holland turned out to be tall, not seven feet, though over six, with a nice smile and touchable hair. He lived about thirty minutes away but said he didn't mind the drive. Not when "you show up in that dress."

The one I'd worn to my sister's shower. The one in my profile pic. He'd told me I was even prettier in person.

He was handsome, if not a little unmemorable, and our conversation flowed easily from one topic to the next. He seemed interested in my farm, asking about crop rotation and growing seasons, but he did throw me off with that one question about how much I made.

Right as our entrées arrived—steak for him, salmon for me —I felt my phone vibrate in my purse. I ignored it, listening to Holland describe his job in insurance, which sounded really boring, but he was into it, so I nodded along when he talked about the company picnic.

I'd briefly wondered what his day-to-day was like if he found excitement from a company picnic. Then I reminded myself that he seemed perfectly nice, and nice guys were often already married. *Or* were on a mission to find a fuck buddy.

When my phone buzzed again a few minutes later, I set down my glass of white wine to check it. There were two texts.

JUDE

Where've you been the last few days? MIA.

JUDE

What time should I pick you up?

Pick me up? For what? We hadn't really spoken this week, not since the incredibly awkward encounter at the farmers market when his date Emma had showed up. I texted him back.

What are you talking about?

He responded immediately.

JUDE

The wedding.

I choked on my sip of wine, and Holland's eyes widened. "Are you okay?"

Coughing a few times, I held my index finger up then pointed to the bathroom, indicating I'd only be a minute. I hightailed it to the restroom and called Jude. "There you are," he said when he answered. "Where've you been? You didn't reply to any of my messages."

I tried not to sound immature when I told him, "Yeah, well, I've been busy."

"Too busy to text me back?"

He didn't believe me. We were well aware of each other's schedules, and he knew it was a lie. No matter how long my midsummer days were, I would never not text him back.

"What's wrong?" he asked after a while, and I faced the mirror, frowning as I lied again.

"Nothing."

He huffed. "Well, what's going on? Are you all right?"

"I'm fine."

"You're not fine, so how about we stop pretending and you tell me what's wrong."

"I'm on a date, Jude!"

He made a rough sound I couldn't interpret. "Sorry. It's just that you weren't talking to me, and I know we're getting down to the wire, and I wanted to get a time so I could let my parents know when to expect the kids."

I curled my hand around the edge of the sink, the porcelain cold under my clammy palm. "You really want to go?"

"Yeah. Why wouldn't I?"

I stared at my reflection, at my furrowed brow and pinched mouth. "I...I figured you wouldn't want to with Emma, and we—"

"Emma? What does she have to do with anything?"

I twisted away from the mirror, unable to look myself in the eyes anymore. "It seemed like you two were—"

"We're nothing. I went to lunch with her, so I could tell her I wasn't interested."

"Oh."

"Yeah. Oh," he mocked. "That why you're on a date right now?"

"Technically, I'm in the bathroom talking to you right now."

"Sorry not sorry."

I sniffed a laugh, covering my smile with my hand even though no one was here to witness my giddiness.

"Take me to the wedding," he said. "Can I please go to the wedding with you?"

"Yes. Of course. I don't want anyone else there with me."

"I don't want you there with anyone else either," he said gruffly, as if he didn't want to admit it.

"Pick me up at three on Saturday," I told him, and he agreed with a hum.

When I didn't say anything else, he asked, "How's the date going?"

I spun back around toward the mirror, a huge, goofy grin plastered across my face, wondering if he could hear it in my one-word answer. "Good."

"What's his name?"

"Holland."

"Like the country?"

"I don't think anyone calls it that anymore," I said, still smiling like an idiot.

"All right. You have fun with the Netherlands or whatever. I've got to pick Seb up from his friend's house."

"Okay."

"Text me when you get home. I want to hear how terrible the date was."

"That's not very kind of you," I teased because I supposed all our pretenses were gone.

"I've come to realize I don't want to be gracious when it comes to your time and attention."

I bit into my cheek. Honestly, I feared my cheeks would crack. "But it would be rude of me not to give him my time and attention right now."

"Arguable, but fine. Text me later."

"I will."

I hung up and took a deep breath, composing myself before heading back out to Holland. I was giddy after that phone call, not because I knew what was happening between Jude and me, but that *something* was happening. He was still my friend—the same guy who would do anything if I asked —but he was also a guy I had feelings for. Big feelings.

When I returned to the table, Holland gave me a questioning look over the rim of his wineglass. "Everything okay?"

"Yeah, sorry about that." I slid back into my seat. "I had to sort out some plans for my sister's wedding this weekend."

We'd discussed our families earlier, and I'd made him aware of Sabrina's big day, but the way he smiled at me made me think he was more than politely interested. Like, maybe, he thought I'd invite him.

He proved my instincts correct when he asked, "Are you bringing a date?"

I refused to break eye contact. Better to get it over with. "A friend, yes."

"Great." He nodded absently a few times, his features going blank as if he needed time to compute. He blinked. "So, I was about to ask if you wanted to order another round of drinks? Or maybe dessert to share?"

"I don't think so."

He nodded again, this time understanding, and signaled for our server. When the check arrived, I offered to pay for my meal, but Holland refused. He walked me to my car, his hands in his pockets.

"It was a pleasure meeting you," I said, hoping to mitigate some of the awkward tension.

"Yeah, you too. I hope everything works out with your friend."

"Oh, it's…" I stopped myself. Because, yes, it was exactly like that, but I didn't know how he knew.

"You looked different when you came back," he explained. "That kind of glow people get when they're in love." He reached out, gently squeezing my elbow with a quiet goodbye, leaving me completely breathless.

Is that what I was? In love?

I'd thought I'd loved Tom, but what I felt for Jude was different. I'd skipped over the butterflies, the will he/won't he angst, already so steady and secure in our relationship. We were friends first, and I guess I'd loved him all along, but only began thinking of him in a different light these past few weeks.

As I drove home, my mind kept drifting back to how Jude had sounded almost…territorial? Possessive? The idea sent a shiver down my spine that had nothing to do with the air vents aimed directly at me.

Still, I couldn't get ahead of myself. Jude and I would have a lot to talk about, though the realization that we would have those conversations settled me. His friendship was the most important relationship in my life, and whatever came from this, we had to keep that sacred. But I knew him—I knew my best friend—and he didn't make any rash decisions, especially when it affected his family. I also wanted to respect the kids and give them whatever they needed, first and foremost. Figuring out our future would be slow and probably not easy, but it would definitely be worth it.

Parked in front of my condo, I headed right upstairs to kick off my shoes and flop onto my bed like a teenager about to text her first crush. Dorothy curled up next to me, and I petted her with one hand while I typed with the other.

Home.

JUDE

That was fast.

You kinda ruined the mojo.

JUDE

Oops.

Yes. I can practically hear the apology dripping from that message.

JUDE

Then you must be high or something.

Smoking might have made the date a little more fun.

JUDE

Damn, honeybee. Harsh.

I sent him a shrug emoji then stood to change into my pajamas. By the time I checked my phone again, I found multiple texts.

JUDE

I want to get your opinion on something.

JUDE

Seb wants to try out for this traveling baseball team. They play through the fall, but then I guess there's another one that plays in the spring too.

JUDE

He loves baseball and I love that for him, but I really don't know if:

JUDE

1. He's ready for that commitment and 2. If he's good enough to make the team. He's finally found something he loves, and I would hate for him to be crushed.

Okay. What are you thinking?

JUDE

That maybe I should come up with an excuse for him not to try out.

I get that protective instinct, but I think you have to let him try.

JUDE

I knooooow

JUDE

But I was really hoping you'd agree with me.

Jude

I feel like I'm losing him.

Babe.

You're not losing him.

You'll never lose him. Or Amelia.

You've all been through some really traumatic and terrible stuff, and as much as they needed you, I think you also needed them. You've held them really close, which is totally understandable, but you have to let them fly. They have to try out for baseball teams and not make them. Or make them and learn it's hard to keep commitments.

My eyes stung as I typed, my heart expanding with the realization of how much I felt for Jude and his children. And I was so grateful for Jude's trust, honored that he would allow me to be his sounding board and support system.

You and Mira made these two beautiful children. They're smart and kind, and you've raised them so well, when other people might've faltered in your same position. You're a great dad. The BEST dad. I am so proud of you.

They'll fail and stumble and mess up, but they'll be fine because of you. Because you showed them how to pick themselves up and keep going even when life sucks.

It was a while before he responded.

JUDE

Thank you.

JUDE

I guess I feel like it's only been the three of us for so long, these little changes with the kids feel huge.

JUDE

I just needed to talk it out.

Happy to be your ear.

When he didn't immediately text back, I moved into the bathroom to remove my makeup and brush my teeth. After I finished moisturizing, I grabbed my phone before taking a seat on the couch to watch TV and smiled at the message.

JUDE

You called me babe.

I did.

JUDE

I liked it.

Me too.

JUDE

I've got to get the kids ready for bed. What are you doing for the rest of the night?

I don't know. Maybe Emily in Paris.

JUDE

Don't you dare start the new season without me.

Uuuggghhhhh. Fine.

I'll watch Derry Girls.

JUDE

I'll allow it since we finished that one.

Thank you for the permission, sir.

JUDE

Sir. Ooh. I like that one. Might have to add it to our list.

I laughed and sent him a checkmark emoji.

Did our dating pact just become a sex pact?

JUDE

Bet your sweet ass it did.

TWENTY
JUDE

assumed I'd be nervous. I hadn't dressed up in a suit and tie in years. In fact, I'd had to run out to buy a new one yesterday since the one I had in the closet had been a tad bit tight when I'd tried it on. Any other time, I probably would've asked Brooke to come along with me, but she'd been wrapped up with the rehearsal and dinner, so it was only me and the salesguy, Ron. I'd put all my trust in him.

Consequently, here I was, knocking on my best friend's door with the intent to take her to a wedding after we'd all but confessed our feelings to each other, in a brand new "pistachio"-colored suit, and I was totally chill.

A moment later, Brooke opened the door, and my breath caught in my throat. She grinned, brushing strands of soft brown hair away from her cheek. "Hi."

"You look…" I allowed my gaze to wander over her face with her adorably crooked smile and chocolate-drop eyes, down her throat to the thin gold chain and single diamond, and even farther, over the pretty floral dress she wore that swayed back and forth with each of her movements. "You're beautiful."

"Thank you." She gestured me in. "You're not so bad yourself."

I tugged on the lapels of the suit jacket then smoothed my hand down my shirt, finding it to be a good omen that I'd decided to go with the patterned shirt with the fine floral print, so we matched. "Ron, the salesguy, told me I didn't need a tie."

She laughed, skating her hands over my shoulders, then plucked at the pocket square. "No, you don't. You look hot, Jude."

Taking that as an invitation, I curved my hands around her hips, pulling her to me, aiming for a kiss, but she ducked out of the way. "I just put on lip gloss."

"I don't care." I closed the distance between us before she could argue. It had felt like years since I touched her, since those too few minutes in my kitchen when everything had changed. Or, really, revealed itself.

It hadn't been like a tectonic plate shift. There was no earthquake or mind-shattering epiphany. It felt more like a curtain had been pushed to the side, and I could finally see clearly for the first time in a long time.

I combed my fingers into her hair, angling her head so I could sweep my tongue over her lips, curling around hers. Uncaring for the mess I made of her hair and lip gloss, I searched for all those sweet corners of her mouth, prompting her quiet, pleading sounds. I didn't stop until sharp pins pressed against my calf.

I jumped back to find Dorothy clawing at me.

Brooke nodded at her cat. "She's been jealous lately, I think. Smells you on me or something."

I bent to pick her up, kissing the top of her head. "Sorry, girl, but you're my second-favorite kitty."

"Oh my god," Brooke shrieked in laughter. I lifted my head, meeting her gaze. "You have…" She swiped her fingers over my lips, presumably to wipe off the lip gloss.

"Your hair," I said with a tip of my chin.

She turned toward the small mirror hanging on the wall and proceeded to release the strands she'd pinned back in a sparkly barrette to redo it. Then she reapplied her lip gloss and fluffed her dress before spinning around, her focus drifting over me after I set Dorothy on the couch. "Oh. You're all full of cat hair now." She dug through a woven basket on her kitchen counter for a minute, brandishing a lint roller. "Come here."

Always.

I stood patiently as she ran the sticky roller over my jacket and then pants, patting it all down when she finished, smiling. Even fixed the pocket square, though it didn't really need it. Her familiar lavender scent wrapped around my senses, pulled me in toward her once again, but she stopped me, her hand in the middle of my chest. "I can't be late, and if you keep kissing me, I will be."

I heaved a sigh, eliciting another smile from her, and I didn't think I'd ever tire of them or the sound of her laughter. She sat on the couch, double-checking her purse, large enough to fit a pair of pale-pink Converse that matched her dress. When she draped the hem of her long skirt over her thighs and opened a shoe box, revealing a pair of heels, I kneeled on the floor in front of her. "Let me."

She gaped at me for a moment, unblinking, and I thought it a shame no one had ever helped her put her shoes on before. I took the box from her hands, and she came back to life with an audible inhale. "Thank you."

I picked up the first shoe, considering the pointy toe and slim heel. "These are gonna kill you."

"That's why I'm bringing the sneakers."

I held up her right foot, grazed her petal-pink-painted toes with my thumb, then slid the shoe on. I set it on the floor with a squeeze of her ankle and permitted myself a caress of her shin as payment before repeating the whole process with her left foot. This time, I doubled my payment with a kiss on her knee. Taking her hand in mine, I towed her up with me. "You ready?"

She nodded, smiling, almost shyly, and I could see she wanted to tell me something. Something *really* important.

Maybe the same something *really* important I wanted to tell her. But now wasn't the time. Like she'd said, she didn't want to be late.

I grabbed her purse and offered Dorothy a farewell pet before leading the way out the door. Brooke locked up behind me and tucked her keys into her bag, looped over my shoulder, before taking my proffered hand. The ease with which we interlaced our fingers was the same ease with which we were making this transition.

Inside my car, we buckled in, and Brooke helped herself to cuing up her playlist on the Bluetooth. "Thanks again for coming with me."

"Like I said, I wanted to."

"I didn't know if…"

I made a left out of the parking lot, following the directions on my phone. "If I wanted to come with you?"

"Yeah. I didn't know if it would be uncomfortable for you because you've only ever…" She trailed off again, and I could guess why.

I offered her a small shake of my head as I followed the on-ramp for the highway. "It won't be uncomfortable. Not with you."

"I don't want you to be sad or anything."

I took my time, waiting until I merged into the middle lane to answer. "No. I spent a lot of time worrying about how I'd feel if I ever decided to try to be with someone again. I thought it would feel like I was betraying her or something, but you and I have been friends for so long that I don't think I could ever feel that way with you. Maybe it would be different—I'd feel different—if it were someone else, but you've only ever made me happy. So, no, I won't be sad. I might get a little emotional because only serial killers remain dry-eyed at weddings, but I plan on having a lot of fun."

When she stayed quiet, I glanced at her again to find her contemplating me with her head tipped to the side. "What about you?" I asked. "Are weddings hard for you?"

She hummed thoughtfully. "Yes and no. Yes, they're hard in that I get a little jealous, but no, because I'm so happy for them. Tom and I weren't meant to be."

"You're goddamn right you weren't."

She bit back a smile. "I'd bought my wedding dress. Did I ever tell you that?"

I changed lanes and placed my hand over her thigh, the thin layers of her dress wrinkling under my fingers. "I don't think so."

"It was a few weeks before I was diagnosed. I found *the* dress," she said with a sad little laugh. "But by the time it came in, I was well into treatment, so my mom went and picked it up then hung it in my closet. Whenever I felt like…" She swallowed, her chin dipping for a moment. "When it got really hard, I'd look at that dress, and it would keep me going. It represented my future. Plus, it was so gorgeous."

"What'd it look like?"

She threw her hand out. "Classic. Ivory satin A-line with—"

"I have no idea what that means."

She drew the figure with her hands in front of her. "The skirt sort of billows out like the legs of the letter A. My dress had wide straps that created this low V neckline," she explained, her fingers meeting in a point at her chest. "And it had an open back and a long train. It was simple, but I loved it."

"What did you end up doing with it?"

She lifted a careless shoulder. "Sold it. Used the money to buy supplies for my farm."

I caught her gaze. "Good."

"What about you? What was your wedding like?"

"Huge. Her family's big and loud, and it took us a while to find a place that would be able to accommodate three hundred people. In Arab weddings, they have a special entrance for the bride and groom." I smiled at the memory. "It's called a *zaffa*, and these guys play traditional drums and perform chants for the bride and groom to enter. They did some sword dancing, and her uncles put me on their shoulders."

"That sounds really fun."

I nodded. "It was perfect. A big party and an even bigger cake."

Brooke laughed. "What did Mira wear?"

"A big white dress. Decked out in sparkles," I said, recalling when I'd first seen her. Like a lump of sugar walking down the aisle to me. "It swallowed her up."

We were both quiet for a while as I followed my GPS to the golf course. It wasn't until I parked that we faced each other, the air charged between us, thick with unspoken longing and words that hovered behind our lips. Slowly, cautiously, I lifted my hand to cup her cheek, marveling at her soft skin.

Her eyelids fluttered closed as she nuzzled into my palm, and I slid my other hand to her neck, sliding under the curtain of her curled hair, and rested my forehead to hers. Her hands found my wrists, holding me in place, and that was when it hit me.

I didn't know if fate was real or if life was simply one big journey of coincidences, but it was wild to think about how the woman who made me believe I could open myself up again to love and marriage was the one woman I'd been introduced to by my wife.

I'd been so fortunate in my life.

To have fallen in love with a girl who gave me everything I'd ever wanted and taught me to appreciate it in her absence.

To have my best friend guide me out to the other side, demonstrating true patience and offering me unending support.

How fortunate I was to have the love of two incredible women in my life.

I thought I'd been cursed with bad luck, but really, it had been the opposite. I'd been blessed.

I kissed Brooke, pressing all of my unspoken thoughts into her lips, hoping she understood the translation. And I thought she did, because when I took her hand once we'd met each other by the hood of the car, she tossed me her impishly crooked smile. "When I get married, I'm not going to wear a wedding dress. It'll be something whimsical and flowery and gold. Like the sunset."

I took her bag from her then positioned her hand in the crook of my elbow. "It should be at sunset. At your farm. Maybe under our tree."

"You'll be there? You think you'll be able to make it?"

My smile slipped, unable to make this promise as if it were a joke. Because it wasn't. What we had wasn't a joke. "I didn't think I'd want to be, but that was before. Now, I know I can be there. Not tomorrow, but eventually."

She stared up at me, her lashes long and dark, fanning around her honey-brown eyes. Eyes that had always seen me clearly. "I can wait."

I kissed her forehead and escorted her toward the hall. Because what couldn't wait was *this* wedding.

TWENTY-ONE
BROOKE

As soon as I entered the venue with Jude, Kim whisked me away with barely a few words. I turned over my shoulder, seeing Jude and Henry, my brother-in-law, shake hands, and I removed my arm from my sister's grip. "You couldn't even give me a minute to say goodbye?"

"Goodbye?" She opened the door to Sabrina's dressing room. "What do you need to say goodbye to Jude for?"

I had no answer, except that those few minutes when we'd spoken outside had moved mountains, and I needed time to learn the new geography of my life. We still hadn't come right out and told each other how we felt, but I didn't need it. Not right now, at least. Now until we could be alone and talk this all through. Until I had the quiet to tell him that I loved him. That I thought I'd been in love with him for a while.

Sabrina spun in her chair, practically glowing. "Brookie!"

I bent to hug her, careful of her dress and makeup. My younger sister was easily excitable, and we'd agreed it would be better for us to get ready on our own, so she could have time for herself before she became a self-proclaimed "emotional mess."

She sniffed in my ear. "I'm so happy you're here."

I petted her shoulder. "Of course I'm here. You aren't getting married without your oldest and best sister."

Kim hip-checked me out of the way to hold out her hand for Sabrina. She stood, and the three of us found our reflection in the long mirror across from us. Sabrina in her bright-white gown, Kim and I next to her in our dresses. Me, in my pink floral dress that wasn't far off from the dress I'd told Jude about getting married in. Kim, in her watermelon-colored dress with pockets. Sabrina had told us to wear whatever we wanted, as long as we could have fun in it.

The three of us smiled, and I didn't feel one ounce of jealousy. Not even a shadow.

"You ready to go see your groom?" I asked, and Sabrina nodded.

"I know he's gonna be so hot in a tux."

Kim laughed. "At least you know why you're marrying him."

With last checks in the mirror, we exited the dressing room so Sabrina and Everett could have their first-look photo shoot. I noticed Jude with Henry and my parents off to the side. I studied him, laughing, telling some story with his hands, how relaxed he was with my family.

How *good* he looked in his suit.

With his chin-length hair pulled back into a little ponytail, a few wisps hung down by his ears, and he tucked them away before running his hand over his beard in that absent-minded way I loved. Maybe because I would have liked to be the one combing my fingers over it.

Kim elbowed me. "What's got you all starry-eyed?"

"Hm?"

My sister pointedly shifted her line of sight from me to Jude, but I played dumb. "Nothing."

She shot me a dubious glare. "You and Jude, huh?"

I shrugged. She didn't fall for it.

She flicked her hand through the air like a queen speaking

to her servants. "I'm not saying I knew it would happen eventually, but it's not like I didn't say it."

"When? To who?"

"Like, all the time. To Sabrina and Mom. You two are—" she crooked her fingers in air quotes "—best friends."

I shoved her shoulder. "We are best friends."

"Straight men and women can't be friends."

"Yes, they can."

She spun to face me, blocking out my view of Jude. "So, you two are doing it?"

I snorted a laugh. "Doing it."

"Well, are you?" She backhanded my arm hard enough to knock me off-balance.

"Ow. And, yes!"

My outburst caught everyone's attention, the bride and groom's, the photographer's, my family's, Jude's. I pasted on a smile, my shoulders up by my ears, and Jude's brows narrowed.

I waved off his worry then flipped around on my sister. "You're embarrassing me."

"Me?" She pushed her hair over her shoulder, as if she would *never* embarrass me, and arched her penciled-in brows. She'd overplucked in college, and they'd never quite recovered. Served her right. "Are you together or what?"

"I don't know, and I'm not talking about this with you."

"Why not?"

"Because, apparently, I can't trust you with any information since you go around gossiping about me to everyone."

"Brina and Mom are not everyone."

I huffed. They were the ones who mattered. Dad, too, of course. I folded my arms over my chest. "It's new, okay? We haven't even talked about what we are or are not, so I'm not going to talk about this with you until I talk to him."

"But look at him over there." She pointed at Jude, and I smacked her hand down. Honestly. A few months home with a baby, and she'd lost all sense of propriety. "He already gets along well with everyone. He's been around so long, he could slip right in. *You*, I guess I should say. Right?"

Her lascivious eyebrow waggle sent me over the edge, but before I could reply, the photographer called us over to take some photos with Sabrina and then Everett's two groomsmen. And before we knew it, we were shuffled back to the dressing room because the guests had begun to arrive.

That was when they cornered me. Sabrina, Kim, *and* my parents.

I held my hands out to head them off. "Yes, Jude and I are here together. *Together* together."

Sabrina shot her finger up. "That was my idea."

"To get them together?" Dad asked.

"No, for him to come with her."

"Well, you two have been friends for a long time," Mom noted, and they all nodded.

Dad shrugged. "I like him."

"Me too," Mom agreed.

Sabrina clapped. "I love him. Do you love him?"

I rolled my eyes.

Sabrina spoke out of the corner of her mouth, purposely not lowering her voice. "She totally loves him."

I popped my hands on my hips. "I told Kimberly I'm not talking about this with you all until I talk to him. We have a lot to consider, okay? It's not like this is some random guy from a dating app—"

"Thank god," Mom said with a wave of her hand.

"And we have a lot of history to sort through—"

"History together is good. A solid foundation," Dad told me with a smile.

"He's got the kids to think about and—"

"And don't you love them?" Sabrina asked, head tilted.

With a sigh, I flopped back into a chair. "You're exhausting. This family is exhausting."

Sufficiently proud of themselves, they kept busy by fixing Sabrina's veil and relating some story about Dad's sister, Aunt Maeve, and all her ailments. Mom guessed she'd have a fainting spell to steal Sabrina's spotlight, and we all placed bets on how early it would happen.

Then it was time for the ceremony.

We were guided down a corridor toward the garden area. The golf course's landscaping was impeccable, with lush green lawns and vibrant flower beds meticulously tended to. An archway covered in vines and white roses marked the ceremony spot, with rows of white chairs fanning out behind it.

The music swelled, a soft strings version of Jason Derulo's "Talk Dirty" because of some inside joke that I didn't want to know about.

Kim walked down the aisle first, and I offered my youngest sister a peck on the cheek before following. Once we were in place, Mom and Dad both walked Sabrina down the aisle as a lovely little break in tradition.

My sister beamed, Everett bit his lip as his chin wobbled, and I coasted my gaze around the area, searching for Jude. I located him in the third row, smiling at me, as if he'd been watching me the whole time. His eyes shone with such tenderness that it rendered me breathless, and it wasn't until my sister handed me her bouquet that I broke our eye contact, needing to focus on this present moment and not the future vision in front of me.

The ceremony was quick, and as my sister and her husband recessed back up the aisle, I found Jude again. His smile was wide and welcoming, only for me, and I bit my lip to keep from grinning too brightly.

With the photos already taken care of, we were free to enjoy the reception, which was held in the golf course's ballroom. As soon as I made my way inside to my assigned table, Jude appeared, his hand at the small of my back.

"You okay?" he murmured, leaning in close.

I nodded, tipping my head back, loving that I could loop my arms around his neck if I wanted, so I did. "Yeah. I'm really happy for them."

He studied me with rapt attention, his eyes drifting back and forth between my own before he seemed satisfied. Then he pressed a lingering kiss to my forehead. "Here." He held out my purse to me, so I could switch my heels for my sneakers, and I moaned in gratitude.

"Better knock that off, honeybee. We're in public."

"You gonna massage my feet later?" I asked, half teasing, but he merely smiled.

"You only have to ask."

I popped a kiss on his lips, tossed my heels into my bag and hid it under the table, and then took his hand in mine. "Come on, let's go get a drink. I fear my family will drive me to get drunk tonight."

At the bar, Jude ordered a beer for himself and a white wine for me. "Why's that?"

"They insist on me telling them everything."

"About us?"

I accepted my wine from the bartender. "Yup. It's Sabrina's wedding, but all she wanted to know about was you."

"Well…" He sipped his beer and exhaled a rough breath as if he had the world on his shoulders. "I can't help that they love me more than you."

I rolled my eyes and thumped him on the chest. He hugged me to him, so I couldn't hit him anymore, both of us laughing into each other's shoulders.

"Don't you two look cozy," Mom said, and Jude and I both turned to her.

"Told you," I mumbled.

"Hi, Sheila. How are you?" Jude asked, releasing me to hug my mother.

"I'm fine, and I take it you're fine too?"

"I'm doing very well. Thank you."

Mom waved her index finger between us with a little wink. "It's about damn time you two realized how good you are for each other."

I downed about a third of my wine while Jude raised his drink to her. "What can I say besides good things take time?"

"That's right." Mom practically danced in place. "I need to go mingle. You two have fun."

But as soon as she left, the bride and groom took her place, and it was the same damn conversation all over again. Then Kimberly and Henry, and then Dad. Even freaking Aunt Maeve got in on the action, only after detailing her gout and bunions. Of course.

As always, Jude charmed each and every person. Not that he hadn't already endeared himself to them. The next few hours passed in a blur of toasts, music, food, stories, and a late-to-the-game fainting spell, which Maeve recovered from fine. When the DJ announced the last dance of the night, Jude tugged me out to the floor and into his arms, holding me flush against him, and I reveled in his warm embrace, spinning in a slow circle to "Maybe I'm Amazed."

"Did you have fun?" I asked after a while, and he nodded, adjusting his hold so his palms lay flat on my back.

"I'm really glad I'm here, and I'm really glad I'm here with you."

His gaze dipped down to my throat, where I wore one of the candy necklaces he'd procured as a favor. He bent, his teeth scraping my skin as he bit one of the hard candies off the string. I felt it *everywhere*.

"*You* better knock *that* off, babe. We're in public."

He chewed and swallowed the candy with a cocky smile, and since we wouldn't be doing a lot of chatting after we ditched this party, I figured we had to have some discussion about us now.

I swallowed a few nerves and asked him outright, "What are we going to do now?"

"Try to sneak out of here without Aunt Maeve seeing us, that's for sure."

"I mean after that."

"After that..." He focused somewhere beyond my shoulder. "It's going to take time. I wish I could give you a concrete answer. I wish I could walk in the front door with you and have the kids be totally okay with it, but I'm... I'm just not sure."

"I get that."

He slanted his head back to me. "Sebastian had tryouts this morning, and he has them again tomorrow."

"Yeah? How'd he do?"

"All right, I guess. I want to get through the next few days with him, and then maybe we can talk about possibly saying something to them?"

"Yeah. I'm fine with whatever you want to do."

"I don't..." He licked his lips and took a deep breath, inching his hands higher up my back, as if he needed something to hold on to for whatever he was mentally hyping himself up for. "They've been through so much, and I don't want to hurt them."

"No, I know. I know. You don't have to explain—"

"You're important to me, Brooke. So damn important. Your friendship means everything to me, and I..." He briefly closed his eyes, and when he opened them again, I thought I could crawl inside for how unguarded they were to me. "I love you."

His words weren't a surprise. Merely a statement of fact. Comfortable and settled. Like slipping on my favorite worn-yet-beloved sweatshirt. That was what being loved by Jude was. Coming home after years in the making.

"I love you too." I slid my hands to the back of his head,

and he pressed his forehead to mine, both of us giggling like we were high. But this one was completely different.

This one wouldn't fade.

We kissed, a breath trapped between our lips, and still, we kept our fingers woven in each other's hair, refusing to move even a centimeter as the song came to an end.

"I love you," he said. "And I can't mess this up—for the kids, for you, but for me too. I can't lose you. I can't go through that again."

"I understand, and you have to know by now that I'm not going anywhere."

He lifted his head, sweeping his thumbs over my cheeks. "I don't know if I deserve you in my life, but I'm sure as hell gonna take advantage of you being here."

I bit back a laugh. "That sounded really sexual."

"Go ahead and ruin the moment. Get your head out of the gutter."

I stepped away from him. "If I'm in the gutter, it's only because I've followed you down there."

He laced his fingers with mine to usher me off the dance floor, slyly patting my butt on the way. "Then let's get you home so I can really take advantage of you."

"Mm. I like the sound of that."

TWENTY-TWO
JUDE

followed Brooke up to her place, my hands on her hips as she unlocked her door. Once she had it open, I had her back against the wall before her purse hit the floor. Her fingers pulled at my suit jacket, mine sought out her zipper, neither of us very careful.

This wasn't an experiment or practice.

This was a culmination. Pure and simple.

We no longer had to pretend we were doing this for a reason. We were doing this because we wanted to. Because we loved each other. Because she was the only woman I'd want to do this with.

After we kicked off our shoes, I chased her down the hall to her bedroom, her dress half falling off, my shirt open, pants unbuttoned. She flicked on her light then threw herself at me like some kind of feral animal, and we tumbled to her bed in a tangle of clothes and laughter.

We kissed until we were nothing more than swollen lips and panted breaths, still not even completely undressed. Brooke's hair was a mess, the sparkly barrette hanging off the side of her head, while I was pretty sure she'd sucked a bruise into my neck. I stood up to toss my shirt on her dresser, followed immediately by my pants as she shimmied her dress the rest of the way off, leaving her in a matching beige set.

My gaze roved over her, my mouth dry. She didn't know how sexy she was as she finally plucked the clip from her hair to throw on her nightstand, letting all of her silky milk-chocolate hair fall over her shoulders. She was long and supple, her muscles gentled with curves, the dip of her waist flaring out to hips I loved to hold and up to breasts I loved to admire. Of course there were her scars, the barely visible one below her right collarbone and the larger one parallel to the line of her underwear. I loved them both. I would love any and every part of her, but especially the marks left behind because she had survived. She was alive.

"You gonna come over here or what?" she asked, all sugar and spice, one leg extended, the other bent in a come-hither pose.

I crawled up the mattress, kissing my way up her stomach, leaving goose bumps in my wake, then helped to remove her bra—because I was nothing if not a gentleman—and bent to suck her nipple into my mouth.

She moaned, her fingernails digging into my shoulders, and I wrapped my hands around her hips, so she couldn't squirm away as I gave the same treatment to her other nipple, licking at the sensitive pink peak.

Her little groans of pleasure were like a shot of adrenaline to my veins, and I couldn't take it anymore. I sat back on my heels to peel her underwear off like I was unwrapping a gift on Christmas morning. Eager to get to it but relishing the anticipation. I curled my fingers around the thin strips across her hips, skimming my knuckles over the outsides of her thighs as I dragged the thong down her legs, revealing her completely.

"You're gorgeous," I murmured, gripping the insides of her knees, not exactly delicate when I pushed them open, creating more room for me to lie down.

But she stopped me from lowering my head. "Wait. I want to talk."

With the tip of my nose mere centimeters away from the thatch of curls between her legs, I heaved a tortured sigh. *"Now?"*

"Yeah. I..." She glanced to the digital clock on her nightstand, the one that lit up in the morning and played nature sounds instead of ringing with an alarm. "You said Sebastian has tryouts tomorrow, right?"

I nodded. "Nine a.m."

"So how late can you stay?"

"Not much later than midnight." My parents were probably passed out on my couch by now. My kids long since fast asleep.

Brooke ran a hand through her hair. "Okay, so that's enough time."

"Enough time for what?"

She moved closer to me, completely naked, all that glorious, creamy skin calling to me, and she wanted to *talk*. A half smile tipped her lips. "We always talk about what I like, what I want to do, but what about what you want?"

"Hm?"

She skated her hands down my chest and stomach to tug at the elastic of my boxer briefs, as if my dick wasn't confused enough as it was. "I want to hear your fantasies. What do you like in bed? What have you always wanted to try?"

My jaw loosened, every possible thought escaping my brain in the moment.

"You always give me what I want. I want to give you what you want," she went on, and I turned, hanging my legs off the side of her bed. She followed, kissing my shoulder. "You can tell me. You know I won't care. I won't judge you."

"I know. It's..." I shook my head because I'd never been asked that question before. Our dating pact had basically morphed into sex lessons, and it wasn't like I didn't need them. I did. I wasn't at all experienced in terms of…kink. I had no idea what I liked. So I told her, "I like what you like."

She sent a shiver down my spine when she breathed a laugh against my ear, and I grabbed hold of her ass cheek, squeezing, eliciting a halfhearted protest. Which really meant *give me more* because she nipped at my ear. I squeezed again, and she whined my name.

I kissed her. "What do you want me to say, honeybee?"

The little minx coiled herself around me, settling on my lap, her hot pussy rubbing over my cock, and I sucked in a breath, seizing her hips. "Tell me what you want," she ordered in a siren voice. "Tell me your fantasy."

Staring down at her naked breasts, swaying with every roll of her hips, and feeling the heat of her… I was done. "I want to use you."

She stilled. Her brows high.

"I want to tie you up and use you. For whatever I want. However I want."

Her top teeth sawed into her bottom lip, and I held her chin between my thumb and forefinger so she'd stop. Only so I could then trap that lip between my teeth. I tugged on it, at the same time I plucked at her nipples.

"Yes," she whispered.

"Yes, what?" I asked, my mouth against hers.

"Let's do that."

I tipped my head back. "Really?"

"Yeah. I trust you. You trust me. So, yes, use me."

I swallowed the boulder in my throat and stood with her in my arms, walking to the foot of the bed, where I deposited her back down to consider my possibilities. Her headboard was plain white with wooden slats. Usable but not super sturdy. I would know since I put the IKEA bed frame together myself when she'd purchased it a few years ago. She'd bought all her bedroom furniture to match. Farmhouse chic, she'd called it.

"I need cables or zip ties or something," I told her, and she slapped her hand over her mouth when she snorted.

"Zip ties? You gonna murder me too?"

I waved her off. "Reading one too many of your dirty books, I guess."

She jutted her chin toward her closet. "You can probably find something in there."

Her walk-in was only a few feet wide, overflowing with hangers and clothes. I searched for a scarf or something long enough to use, but the only thing available was a black leather belt. I held it out for her, and she shrugged.

"Lie back," I told her, and she scooted up the mattress, extending her arms above her head. I wrapped the belt around her wrists and quickly realized it wouldn't work. I couldn't cinch it. I took the end out of the buckle and attempted to wrap it around a few times, but that didn't work either. "How do you do it?"

She tipped her head back, checking out my work upside down. "Maybe loop it around the frame first."

So, I did that too. "Why is this so difficult?"

She sat up. "My books always make it seem so easy. Look it up."

We both found our cell phones and brought up our own searches, coming back together on the bed, peering over each other's shoulder to see what the other found.

"I got a YouTube video from some…is he Russian?" I turned the volume all the way up. I couldn't tell what Eastern European country he was from, but that accent meant business.

"Reddit says to make sure the insides of my wrists are facing each other, and you should be able to get a finger between the restraints."

I nodded at Brooke's notes as I viewed the video again, making sure I understood how to loop the belt.

"Ooh, we could use ACE bandages."

I glanced over my shoulder at her. "You have ACE bandages?"

"No." She shrugged with a laugh. "But good to know for next time."

I growled and stole her phone from her hands, placing it on the floor along with mine. "Enough fucking around." I flipped her over on her stomach and smacked her ass. "Time to get to work."

She wiggled away, her butt cheeks jiggling, and I prodded her to crawl up the bed as I started in on the makeshift hand-cuffs. Once she was on her back, she slid her hands through the loop I'd created, and I pulled it taut. "Okay?"

"Yeah. It's good."

I waited until she got herself comfortable then circled the long end around one of the slats in the bed frame and pushed it through the handcuffs. One good tug, and it would come undone from the frame, but with how Brooke's nipples pebbled and her skin flushed, she liked this game as much as I did.

With her sufficiently bound, I stood up to observe my rather shoddy handiwork. "We'll have to do more research."

"Yeah," she agreed, hips and legs absently swiveling. "We will."

We will.

That was all I needed. Us.

I settled on the bed, nudging her thighs apart, even as she raised her head. "I thought you wanted to use me."

"Yeah. I do. So shut up and let me use my mouth on you like I want."

"Well, if you insi—" Her laugh cut off with a gasp when I licked up her slit. She thought she was clever with her sassy attitude.

I'd leave her a mess, too tired to even smile when I was done with her.

I draped her legs over my shoulders, winding my arms

around her hips so I could hold her soft flesh open with my thumbs, sucking on her clit, and her thighs clamped down around my ears. By now, I knew what she liked, and I didn't hold back, flicking the tip of my tongue over that little sweet spot. The tension in her muscles built slowly and steadily, exactly like her soft pleas, and I reached my right arm up to grip her breast, squeezing it roughly. I rolled her nipple between my fingers, rubbing my tongue over her at the same time, not letting up until I felt her contract, every part of her coiled tight, and then release, and I lifted myself up above in time to catch the flush in her cheeks.

"How was that?"

She licked her lips, blinking into awareness. "So good."

"I think you like being tied up."

"I might."

I bent, dragging my tongue up her throat. "You have a vibrator?"

"In my drawer."

I wasted no time opening her nightstand, rummaging around reading glasses, chargers, eye drops, hair ties, and lotion to finally find some lube and what appeared to be a penguin with a suction cup in place of a head. I held it up, my head angled in silent question.

"I thought it was cute."

I pressed the power button, and the thing came alive in my hand. "Oh, it's cute, all right."

Positioning myself back between her legs, I squirted a tiny bit of lube on my index finger, smearing it over her clit before placing the vibrator against it, and Brooke's legs immediately spasmed.

"This guy's got some power," I said in amazement, and it wasn't long before she was on the verge of coming again. I placed my hand on her hip to keep her still, my cock practically pulsing at the way her neck arched, her feet scrambling for purchase. Her belly quivered, and I loved how she didn't seem to be in control of herself anymore. Especially with the high, keening sound she made when she orgasmed again.

I hit the power button, giving her some time to catch her breath, and so I could take off my underwear, a wet spot marring the cotton from where my dick reminded me of its need. It would have to wait.

I brushed strands of hair off her face, slid my palm over her damp brow, cupping her cheek as I kissed her, drinking in the salty taste of her skin when I dipped my tongue into the hollow of her collarbone. "You ready for another one?" She didn't answer, so I did it for her. "Yes, you are."

I situated her legs outside of my thighs so she couldn't move them as much then skated my hand over her torso, teasing at her nipples. "You told me I could use you. So I am."

"You're going to kill me."

I wrapped my hand around her throat, letting her feel the weight of my fingers over her pounding pulse. "Not quite yet."

Powering on the penguin once again, I settled it on her clit, and I knew it wouldn't take long, she was already so keyed up.

"Oh fuck," she groaned. "Oh my god."

I drank her in. Her face flushed, her eyes shut, her skin pink and glistening with sweat, and I couldn't stop myself from pushing my knees wide, holding her open, as I released her throat to circle my hand around my cock instead. I gripped it roughly, cutting off the growing strength of my own orgasm. I couldn't come yet. Not until I was buried deep inside her.

Which wouldn't be much longer.

She thrashed her head side to side, mumbling nonsense, her hips jerking off the mattress without my hand to hold her down, but I kept that little son of a bitch penguin sucker on her, carrying her through her high, waiting until she settled back on the bed to power it off.

That was when I popped open the lube, squeezing some onto her and on my fingers. I spread it down the length of my cock then rubbed the bit on her over the seam of her pussy and into her, giving in to my impulse to make her come *just one more* time.

She moaned, her body jolting when I found her most sensitive spot. A few strokes of my fingers, and she went off like a bomb, cursing and gasping, and then *I* was the son of a bitch, driving my cock into her before she had a chance to rest. I hoisted her legs straight up into the air, holding them against my chest, as I found my rhythm.

She fought the binding, writhing in earnest, and I couldn't help but grin into her calf. Her eyes snapped up to me when I nipped at her ankle.

"Who's going to replace me after you've killed me?" she asked, her breasts bouncing with each of my thrusts.

"One of the boys. Probably Nate since I've known him the longest."

"He—ooh!" It took her a few seconds to return to her thought. "He won't fuck you as good as I do."

"No." I released her legs, the burn at the bottom of my spine too hard to ignore anymore, and I held myself above her with my hands on either side of her shoulders. "He probably won't. Guess that means I have to keep you around."

She bent her knees, hitching her legs around my hips, the sweetest "Please, Jude" dripping from her lips.

But I'd freely offer her anything. Everything. She never even had to ask.

She could take all of me.

I curled my hand around her hip to press up against her lower back, changing her angle, and she cried out, both of us falling over the edge at the same time.

Relaxing my grip on her, I eased my cock in and out of her a few times, allowing both of us moment to float back to earth, to calm our racing breaths and heartbeats. Before slipping out of her entirely, I undid the belt from around the headboard and her wrists, placed a quick kiss on her lips, then hopped off the bed to clean up in her bathroom and wet a washcloth with warm water.

When I returned to the bed, Brooke was rubbing at her wrist.

"Are you hurt?"

"I'm fine."

To see for myself, I picked up her left wrist, examining it, and when I found nothing except for a faint red mark, I kissed it then checked out her right wrist, skimming my nose over the thin skin there. "Did you enjoy that?"

"I did."

I kissed her wrist and placed her hand on the bed, nudging her legs open so I could wipe the cloth over the insides of her thighs and between them. After a few swipes, I folded up the washcloth and chucked it into her laundry basket, set outside of her closet.

Facing her, I kissed the slope of her shoulder. "Didn't use you too hard, did I?"

She smiled sleepily. "It was perfect."

I hummed an agreement against her throat and tunneled my fingers into her hair, holding the back of her head, so I could kiss her mouth, lazy and long. Leaving her on the bed, I dressed then dug through her drawer for a T-shirt, which I held out for her so she could slide her head and arms through.

"You want underwear?"

She shook her head. "Just shorts."

After finding a pair, I knelt so she could step into them and got in a kiss above her pubic bone before I covered her up completely. I stood, gathering her in my arms. "I love you."

"I love you," she said against my throat, and it struck me again how weird it was that it wasn't weird.

This was the easiest relationship of my life.

I hoped it stayed that way.

Holding hands, we walked to her door, and she told me to let her know how the tryout went tomorrow. I agreed with one last kiss. "Sleep well."

She offered me her crooked smile. "Night, babe."

I tapped her nose. "Night, honeybee."

TWENTY-THREE
BROOKE

JUDE

Seb finished with the tryouts.

How was it?

JUDE

Good. I think.

JUDE

But it was so bizarre. Parents were sitting around watching like it was professionals or something.

Yeah, I remember when I played travel soccer as a kid. Parents can be intense. Did you feel uncomfy?

JUDE

Yep.

JUDE

Me and Lulu took a walk. I didn't think Seb would like me looking over his shoulder. And it's not like a game, where I can cheer him on.

JUDE

It's nerve-racking.

Totally.

What are you doing now?

JUDE

Going home to change and grab lunch then meet the guys at Imagination for a playdate.

I think you guys enjoy your playdates more than the kids.

JUDE

High probability.

JUDE

What are you up to today?

I'm at the farm, doing some banking. Nicole ran the stand at the market by herself yesterday so I'm giving her a few extra bucks in her envelope next week, and Gunner should be here soon so we can pack up this week's co-op deliveries.

JUDE

Got anything not green?

Some red bell peppers.

You need to start eating better.

JUDE

No thanks.

Listen, pal.

JUDE

They don't taste good.

I need you around for a long time. You better start eating some greens, or I'm gonna shove them down your throat.

JUDE

So violent.

The problem is you don't know how to cook them. Wait until you try my sweet-and-spicy chicken and brussels sprouts.

JUDE

I'll eat the chicken.

Your insides must look like rock candy.

JUDE

Most definitely.

———

Three hours later…

JUDE

FYI

JUDE

I gave Liam your number because Kennedy is interested in joining the co-op.

JUDE

How much of a cut do I get for that?

I'm paying you in free vegetables.

JUDE

That's literally the worst payment plan anyone could have.

JUDE

I'm taking the kids out for dinner. Might ease into the idea of you.

Good luck.

———

Five hours later…

Since you never texted, I'm assuming it went badly.

JUDE

It didn't really go at all.

JUDE

I asked them what they thought of you. Amelia said you have pretty hair and that you're really good at Go Fish. Seb asked why.

JUDE

I told him that you're my good friend, so then he said it's weird you and me are friends. He said, and I quote:

JUDE

"Your friends are Uncle Nate, Uncle Dylan, and Uncle Liam. Do you want us to start calling her Aunt Brooke?"

I think I just got the same feeling in my stomach that you get when you eat anything green.

JUDE

Yeah. So I dropped it for now.

JUDE

What are you up to?

Nothing.

Stressing.

JUDE

Over what? Sebastian? Because it's fine. It'll
be fine.

No. I know that. I'm stressed over my
appointment tomorrow.

JUDE

What appointment?

My oncology check-in.

JUDE

You didn't tell me you had an appointment.

Well, between all the BIG FEELINGS this
weekend…

JUDE

Don't forget the BIG SEX.

Yes. Of course. So between all of that, when
was I going to tell you?

But it's not a big deal. Only my annual
appointment to make sure everything looks
good. No reoccurrences. I'll probably get a
blood test.

JUDE

I love you.

I know.

JUDE

Make me the brussels sprouts. I'll eat them.

Ok.

I love you.

JUDE

I know.

————

An hour later…

JUDE

Are you asleep yet?

Nope. Can't sleep.

JUDE

Come over.

What about the kids?

JUDE

They're asleep. Come sleep with me. We'll set the alarm to wake up before them.

Be over in a bit.

parked in front of Jude's house, seeing every light in the house was off, confirming that the kids were indeed fast asleep. The tight knot of nerves that had taken up residence in the pit of my stomach loosened as I opened my car door, and it almost completely dissipated when I spotted him standing at the front door, waiting for me, haloed by a single porch light.

Late-night sounds of crickets and the rustle of wind sent goose bumps down my arms, even in the hot August air, as I stepped out of my car. I made my way up the sidewalk leading to the front door and rubbed my hands over my biceps. It didn't occur to me until right this second that as soon as Jude told me to come over, I'd hopped out of bed, not bothering to change or throw anything over the overly large T-shirt that hung off my shoulder and the tiny cotton shorts I wore. I'd merely slid into a pair of flip-flops and snatched my bag from the kitchen counter.

"You cold?" Jude asked as I reached him.

"I didn't think about putting on different clothes, and now that I'm here, I—"

"You're fine." He cupped the back of my neck and brought his lips to mine in a searing, breathless kiss that obliterated every last ounce of self-consciousness. I rose up onto my toes, winding my arms around his neck.

Had it been last night he'd left my condo after tying my wrists together?

Felt longer.

And like only five minutes ago.

I supposed it had been a long time since I'd wanted to only ever be around one person. Not since I was a teenager and a twentysomething. Not since I didn't have much to lose.

Now, we were real adults with a lot of responsibilities. There didn't seem to be enough time to work out this new, clawing need that had suddenly taken root. Nothing but his familiar scent and taste would relieve it.

When we finally broke apart, a lopsided grin slid across his face. "I missed you."

I touched three fingers to my mouth, agreeing with a hum. "Feels like it."

His rough midnight laugh soothed me, and I wrapped my arm around his waist when he looped his arm around my shoulders. "Come on. Let's go to bed."

The kids' rooms were on the first floor, so we had to be quiet as we snuck up the creaky staircase. We crept into Jude's bedroom, and as soon as we turned the corner, he closed the door and pulled me into him, lifting me up in a bear hug.

The ultimate teddy bear of a man. As squishy on the inside as on the outside. I tucked my face into his neck, the bristles of his beard tickling my temple, my new favorite spot, where I could enjoy his warmth and hear his gentle breathing, feel his heartbeat.

"You all right?" he asked, setting me down.

I backed up, my palms on his pecs. "I am now."

He kissed my forehead and gestured for me to get into bed, so I did, though it didn't escape my notice that this was the same bed and bedroom he had shared with Mira.

"Is this okay?"

He shucked off his mesh shorts along with his T-shirt then hit the light and crawled in next to me in only his boxer briefs. "What do you mean?"

We rolled toward each other in the dark. "Me being here. In your bed."

He understood my meaning and exhaled audibly as he lay on his back. I held my head up in my hand, my sight acclimating to the darkness as I waited while he gathered his thoughts. I drew my fingertips over his beard to rest at the base of his throat, feeling the vibration when he spoke.

"I like that you're here. I want you to be here, but yeah, it's…different."

I heard more than saw him scratch his jaw, his fingers moving over the bristles.

"No one has slept in bed with me since Mira died. No one outside of my kids. How do you feel being here?"

Scooting over to lay my head on his shoulder, I placed my hand over his heart. "I didn't know if you'd ever invite me over like this." I swallowed, thinking about my wording. I didn't want to hurt his feelings, but we also needed to have this conversation. "I know Mira was a huge part of your life. She still is. I know you love me, and I don't think I'm a particularly jealous person, but… It's impossible for you, for the kids, even me, to forget about her, and I don't want to be compared to a ghost."

Jude rubbed his hand up and down my back, remaining quiet, and I lifted my head. "Am I the asshole? I don't want it to sound like you can't—"

"You're not the asshole. It doesn't sound like anything besides honesty, and that's what we need."

I tucked my head back down, listening to his heartbeat

and then the low rumble of his voice. "I don't compare you, if that's something you're worried about. What I had with Mira is totally different and separate from what I have with you. And I guess, sometimes it is easy to romanticize it because we had a good life. My marriage was good. I loved her very much, and in some ways, that love is still very real. I'm sure that's probably really hard to hear, and I'm sorry."

I blinked at the sting in my eyes, and he kissed the top of my head. "Sometimes I think about different timelines. Alternative lives, you know? Like, in another timeline, Mira is still alive and we're still married and everything is great. But in another one, Mira and I were never even together because I never got up the guts to ask her out in high school, or she would've said no, or her parents wouldn't have allowed us to go out. Her parents were really strict," he said, almost as an afterthought. "But in this life, the only one I've got, Mira isn't here anymore. You are. And if she hadn't died, I probably would've never become so close to you. I'd never have learned how wonderful you are. How smart and kind and brave you are. If there is anything I can promise you, it's that I am not comparing you to the past. You are truly the one person to remind me to keep living for the future."

He cupped the back of my head, tangling his fingers in my hair. "You are my future, Brooke. For as long as you'll have me and for as long as the universe allows, I want to be with you."

I dabbed at the tears on my cheeks, nodding, because I couldn't speak.

"I don't think it'll be easy. But I do think it'll be amazing." He rotated us so he was above me, his thumbs swiping under my eyes. "I love you."

"I know," I croaked.

"I'll need you to be patient."

"I know that too."

Even in the dark, his grin glowed. "I've been thinking

more and more about this house. It was never the plan to stay here. It's small, and the kids are getting bigger, and only having one full bathroom sucks."

"So you think you'll be moving soon?"

"Soonish." He shrugged. "Maybe."

I sniffed a laugh. "I love you."

"I know." He bent to kiss me, but my yawn interrupted him. So he redirected his kiss to my cheek as he lay on his side, sliding his arm around my waist. "Sleep now, honeybee. I got you."

And he did. So I closed my eyes and slept.

TWENTY-FOUR
JUDE

Banging on the staircase woke me, my eyes shooting open. It was Seb. He always sounded like an elephant stomping around.

"Dad! Wake up! You have to check your email."

I sat up, the bedsheet shifting with my movement, revealing Brooke's shoulder, and multiple things hit me at once.

Number one, we'd forgotten to set an alarm last night.

Number two, it was after eight o'clock in the morning.

Number three, Sebastian was about to see Brooke in my bed.

And right on cue, he flung open the door, popping his head about the frame. "Dad, I was messaging with Landon. They sent out the email for who made the team. You have to check to see—"

His attention slanted from me to Brooke, and I had no time to do anything.

"Seb," I started at the same time Brooke lurched awake next to me, jackhammering up in bed with wide-eyed confusion. My son's face drained of color, and I lifted my hand. To do what, I didn't know. "Buddy, I—"

"I hate you!" His face went from pale to bright red in less than a second. "I hate you!" He fisted his hands at his sides, his head toggling back and forth as he screamed at Brooke and me. "I fucking hate both of you!"

Then he pivoted and ran.

By the time I pulled myself together and out of my state of shock, the front door slammed. I leaped out of bed, tugged on my shorts and shirt from the floor, and raced outside but didn't see him anywhere. Running around to the back of the house, I searched the backyard, but he was nowhere to be found. I called his name, shouting for him, but even if he heard me, I doubted he'd answer.

"Shit. Fuck." I jogged back inside to find Brooke in the kitchen holding Amelia, who waved Seb's iPad at me.

"Brother forgot this in my bed. He-he said we could watch Bluey together."

I ignored her, telling Brooke, "I don't know where he went. Can you stay with her so I can go look for him?"

"Yes. Of course."

I started to my room, though she stopped me with a soft, almost pained, "Although I can't stay long. My appointment's at ten."

I thumped the side of my fist against the wall as I silently cursed. "Okay, lemme... I'll figure it out."

I slipped into my sneakers and ran the toothbrush over my teeth for a few seconds before splashing cold water on my face. I needed to think. Needed a plan. I needed help in finding Sebastian. The idea that he'd run away from home terrified and shamed me. He could literally be anywhere, have gone anywhere, been taken...

Keeling over, I put my hands on my knees to catch my breath before I had a panic attack.

"Hey, it's going to be all right. We'll find him." Brooke stood in front of me, her bare feet in my line of sight.

"What if... I didn't..."

"Don't think of the what-ifs. He's upset and ran away. He won't be able to get that far. He might even come back after he runs it off."

Standing up straight, I wiped at my face. "How long can you stay here?"

She checked the time on her phone. "Half hour. Maybe a little longer. But I need to go home and change. I'm really sorry I can't stay. I would, but rescheduling is a nightmare and—"

"It's fine. It's fine." I rushed past her after a quick peck on the forehead.

I was being pulled in different directions, torn apart. Sebastian was out there alone somewhere because he'd been blindsided. And Brooke needed me, needed my support for her oncology checkup that could determine…everything.

Guilt and fear waged war inside me, and I raked my hands through my hair. How had I let this spiral so quickly? I should have been more careful, more considerate of Sebastian's feelings. Introducing Brooke into our lives was going to be a huge adjustment, and I'd naively thought I could control the situation.

I drew my phone from my pocket with trembling fingers, firing off a text to the group thread.

> Seb saw Brooke at my place this morning and ran off. I need to find him, but Brooke has a doctor appt she can't miss. Nate, I need you over here to stay with Amelia ASAP.

NATE

Omw

DYLAN

Duck

DYLAN

FUCK

DYLAN

i'm at work but Gen's home with the kids if u
need anything

LIAM

What can I do?

I dropped a kiss on Amelia's head as she ate breakfast in the kitchen before heading out to my car and sent off another message.

Start thinking of a list of places he might go?
I don't know.

I'm freaking out.

NATE

8 minutes away.

LIAM

Try to stay calm. Call your parents. He might
go there.

I turned the ignition over and set out, determined to drive in consecutively larger circles, like a bull's-eyes with my house at the target. Brooke was right. He was on foot; he wouldn't be able to get *that* far.

Though he was pretty fast.

As I drove, I called my mom then Youmna, telling each of them the same thing. First, not to panic—which, of course, made them panic and set mine to an even higher notch—and that I would explain everything later, but Seb had run away and to let me know if he showed up at their house.

Mom immediately put me on speaker and ordered my dad to get in the car to start looking.

Youmna immediately started yelling at George in Arabic. I assumed to get in the car and start looking.

Both of them were worried for Sebastian and for me but were understanding. A little too understanding.

I might have felt better if they got mad at me. Screamed at me for being a bad parent.

Neither of them did so.

And I'd never felt more guilt and humiliation than when I hung up with them. I'd messed up. Messed up so bad my kid had run away.

My vision blurred, and I slammed my hand on the steering wheel, accidentally honking the horn, before I pulled over. I had to clear my eyes and head, and once I parked, I stepped out of the car, only to kick the tire, letting myself cry and curse and free all of my anger.

Sebastian had been begging me for a cell phone, but I'd held off, reasoning he could use his iPad to communicate with his friends. He didn't *need* a cell phone. He was too young.

Well.

He needed a cell phone now.

He had no way of calling or texting me. No way of letting me know where he was. If he needed me. If he was hurt. If…

I hung my head, crying into my hands, praying, asking Mira to help.

I'd lost our son.

I'd hurt our son.

This was my fault, and I needed to fix it.

Mira didn't answer my silent pleas, and I wiped the collar of my shirt over my face. Sniffling a few times, I sat back behind the wheel once again and set off.

My heart pounded in my ears as I drove aimlessly, scouring every street and park for any sign of Sebastian. Each minute that ticked by ratcheted my anxiety higher, but I found my mind drifting to Brooke.

By now, she was probably in the waiting room, and I

hoped to God everything went well. I couldn't handle one more bad situation.

With no messages from her or Nate, I figured everything was still good at home, so I focused on finding Sebastian.

I had to find him. Had to find my son.

After driving for another hour with no sign of him, I picked up my phone, intent on calling my mother again to let her know I was going to call the police, but a text popped up.

DYLAN

maybe he went to the baseball field

Baseball.

Fuck.

I opened my email app to find one from the coach of the traveling team. I scanned the short paragraph. Sebastian didn't make the team.

Chest aching, I hooked a right turn, speeding toward the community baseball fields on the west side of town. A few minutes of hoping and sweating gave way to the familiar view of the park and field, surrounded by a chain link fence.

I pulled into the empty parking lot, haphazardly throwing the car into park before scrambling out. My feet pounded against the pavement as I raced to the baseball diamond, scanning the bleachers in desperation.

And *there.*

There he was.

Huddled on the bench in the dugout.

My boy.

TWENTY-FIVE
JUDE

"Sebastian."

At my voice, he startled, uncurling from his balled-up position, whipping his head in my direction, features twisting into a wounded glare.

I opened my mouth to speak, but he stopped me.

"Go away." He swiped the backs of his hands over his cheeks in a jerky, furious motion. "Just leave me alone."

I paused my steps toward him, words of comfort dying on my tongue. The rush of traffic from the nearby road filled my ears like a dull roar, my chest empty. It was true. Whoever said it. That kids are our hearts, walking around outside of our bodies. Because I didn't feel mine at all.

I watched mine cry instead.

Slowly, cautiously, I crossed the final few feet and lowered myself onto the bench beside him. "Buddy, I'm sorry, but that's not what I'm gonna do. I'm not going to leave you alone."

He tucked his legs in again, wrapping his scrawny arms around them, hiding his face from me against his knees. Like he used to do when he was little.

"I've been worried all day," I murmured, voice barely more than a rumble. "I know you're upset, but I wish you wouldn't have run off."

He cocked his head, as if about to tell me off, but I didn't let him.

"I don't want to treat you like a little kid. You're not a little kid. You're mature and smart and…I would be devastated if anything ever happened to you. If you were hurt or…" I stared at the ground, where I absently dug the toe of my sneaker into the dirt. "This is my fault."

He didn't speak, his face hidden once again. I placed my hand on his back, and when he didn't move away or mention it, I inched even closer to him. "I know you want me to treat you like a big kid, because you are, but it's hard for me to accept. That's not on you. That's on me. You're going into fifth grade, but it's hard for me not to think of you as a five-year-old. As the kid who cuddled with me during movie nights and wanted to ride on my shoulders as we walked home from the school bus stop. You are my whole life, and I'm so afraid of messing up that I'm not treating you like I should. Like the caring and thoughtful ten-year-old you are, and I'm sorry."

I saw the muscle jumping in his clenched jaw and nearly wilted at the hurt radiating off him in waves.

"Buddy, I'm so, so sorry I lied to you. I shouldn't have. It's not an excuse, but I want you to know that when I told you I wasn't going on a date, I thought I was protecting you. I assumed you wouldn't be able to handle it."

He heaved out a breath, his shoulders shaking as he started to cry.

"Maybe you can't handle it, and that's okay, but I should have talked to you about it. I'm sorry I didn't. I love you so much, and I'm sorry I lied to you. I'm sorry you were blind-sided this morning. I'm so sorry."

He shuddered, and I pulled him into me, holding him tight as he cried for a long time. I suspected he had a lot to say to me but didn't quite have the words yet, and I made a mental note to call our family therapist to get back on the schedule.

Minutes later, when he finally settled, I wiped his face clear of tears and snot with the bottom of my T-shirt then hauled him back into me, kissing his head. "Mommy and I were both really excited when we found out we were going to have our first baby, but your mom, she was *really* excited. And she loved being pregnant. She took a picture every week to see how big you were growing in her belly, and she would sing to you, rubbing where she thought your head was. Sometimes people say women glow when they're pregnant, and that was true for your mother. She lit up."

Sebastian sat back, interested, so I continued.

"She second-guessed everything, the color of your nursery, the sheets on the crib, the clothes, the books, even the little washcloths and bath stuff. She was afraid you'd be sensitive to this thing or that thing, had bought three different kinds of diapers because she wanted to make sure you wouldn't develop a rash on your tiny butt," I said, earning a ghost of a smile from my son.

"And I'll never forget the day you were born as long as I live." I smiled at the memory. "It was the middle of the night when your mom started feeling like she was in labor, and I got us packed up and in the car right away. But the nurses at the hospital told her she wasn't in labor. It was Braxton-Hicks." I looked at my son, explaining, "That's what it's called when a mom might think it feels like labor, but it's not. She feels pain, but not real contractions. So they sent us home, and your sweet, darling mother cursed up a storm. Dropping f-bombs all over the place. Cursed out the nurses, even the guy who brought up the wheelchair for her. She was pissed."

Sebastian snickered. "What happened?"

"I brought her home, and a couple hours later, we went right back to the hospital. It wasn't Braxton-Hicks contractions. They were real contractions, and you came screaming into the world as Mommy screamed at the doctors and nurses that she f-ing knew what she was talking about."

He laughed even harder, and I ruffled his hair then dragged my hand down his cheek, admiring him like I used to in his crib. "When you cursed at me this morning, that's what I thought of. Even through all the worry and fear of you running away, I thought of your mom cursing in labor at everyone who crossed her path. And I thought of how she loved you."

I held on to him, both of my hands around his face, his features a perfect mixture of Mira and me. My two children, the living reminder of her, of some of the best times of my life, and I supposed I should let them in on more. They should know more about her, more of the memories I'd been so afraid to share with them. Afraid for them and for me. I didn't want to fall down into a hole that I wouldn't be able to climb out of.

But I was out. I was out now, and I had to keep my eyes open for my kids.

My perfect, beautiful children.

"Your mom loved being a mom more than anything. And she loved *you* more than life itself. That love will never change or diminish, no matter what. Even though she's gone, she's still in here—" I tapped my fingers on his forehead then lower over his chest "—and here."

Tears streamed down Sebastian's face anew, but he nodded, seeming to take some solace in my words. I cried too.

"Your mom will always be your mom. Nothing can ever change that or take that away. I promise you. No matter what happens, that will never change. Your love for her and her love for you is forever. You hear me?"

Another nod, this one accompanied by a tiny, tremulous smile and sniffles.

"We can talk about what happened today another time, but I want you to know how much Mommy and I love you, and even though she's not here in person, you will always have her love. I'm proud to be your dad, and *that* will never change either. I love you."

I searched his eyes, willing him to understand the depth of my words, of my commitment to him and his well-being, above all else. After an endless stretch of silence, he seemed to deflate with a sigh.

"I love you too," he said and hugged me, accepting all the kisses I laid over his head.

I wiped at my own eyes and stood, motioning toward the parking lot. "You ready to get out of here?"

He stood and started toward me, but he stopped after half a step. "The email. Did you get it?"

I tried not to physically react. "Yeah, buddy, I did."

He stared at me, understanding. "I didn't make it."

I shook my head. "I'm sorry."

He swung back around, kicking at the dirt.

I closed the distance between us and kicked the dirt too. "Damn it."

He paused and furrowed his brow at me, so I shrugged, allowing him to follow my lead. I tried not to curse to be a good example, but if there was ever a time to let it fly, today was the day. He stomped his foot. "Son of a bitch!"

I nodded. "Assholes!"

"Motherfuckers!"

"Hey, whoa, okay." I grabbed hold of him, towing him into my side with a chuckle. "That's enough for now, all right?"

We walked together back to the car, my arm over his shoulders, both of us quiet in our thoughts. The car ride home was quiet too, and while I was beyond relieved to have found

Sebastian, this was only the beginning. We had a long road ahead of us.

Once I parked, Seb headed right inside, not waiting on me, so I stayed in the car to call my mother then Youmna, letting them know I'd found him safe and sound. Of course, they both wanted to come over, but I asked them not to. Told them Sebastian and I both needed some time, and that we had a lot to work through. Neither one of them was happy about my boundary, and I was positive they were already texting each other about me. Wondering if I needed to seek medical attention.

No, but maybe a few beers would help.

As soon as I stepped into the house, Amelia tore down the hall. "Daddy!"

"Hey, Lu." I swung her up into my arms and kissed her temple. "What are you doing?"

"Un-uncle Nate lemme do his makeup."

"Makeup?" I carried her to the living room, where Nate sat with his back to me. "Where'd you get makeup?"

That was when he faced me, his cheeks covered in what I could only guess was red marker. Shapes drawn on his face in thick blue lines.

I tickled my daughter's side. "What did you do?"

She shrieked in laughter. "Makeup!"

Nate held up one of the markers. "Says it's washable."

"Yeah." I agreed. "But it'll take a whole lot of scrubbing."

I put Amelia down with a pat to her butt. "Go get your iPad. You can go on it in the kitchen while you have a snack."

"Ice cream sandwich?" she asked in her cutest squeaky voice.

"Yes. You can have an ice cream sandwich."

"Yes!" She ran off to help herself to an ice cream sandwich from the freezer with the stool I kept specifically for her.

I plopped onto the sofa with a groan and rubbed my hands over my face. "I'm exhausted."

Nate leaned forward to take his cell phone from the coffee table, tapping on it for a minute.

I apologized. "I'm sorry, man. I'm sure I ruined your plans for the day."

"Nah." He kept his focus on his phone as he texted. "You know I'm always here for you. Tabitha's got the bar covered."

"I suspect she got her raise?"

"Yeah." He huffed a laugh, an odd, almost wondrous smile on his face.

"What?"

He shook his head, and for a moment, I thought he wouldn't tell me. But this was Nate. He wore all his emotions on his sleeve and had no problem talking about them either. "We were closing the other night. Just me and her, and I asked why I never see her drink or hang out with anybody there. I've never met any of her friends. She said Walt's not her scene."

"Funny since she's been working there for a decade."

He raised his palm. "That's exactly what I said."

"What is her scene?"

"I asked her that, and she said someplace quieter where she could have a glass of wine and eat a nice dinner."

I crossed my arms, giving in to a smile. "So why do you look like that?"

"I don't know. Got me thinking, I guess."

"About what?"

"Walt's has done good business for me, but I'm not a young buck anymore."

That dragged a laugh out of me. "No. None of us are."

"I'm not interested in being up until three in the morning, making sure everything is closed up."

"That's what you have Tabitha for."

"I don't want that for her either. She's got a lot going on and… I don't know. Maybe it's time for me to switch things up."

"What are you thinking about?"

"Opening up someplace quieter, where someone could have a glass of wine and eat a nice dinner."

This guy. If my own life weren't a mess, I'd tell him to clean up his act to see what was right in front of him. But I couldn't, so instead, I said, "Yeah, might be nice. If you got the funds and plans."

He nodded, eyes glazed over and lost in thought for a moment, and then he snapped out of it with a whack to my arm. "So, what happened this morning?"

I stretched my arms behind my head and leaned back, my gaze on the ceiling. "Brooke was anxious about her doctor's appointment today, so I told her to sleep over last night since it would make me feel better about it too. I said we'd set an alarm, but I never did."

"And Seb walked in."

"And Seb walked in," I repeated. "I found him at the baseball field. Torn up. I really messed up."

"Hey. Hey." He waited until I looked at him. "You're a good dad."

I pinched the bridge of my nose, and Nate threw his arm around me, patting my back a few times. "He loves you. You raised a great kid. Two great kids."

I sniffed and cleared my throat. "Thanks."

"Love you, man."

"Love you too."

He sat back. "You want me to stick around or…?"

"No. Go do what you need to do. Seb didn't make the travel baseball team either, so…"

He winced. "When it rains, it pours, huh?" He stood with a pat to my leg. "Why don't you come to the bar tomorrow night?"

I shrugged my answer, doubting I'd feel like doing anything in the next few days. He let himself out, and I stretched out on the couch.

Some days I didn't know what the hell I was doing. Today was one of those days.

"Daddy! I need help!"

"Yeah, be right there." I stood with a grunt. I didn't know what I was doing, but I had to keep on going.

TWENTY-SIX

BROOKE

Jude told me he didn't want me to bring anything, but I stopped at the store anyway and purchased a few items I thought he and the kids would like: rocket pops for Amelia, Tastykake cupcakes for Sebastian, and A-Treat for Jude.

Parking in front of the house, I took a steadying breath then killed the engine and climbed out of my car. With the shopping bag in hand, I made my way to the front door, and it swung open before I even had a chance to ring the doorbell.

"Brooke!" Amelia flung herself at me, hugging my legs.

"Hi, girlfriend." I tugged on her hair, tipping her head back. She grinned her gap-toothed smile at me. "I brought you some treats."

She danced in place, screeching, "Treeeeaaaats!" I opened the bag so she could see, and her voice rose another octave. "Rocket pops! Brother! Come see! Come look at the treats!"

Sebastian stalked into the hall with Jude trailing a few steps behind. As soon as the younger Gray saw me, his lip curled in disgust. "What are you doing here?"

Amelia shook the box. "Look! Treats!"

Jude reached for Sebastian's shoulder, but he shrugged him off, telling me, "Go away."

I stepped toward him. "Seb—"

"No one wants you here."

I made sure to keep my face devoid of emotion even as my heart broke for the boy in front of me. Even as Amelia clung to me, shaking her head. "Don't go."

Jude gripped his son's shoulder. "Stop."

"Get out!" Sebastian pointed at the door. "Go!"

"Enough!" Jude spun him around. "That's not how you speak to people. Apologize right now."

Sebastian balled his fists, refusing to look at me or his dad. "No."

When Seb didn't move, Jude hunched over, nose-to-nose, seething. "I told you we'd talk later, but I've about had it with you today. You want to treat people with disrespect, you'll get it right back. Go to your room so I don't lose my temper and start smashing up every game you have."

I picked up Amelia, hating that I was the reason for so much drama and heartache. I'd never seen Jude raise his voice to his kids. Both of the children were well-mannered and polite. Sure, they'd thrown the occasional tantrum or had a meltdown, but for the most part, Jude was a mild-mannered parent.

Until now.

And it was my fault.

As if Seb could hear my thoughts, he sneered at me then stomped off. Jude turned his back to me, tunneling both of his hands through his hair, obviously upset. Giving him some space, I carried Amelia into the kitchen and got her settled at the table with a popsicle and a plate in case it dripped. I sat with her, making small talk about the kind of backpack she wanted for school. Unicorn, obviously.

"I'm sure your daddy will find one for you," I said, only for her daddy to speak up behind me.

"I promised we'd go shopping for one."

I spun in my chair to find him leaning against the wall, his thick arms across his chest, his eyes a little bloodshot. It had only been this morning he'd rushed out of the house, yet he looked like he'd been through a storm for days.

"You okay?" I asked, standing up, and he nodded.

"Lulu, me and Brooke are going to go sit outside. You hang out here until you finish your popsicle, okay?"

She gave him a thumbs-up, her attention zeroed in on her iPad. I assumed she'd already had *a lot* of iPad time today. Then he motioned to the front door, so I followed him out. As soon as the door closed, he pivoted to me, his hands in my hair, his lips on mine. "How was your appointment?"

I curled my fingers into his shirt. "Good. Everything is good."

"Thank god," he rasped, tugging me into him, holding on to me like a lifeline in the water.

I couldn't believe after everything that had happened today, he wanted to talk about me. I told him so, and he huffed gruffly in my ear. "I was worried all day."

"You shouldn't have been worried about me. You have enough to deal with here."

"Like I can't multitask?"

"Yeah, but I don't want you worrying about me."

He held me away from him, brow furrowed, offended almost. "You deserve someone worrying about you."

As if his simple statement didn't take my breath away, his kiss did. With his hands bracketing my face, he kissed me like he had something to prove. And maybe he felt like he did, but that was the problem. He had nothing to prove to me. I knew he loved me. Like I loved him.

There were no conditions.

We eventually pulled apart and sat on the stoop, my right leg against his, neither of us talking for a while.

So, I started. "I'm sorry."

"You have nothing to be sorry for. None of this is your fault."

"I shouldn't have come over last night," I said, a pit in my stomach because I'd caused such turmoil in his family.

"Brooke, none of this is your fault."

I swallowed down the guilt lodged in my throat. "Feels like it, though."

He rubbed the heels of his palms against his eyes, and I instinctually cupped the back of his head, scratching his scalp and the column of his neck. He groaned and leaned toward me. "Sebastian shouldn't have yelled at you like that."

"He's upset."

"That's not an excuse."

"He's ten. He saw me in bed with his dad. Of course he wants to yell, and since he's not going to yell at you, he's going to yell at me."

Jude folded his arms over his bent knees, resting his forehead on them, and I let my fingers drift to his back, scratching up and down his spine as defeat echoed in his words. "I'm the one who screwed up here. I'm the parent. It was my responsibility to be upfront with Seb about my relationship with you from the very start. Instead, I tried to control the situation, thinking I could protect him from any fallout. I didn't give him nearly enough credit. I messed up."

I twisted my hands in my lap. He didn't want me beating myself up. Well, I didn't want him beating himself up either. "You did what you thought was best."

He grunted and shook his head like he didn't want to hear it. Didn't want to be comforted. "We had a talk at the baseball fields after I found him. I thought… I didn't think he'd take it out on you."

Hearing the shame saturating his words was like a hundred tiny lashes against my heart. My throat tightened, and tears pricked my eyes.

"I hate to say it, but I think he's going to keep taking it out on me. He probably thinks I'm trying to replace his mom."

"I know, but..." His shoulders drooped even farther.

That was the issue right there. Sebastian had some things to work through, and until he did—until they all did—he wouldn't be able to accept me in his life, and I refused to be the source of more trouble. I wouldn't let myself be put in the middle. Because Seb would continue to take his anger out on me, Jude would defend me, the cycle would repeat, and poor Amelia would be dragged down by having to live through that.

"Jude, I don't—"

"No." He stopped me with two fingers to my lips. "Please don't say what I think you're about to say."

"You know it's the right thing to do," I murmured behind the pads of his fingers. I held on to his wrist to kiss then held his hand between both of mine. "We can't be together right now. Not until everything is worked out with you and the kids." He shook his head, but I went on anyway. "I don't want to be the evil stepmother, so please don't make me that."

"I won't."

"You will. You'll put me in that position. He's not ready."

"But I am. And I've always put the kids first every time." Jude gripped my shoulders hard as if trying to keep me from running. I wasn't running. I was staying...at a distance.

"I know." I smiled through the stinging in my nose and eyes. "That's what I love about you. You're willing to do the hard things."

He closed his eyes and rested his forehead against mine. "I don't want to do the hard things anymore. I've done them for so long. I don't want to do them anymore. I want easy, and that's what being with you is."

"I know." I lifted my head and met his gaze, both of us glassy-eyed. "But I never want to be the issue between you and the kids. They're your first priority. And mine," I said with a laugh about that realization. "I love them and love you enough to know you need some time and space to focus on them. We can't throw this at them and expect everything to be fine."

His lips formed a tight line as he nodded eventually, his voice barely a rumbled whisper when he said, "I know." He lowered his chin to his chest. "What do we do now?"

"We give them some time."

"I've already left a message for the family counselor we used to see."

"That's good." I dragged my hand over his hair and beard. "So, you start there and keep me updated and…"

I felt the hot splash of a tear on the back of my hand, realizing it came from Jude. I kissed his temple, his cheek, his mouth. "I always do the right thing," he rasped. "I do everything I'm supposed to, and this one time, I want to be selfish… It feels like the universe doesn't want me to be happy. It's not fair."

A spike drove through my heart because, no, it wasn't fair. It wasn't fair that Mira had died. Or that he was a single dad. Or that his kids were young and didn't understand love yet. At least not enough to know what their father would give up for them.

But this was the right thing to do, and Jude always did the right thing.

"I love you," I told him.

"I know," he said and kissed me.

"I'm not going anywhere. And we'll talk every day. We'll see each other at the market."

He traced my mouth with his thumb. "School starts soon and—"

I inhaled sharply when the idea hit me. "Did Seb make the team?"

Jude shook his head.

"Shit."

"I'm sure that's part of the reason he yelled at you. He didn't mean it."

"No. I know. I know. And it's more of a reason for me to back off. He needs you more than I do right now."

He wrapped a lock of my hair around his index finger. "I need you, though."

I couldn't answer him. Because I needed him too. Instead of telling him that, I held on to his wrist to kiss his palm then stood, tugging him up with me. He escorted me to my car with his hand on my back and opened the door for me.

"I love you," he told me.

"I know."

I stuck out my hand, smiling. "Friends?"

He smiled, smacking his palm against mine. "BFFs forever."

I laughed despite the pain beneath my ribs. "The last F stands for forever."

He shrugged. "Double forever. Infinity."

"Double forever. Infinity," I agreed.

TWENTY-SEVEN
JUDE

'd been a kid when I'd met Mira. We fell in love as teenagers and learned about life together, grew up side by side into the adults we eventually became.

But what Brooke and I had was different—a friendship forged from the broken shards left in the wake of death and sickness. Funny that, in marriage, people promised to be together in sickness and in health, but it was the people who never promised me anything who showed up for me after that. Who picked me up when I needed it. Brooke was one of those people.

I hoped I was one of those people for her too.

We both had pasts. We had dents and flaws from lives that had, at times, been well-lived and, at others, brutally unfair. But we'd survived all that life had thrown at us, and didn't we deserve to be happy in the end?

Didn't we deserve to enjoy our peace?

Sitting next to Brooke as she'd suggested we take some time to slow down had felt like I'd been forced to swallow cough medicine. Or eat that godforsaken kale she told me was "actually really good." Sure, it was good for me, would make me better, but that didn't mean I wanted it. Didn't mean I liked it.

I respected and admired her protective instincts that drove her to make a sacrifice for Sebastian's and Amelia's well-being—hell, I loved it. Because that was what made Brooke so perfect for me. She understood what it meant to be a parent.

But on the other hand…fuck that.

I'd been living a brittle existence for years, surviving but not thriving. Brooke had sprinkled some Miracle-Gro on me, and I flourished under her sunshine. And now, she wanted to go and do the noble thing? She wanted to force me to cut us off at the roots?

No.

No.

No.

And yet…

"Daddy!"

I spun around from where I stood in the road, the brake lights of Brooke's truck long gone, and caught Amelia when she ran to me. "It's getting close to bedtime. You ready for a bath?"

"No. I want to take a shower."

"Yeah?" I closed and locked the front door then put her down. "You took a shower last night and basically wasted all the hot water."

"I-I won't waste water." She folded her hands together and stuck out her bottom lip. "I swear."

"You swear?" I laid a smacking kiss on her cheek. "You swear?"

She squealed. "I swear!"

"Okay. Shower it is." While she skipped into her bedroom to dig through her pajama drawer for the ones she wanted, I turned on the shower for the water to warm up then sat on the toilet while she showered because she still needed help. I needed to make sure she washed everything, including her "pagina."

"Daddy! Are you out there?"

"Yes," I droned, typing out a text to the boys to fill them in on what had happened today.

"Can you open the-the shampoo for me?"

"Yeah." I flicked the cap open for her and squirted some into her palm, waiting until she washed that out since she'd need help with the conditioner too. It took eight more minutes and a dozen reminders on my part, but she finished up, leaving enough hot water for her brother. I wrapped her up in her towel and pointed her to her bedroom, so I could talk to Seb.

"Hey."

He ignored me, his focus on the Switch in his hands.

"Sebastian. Put it away. Time to get ready for bed."

He set it down and rolled off his mattress, still not speaking to me.

"How long are you going to give me the silent treatment?"

"How long are you going to let her sleep in your bed?" he shot back, and I briefly wondered if some of his anger sprouted from the idea that he wouldn't be able to sleep in my bed anymore if Brooke was in it.

"Actually," I started, setting my elbow on the top of his dresser when he closed the drawer, "she said it would be better if we didn't see each other right now." I didn't want to make him feel bad, but I also kind of did.

How shitty of a parent did that make me?

That I wanted to force him to acknowledge what I had given up and continued to give up for him?

He froze, only for a moment, probably expecting a fight. He wanted an outlet for his pain. I understood that.

Then he turned his chin up to me. "Good."

"Good? You're happy that Brooke and I aren't going to be together?"

"Yeah. You married Mom. And you told me—"

"I told you nothing would change the love you had for her. Because Brooke doesn't want to take the place of your mom. But she loves you too. She wants to be there for you, be your friend. And I don't know why, all of a sudden, you supposedly hate her. You always liked Brooke."

He grumbled something I didn't quite catch, but I received the message anyway. He hated her now that I wanted to be with her.

I didn't have the energy to keep this conversation up. Especially when he wouldn't listen. He wanted to be mad, so I'd let him. "I love you, Sebastian, and you won't understand until you're older, but it's possible to love lots of people in lots of different ways. No one is replacing your mother."

I left it at that and trudged out of his room, fatigue weighing each of my limbs down. I flopped onto Lulu's bed, rearranging the hundreds of stuffies to get comfortable while she took three times longer than it would take a sloth to get dressed. I combed her hair and reminded her to brush her teeth, which she could do completely independently. So I stayed in her room while she went to the bathroom. I heard Sebastian in the shower and Amelia's squeaky voice say, "Brother, listen to me. I'm-I'm good at math. One hundred plus one hundred is two hundred and, and, and… If you make it to a million, there's no more numbers."

"Yes, there are," he told her. "Numbers go to infinity."

"Infifty?"

"Infinity!"

"Oooh, infinity. Yeah. What's that?"

"It goes on forever."

Little did he know, he'd just defined what Brooke and I had promised to each other tonight. Best friends for infinity.

Next morning…

BROOKE
How did last night go?

Seb ended up in my bed in the middle of the night.

I'm pretty sure he feels bad but doesn't know what to say.

Me either.

BROOKE
You'll get there.

————

Friday…

The only time the family therapist could fit us in is for Saturdays. I won't be at the market for the next few weeks.

BROOKE
I guess I'll have to give all the squash I was saving for you to someone else.

Damn. What a shame.

BROOKE
I'm sure you're devastated.

Very.

————

Saturday…

BROOKE

Saw your parents today at the market. They couldn't figure out your POS system.

BROOKE

I gave them your squash.

BROOKE

I love them. They're so sweet.

BROOKE

Hope therapy went okay.

Sorry, I'm just seeing this now. I took the kids to a movie after our appointment.

I actually don't know how it went. We started chatting with the three of us, and then she asked to talk to the kids alone. Nobody cried. Lulu said she played with the train set.

BROOKE

That's good, I guess...?

Yeah. I guess.

I feel like I'm grasping at straws here.

And I'm looking at the report from this morning now. I don't know what my parents did, but they didn't put in any of the sales.

BROOKE

I'm pretty sure at one point, they started taking cash and giving out freebies with every sale.

Great.

———

Days later…

This is stupid.

I'm going to drop the kids off with my parents and come over.

I want to see you.

BROOKE

I'm not even home.

BROOKE

I'm in Philly helping Sabrina and Everett move in to their house.

BROOKE

She texted me this morning that they needed help.

BROOKE

But even if I were home, what would you tell Seb?

That I miss you. That's what I would tell him.

BROOKE

I know, babe. I miss you too.

———

A week later...

BROOKE

Don't panic. I'm fine.

No one in the history of ever has NOT panicked when someone says not to panic.

BROOKE

I'm in the hospital.

I'm panicked. What happened?

BROOKE

A little mishap on the farm. Gunner's with me. I'm getting checked out to make sure my ankle isn't broken.

I'm coming. I need to drop the kids off, and then I'll be there.

BROOKE

No. It's fine. You don't need to come.

Don't tell me that.

I called Brooke, and she picked up immediately. "Don't tell me you're in the hospital and then not to come."

"I'm fine, really."

"And I really don't give a shit."

"Oooh, Daddy, you said—"

I covered Amelia's mouth with my palm so she couldn't repeat the curse, and Brooke's breathy laugh in my ear hit me at the same time a kid hit the ball out toward third base.

"Where are you?" Brooke asked, and I placed my elbows on my knees, holding my cell phone closer to my mouth as if that would help block out the sound.

As if I didn't already know what she would say when I told her, "Sebastian's baseball game. It's his last one for the summer."

"You definitely can't come."

"Br—"

"No. I'm fine. Really. Gunner's here with me, and as soon as I talk to the doctor, I'll text you."

"I love you."

"I know. I love you too."

———

Hours later...

BROOKE

Only a sprain. I have to stay off it as much as I can for two weeks, and I got a nice-looking little bootie to wear.

Thank god it's not broken.

BROOKE

No, but I'm not happy about not being able to be on the farm right in the middle of a big harvest.

I could help.

BROOKE

Please don't offer something you can't follow through on.

I called her once again. This time at home in my bedroom so I was alone with the quiet and I could hear the waver in her voice when she picked up, saying, "I know this is hard. But, please… You'll make it harder for me. You'll come over and take care of me, and I won't want you to go. I'll say something and you'll give in, and we'll be back where we started. So, please, don't come over."

I took my frustration out on my pillows, punching and folding them behind my head. "Then at least talk to me."

She sniffled, and my heart ached so much I had to turn on my side to relieve some of the pressure. "Who did this to you? Tell me what vegetable patch I need to take out."

She laughed so sweetly my eyes burned with a need to see her for myself. Make sure she was okay. "It was the sweet potatoes. Tripped over a box and twisted my ankle in a ditch."

"Send me a picture. I need to see what your ankle looks like."

The photo came through a few seconds later, her ankle purple and angry.

"I'm gonna kill every last one of those sweet potatoes."

"My hero."

Two weeks later...

How's the ankle feeling?

BROOKE

Good. I'm actually going to go out on the farm today.

BROOKE

I hope the kids have a good first day of school. Take pictures so I can see Amelia getting on the bus.

I will.

How about I come over? I can help you. Since the kids are gone all day.

BROOKE

Please don't. I have a lot of stuff I need to get done today.

BROOKE

And please don't call me right now. I won't have the energy to refuse you. And I don't want you unless I can have you.

BROOKE

I love you.

I know. I love you too.

TWENTY-EIGHT
JUDE

t had been one month. One miserable month since I'd seen Brooke in person, and I finally had a night out by myself to head to Walt's.

When Nate spotted me from behind the bar, he tapped Tabitha on the shoulder, said something to her, then hopped around to the other side, clapping my hand to pull me into a hug. Tabitha slid two pints our way, and I murmured my thanks.

She offered me a jut of her chin in return then pivoted away from me to fill two more pints.

I lifted the beer to my lips. "She doesn't talk much, huh?"

"Tab?" He slung a lazy arm over the back of his chair, eyeing her. "Takes her a bit to warm up."

She placed the other two beers on the bar top, obviously for Dylan and Liam, who hadn't arrived yet. Then she slanted her dark eyes to Nate, who grinned at her. "Thanks, tabby cat."

She didn't return the smile. "Be a good little boy and take your party over there. Leave these seats for the paying customers."

Nate clucked his tongue at her but picked up his pint and

Liam's Guinness, so I took my lager and Dylan's Sam Adams, and we stood in the corner around a high-top like the apparent good little boys we were.

A minute later, Liam ambled in, appearing like he was coming right from work at the university and accepted his beer from Nate with a pat on the back. Then he proceeded to down about half of it.

"You all right?" I asked, and he thumped the pint glass down on the table with a nod.

"I got stuck teaching a one-hundred-level intro to poli-sci class, and they're driving me nuts. They email me like they're texting their friend. One of them sends his assignments in as screenshots. Another doesn't format her papers correctly."

"Formatting her papers incorrectly, oh no," Nate mocked.

Liam swiped his hand over his hair, looking exhausted. "Plus, we're trying to get Finn tested for ADHD, and that's a whole thing." He blew out a breath. "Everyone's like, he'll grow out of it, he'll grow out of it. You just have to be stricter with him. He's not growing out of it, and we don't have to be stricter with him."

"Be stricter with who?" Dylan asked, appearing at the table with a backward baseball hat and red lipstick on his jaw.

I tapped my chin, subtly letting him know about the makeup, but Nate noticed first.

"Don't tell me that's my sister's lipstick on your face."

Dylan shrugged. "Okay. I won't."

"So what's up with Finn?" I asked, trying to get back on track.

Dylan scrubbed at the red lipstick with his palm while Liam explained, "The wait list for pediatric psychologists is a mile long."

It had been hard enough for me to find a therapist for my kids when Mira'd died; I suspected child psychologists were as busy, if not more. "I know how that is. I'm sorry, man."

Liam pushed up the sleeves of his sweater and rolled his

shoulders as if shaking off the day. "Eh, it'll work out eventually. What about you?"

I wagged my head side to side. "Okay."

My three friends stared at me.

"Amelia loves kindergarten."

They waited.

"Sebastian's struggling in his math class a little bit."

And waited.

I reclined against the wall, attention on one of the televisions. Some car commercial.

"What about you and Brooke?" Nate asked.

I took a sip of my beer, watching a couple kiss on screen, all happy and smiles. "We're fine."

"Yeah? Why do you look like you haven't slept in weeks?"

I wiped my fingers over my eyes. "Because I haven't."

"What? You two break up already?" Dylan asked into his pint.

I heaved a sigh. "Never even got a chance to get started."

"Seb's still not coming around?"

I lifted a heavy shoulder. "He's still got a lot to work through. Delayed grief." I thought about the days he'd spent in silence with me over the last few weeks, especially after his counseling sessions. "Amelia, she's…" I laughed, despite the nights I'd spent angry at my son, at myself, at the past, at Brooke, at having something amazing barely out of reach. "All she knows is her brother's been sad, and I've been—" I bent my fingers in air quotes "—throwing a lot of tantrums."

Nate slapped the table in amusement. "Throwing tantrums?"

"I've been…impatient lately."

Dylan smirked. "I'd be impatient too if my kid was cockblocking me."

I shot him a glare. "You know it's not that."

"So what is it, then?"

"It's everything." I gestured vaguely with my beer. "I'm

trying my best to keep it together and always do the right thing, but between Seb's attitude and missing Brooke, it feels like I'm gonna lose it at any second."

"So tell Brooke," Liam suggested. "She's—"

"I've told her I wanted to see her, but she said she doesn't want to see me until she really has me. She said it would be too hard, and… I don't know." I rubbed my beard. "Sometimes I think she's right, and sometimes I think I should club her over the head and bring her home to my cave."

Nate made a noise of agreement. "Not the worst idea I've ever heard."

"It is if it's only going to piss Sebastian off and make Brooke uncomfortable." I set my beer down then looked all my friends in the eye. "I never thought I'd get a second shot at having a woman in my life again, and I don't want to mess it up. I can't lose her." I sliced my hand through the air. "If there's any chance that my kids aren't ready for me to bring her home, then I'm not gonna do it, because Brooke is going to be in my life forever. I need everybody on the same page."

Dylan raised his glass as Liam slapped my back, muttering a quiet, "Good for you."

Nate smiled. "I love when you go all Papa Bear."

"'Cause you love that Dad energy."

He flicked his hand in front of his face as if something smelled bad. "You're gonna curse me talking like that."

Liam folded his arms over his chest. "When are you settling down? Haven't heard anything from you lately."

"Not much to tell." Nate opened his arms. "Ruling my kingdom."

"More like the court jester," Dylan shot, and Nate shoved his shoulder.

I searched my brain for the last time he'd mentioned anything about a girl. "Weren't you hanging out with a Russian chick?"

"Czech, and she had to go back home."

Dylan snapped his fingers. "You hooked up with that girl on your birthday."

He brushed that off. "One-night stand. Barely remember her."

With a glance to the dark-haired bartender, I told Nate, "I feel like you're looking in all the wrong places."

"I'm not looking at all," he said and flipped his cell phone out of his pocket, looking at Liam. "Where's your brother working now?"

"Which one?"

"Whichever one is the chef."

"Collin. Who the hell knows with that guy? You two would get along great."

Nate wagged his cell. "You think he'd mind me contacting him about possibly working together?"

Liam shrugged and pulled out his cell phone, texting Nate his brother's contact. "What are you planning?"

Nate explained his possible plans for a wine bar and bistro, but my palm itched with the desire to take out my cell phone to call Brooke. I loved hanging out with my buddies, but I loved hearing my girl's voice even more.

As soon as I closed my car door at the end of the night, I called her, but she didn't answer. Probably already asleep. I left her a voice mail. "I'm just calling to say goodnight and I love you. I hate not being able to see you, but you giving me this time to get everything sorted with the kids proves that you were meant for me. You're it for me, Brooke Fraser, and when the time is right, I'd like to make it permanent. So, thank you for allowing me to figure it out now, so that we can be happy later. We will be happy later. I promise you that."

TWENTY-NINE
BROOKE

The early morning air was crisp and cool as I set up my produce stand at the farmers market. I tried to keep my movements brisk and efficient to stay warm in the chill air. As much as I loved autumn in Pennsylvania, those first few weeks could be brutal with the change in temperature.

I had just finished arranging the last basket of zucchini when a familiar voice made me freeze.

"Daddy, can I get a cupcake?"

My heart stuttered in my chest. I looked up to see Jude approaching my stand, flanked by Sebastian and Amelia. My gaze drank in the sight of him hungrily after so many weeks apart. He appeared...not good, if I was being honest. Tired and stressed, with his brow furrowed and shoulders slumped.

But then his eyes met mine, and I felt that familiar jolt low in my belly. The same longing and love I'd felt for him since the beginning. Clearly, the separation had been affecting him as deeply as it had me.

Sure, we'd talked every day, if not multiple times a day through texts and phone calls, but this last month had been the longest Jude and I had gone without seeing each other in…well, since Mira had been alive. We'd been mere friends then, acquaintances who chatted when we saw each other. Since then, we'd grown, become woven so deeply into the fabric of each other's lives there was no way we could unravel it.

I didn't want to unravel it.

I knew he didn't either.

Especially after that voice mail he left me last night.

I forced myself to turn away from the sight of Jude and his kids talking to someone two tables down before I did something reckless, like vault over my veggies to throw myself at him. Instead, I busied myself with getting ready. People were already strolling through the tents, and if it weren't for Nicole, I'd be way late.

I'd been feeling congested the last few days, so I'd taken some nighttime cold medicine last night and was out like a light. Which meant I'd missed Jude's call and my alarm this morning.

Although the feel of a hand on my back now was its own wake-up call. A straight shot of adrenaline. I recognized the warmth and feel of Jude before I even turned around.

He stood in front of me, his hand extended with a cup of coffee and a cupcake. "I got your usual order from Diane, plus a cupcake from that new stand."

I accepted them reflexively. "I didn't know you'd be here today."

He sipped his own coffee. "There're only a few more weeks left," he said, referring to how the farmers market closed for the winter. "And I wanted to make sure my parents knew what they were doing, so we stopped here for breakfast before we go to our appointment."

"Brooke!" Amelia waved at me, icing all over her mouth and fingers.

I bent to her. "Hey, girlfriend. You sure demolished your cupcake fast."

"You gonna eat yours?"

"Why? You think I'm going to give you mine?"

She batted her eyelashes at me.

"You're cute, but not that cute."

I popped the plastic lid and lifted the cupcake to peel the wrapper. After taking a bite, I held it out for Amelia to do the same. She bit into it like a lion attacking a gazelle, and I snorted a laugh. "You're an animal."

Trying and failing to wipe her mouth clean with my fingers, I searched for something to help, and Jude held out a napkin. I took it with a quiet thanks and wiped Amelia down before standing up straight to finish the rest of the treat. Holding it out to Jude, I offered him a bite, which he declined.

His focus pinned on my mouth as I finished the rest, licking my lips, and he shook his head as if coming to. He blinked down to Amelia. "Didn't you say you had something for Brooke? What did you do with it?"

She held up one of her unicorns—Purse, I believed—but didn't have whatever the thing was she'd apparently brought for me. "I-I-I think I forgot it at your table." She stuck her finger up at me. "Be right back."

"Amelia!" Jude took off after his sprinting daughter, leaving me with only Sebastian.

He pointedly ignored me, his foot scuffing the macadam, so I tried an easy greeting. "How's it going, Seb? Do you like fifth grade so far?"

He nodded, answering with a mumbled, "It's good."

"Good. I'm glad." After a few moments, I tried again. "You didn't want a cupcake?"

He shook his head.

"Why not?"

He combed his hand through his hair the same way Jude did and chanced a peek at me. When I offered a small smile, he told me, "Dad said I could have a cupcake now, or he'd take me out later, just me and him, for something."

"Oh? That's great. Where are you going to go?"

"Probably for ice cream."

"That'll be nice. I'm glad you are having some one-on-one time with your dad. I think you two need it."

He studied me under dark, thick lashes, frowning. I started to turn away since, obviously, today was not the day to bury the hatchet, when he said, "I'm sorry."

I flicked my gaze up to find Jude and Amelia on their way back to me, but when he caught my pointed look, he stopped to check out Sarah Ann and Tori's soaps, easily redirecting Amelia.

I gestured for Sebastian to follow me behind my table, out of the way of people, and we sat on the two folding chairs while Nicole took care of any customers. Facing each other now, Seb couldn't avoid me. I leaned forward, lightly tapping his knee. "I'm sorry too."

His throat bobbed on a swallow, his gaze down at where he picked at his thumbnail. "What are you sorry for?"

"I'm sorry if I made you feel uncomfortable in your own home. That is the last thing I want to do, and you're smart, so I won't pretend like you don't know what it means that I was in bed with your dad."

He folded his arms, nodding a few times, and when he didn't respond, I figured I could keep going.

"I want you to know that I love your dad. I've loved him like a friend for a very long time, and I recently realized that I love him as more than a friend. I also want you to know that I understand you and your sister are a package deal with him. I would never ever want to hurt you, not only because you're part of the package deal, but also because I really like you. I think you're a pretty cool kid."

He finally lifted his head, reluctantly meeting my gaze. I considered that a win.

"I like that you're a great big brother, protective and kind. I also think you're brave for going after what you want and trying out for the baseball team." When he opened his mouth to speak, probably to argue that point, I stopped him with my hand on his shoulder. "It takes a lot of courage to put yourself out there. A lot of people won't try things because they're afraid to fail, but you tried. I know you were really upset you didn't make it, and I was upset for you too. I wish you would have made the team, but I also know you're going to try again next year, and I'm really proud of you."

He seemed amazed that I knew all of that.

I smiled. "Your dad told me you're still practicing in the backyard, and that Uncle Dylan is coming over to help sometimes."

He nodded. "Yeah. I have to work on my mechanics."

I didn't know what that meant, but I was happy he was even talking to me. "Well, good for you for doing that."

He sat up from his slouched position and rubbed his hand over his jaw, *exactly* like his dad. I imagined Sebastian twenty years from now, rubbing his hand over his bearded jaw. "Did, uh, did my dad tell you that he's making me talk to a therapist?"

"He told me you all are."

"Yeah, but it's mainly me."

"That's okay, though. Lots of people go to therapy. I did. It helped me a lot."

"I started going after my mom died," he admitted, and he might as well have reached into my chest to rip out my heart. No ten-year-old should ever have to utter those words, though I stayed quiet, waiting to see where this conversation was headed.

"But then I stopped for a while. I guess Dad didn't think I needed it anymore, and I didn't."

I filled in the blank. He didn't need it until he saw me in bed with his dad.

Relatable.

What kind of therapy would I need if I found my parents in bed? I once saw my dad squeeze my mom's boob when I was little and nearly threw up.

"Do you think it's helping?" I asked and held my breath until he answered.

"I guess."

"Good. That's good. That's really good."

A few moments passed before Sebastian cleared his throat, his gaze flitting up and down between mine and where he scratched a stain on his jeans. "Sorry for yelling at you that day."

"I appreciate that, but I know you were upset, and sometimes when people are upset, they react without thinking."

"You've always been really nice to me and Lulu, and…I'm sorry."

"Thank you."

When he looked up at me for more than half a second, I opened my arms. "Could I have a hug?"

He thought about it, chewing on his lip, and then nodded. I reached over, folding him in my arms and, after a few seconds, felt his hands wrap around my back. "I'm sorry, Sebastian. If I ever do anything to hurt your feelings, I hope we can talk like this. Or even if you want to talk about anything else going on in your life. I'm here for you. I hope you know that."

He nodded, and I swore I heard a tiny sniffle. I hugged him tighter. "I love you."

He didn't respond, but I didn't mind. Not when I felt his hands lock in place at my back and his face tuck into my shoulder.

I smiled against his temple. "When you're ready—when you *and* your sister are ready—I would really like to play Go Fish with you. All of us, me, you, Amelia, and your dad."

He backed away from me, his solemn eyes taking in me

and my offer. He understood, because like I said, he was a smart kid. He smiled then, and I knew we'd be okay. All of us would be okay.

"Here you go!" Amelia skipped around the table, waving a piece of construction paper at me, grinning widely enough to show off how her front tooth was coming in.

I crouched down to meet her and take the paper from her hand. "What's this?"

"I made it at school."

I made sure to keep the smile on my face as I admired the…face? made out of macaroni.

"We-we're doing shapes and fractions!"

"Lu, take the volume down," Jude said, tugging on one of her curls.

I held the paper out in front of me so everyone could see the Picasso. "And you made this for me?"

She hopped on her toes, all proud and innocent, and god, I loved her too. I towed her into me with one arm. "I love it so much. I'm going to hang it up at home. Thank you."

Pleased with herself, she hugged me back, wrapping her arms around my neck. I picked up the little pixie and kissed her cheek. "Love you, girlfriend."

"Love you too!" she squealed in my ear.

Even though she might have burst my eardrum, I still heard Jude's low rumble of a laugh. He stared at me, wordlessly speaking.

I love you, he told me.

I raised my brow at him. *I know.*

"Come on, little one. We gotta get going." Jude took Amelia from me and motioned Sebastian over to him.

I waved to them. "I'll see you guys later."

"Bye, Brooke!" Amelia shouted while Seb lifted his hand.

Jude grinned at me, the sparkle back in his eyes, and I couldn't have been happier to see it.

It was worth the wait.

We were worth the wait.

THIRTY
JUDE

September sailed into October with cold winds, and I stared outside the window at the small whirlwind of fallen browned leaves in the grass. It was a Sunday, and while I'd let the kids run themselves ragged at the park this afternoon, they were still all hyped up. Most likely because they didn't have school tomorrow.

It had been two weeks since I'd seen Brooke at the farmers market. Two weeks since my mother had whispered about how much she thought Brooke was great for me. Two weeks since my father had told me how proud he was of me. Two weeks since I'd witnessed Sebastian let Brooke hug him like it was the most natural thing in the world. Two weeks of Amelia asking if I thought Brooke really hung up her ugly macaroni face.

I didn't know that kindergarteners learned fractions, but I guessed if one-half a face was made out of red macaroni and the other half yellow, I supposed a five-year-old could understand that was ½. Either way, the thing was a nightmare. But yeah, "I'm sure she hung it up."

I knew by now my kids had sensed a shift in my demeanor since that fateful morning. I had needed to touch her, hear her laugh, see her smile in real life to reenergize myself. We had spent these weeks apart so I could focus on my kids, to make sure they were mentally and emotionally healthy, so that when I did take the next steps with Brooke, we would all be able to be happy together.

But it had been killing me. And the kids knew that. They'd been on the receiving end of my occasional outbursts and short fuse. I wasn't like I'd hidden why we were doing this. At least, not after the farmers market.

Even Amelia asked why I hadn't hugged Brooke goodbye.

Seb had stayed silent about his interaction with her, and I hadn't pushed him when we'd gone for ice cream, but I made sure to bring it up in our counseling session, talking about what the future might look like for all of us. The kids drew pictures of what they wanted for themselves now and when they grew up.

Our therapist, a lovely young woman by the name of Dr. Heidi, explained to the kids that I also had certain things I wanted: a house, a family, to be married. And even though I wanted those things, it didn't mean what they wanted would change, now or when they grew up.

It had been a big breakthrough for everyone.

So it shouldn't have surprised me when Sebastian shuffled up next to me by the window. "Hey, Dad?"

"Yeah, buddy?" I glanced over my shoulder at him, stopping short at the serious expression on his face.

"Can I ask you something?"

"Of course." I turned away from the window and directed him to sit at the kitchen table. I'd finished loading the dishwasher from our early dinner when the leaves had caught my eye. But now, I gave my son my full attention. "What's up?"

He chewed on his lip for a few seconds, an inherited nervous tic from Mira. "Are you, like...sad? Because you haven't seen Brooke in a while?"

The question tugged hard at my heart. I exhaled wearily,

running a hand through my hair. "Yeah, I am. I was really sad before, but since we saw her the other day, I feel a little better."

"Are you mad at me for it?"

"No, buddy, no." I held his shoulders. "I'm not mad *at* you. You know how sometimes you feel like nothing's quite going your way, and you don't know who to be mad at? Like, you have a lot of bad luck?"

Seb nodded.

"That's how I feel. I've had a lot of bad luck in my life, and sometimes it's easy to ignore and sometimes it's not. It hasn't been easy lately."

His nose twitched as he contemplated that. Always so thoughtful, my kid. "You really miss her, though?" he asked, nose twitching again, and I assumed this time it was more about emotion and less about making connections in his brain. "You miss her more than you miss Mom?"

I released my grip on him. It wasn't a tough question to answer, but it was tough to explain. "I miss her differently than I miss Mom."

"Brooke told me she loves you."

"Did she?" I tried to keep the shock out of my voice. "When you talked to her?"

He nodded. "She said…"

I noticed his cheeks bloomed red as he blinked a lot. Yep, he was going to cry. I grabbed a tissue from the box on the counter and put it on the table. Because Sebastian hated when people noticed him crying. So, I pretended he wasn't.

"She said she was proud of me."

I scooted my chair closer to his, allowing me to rub his back. "Are you upset about that?"

He shook his head. "I liked it."

"Okay, well, that's good. That—"

"I feel like I shouldn't like it."

It took me a minute, but I got it. I understood.

"I get it. You're feeling guilty?" I guessed, and when he answered with a tip of his chin, I went on. "I loved your mother for a long time, a really long time, and it took me a while to realize I can still love her and have fun doing things I want to do. I can still love her and love other people. Even though Mommy's not here anymore, you still like to hang out with me, right?"

He picked up the tissue to blow his nose and nodded.

"And I'm pretty sure you still love me, right?"

He laughed, nodding once more.

"You can love other people and still love Mommy. You can live your life even though she's not here, and you know what?" I waited until Sebastian met my gaze to continue. "Mommy would want you to. She wouldn't want you to always be sad about her and always hold back from doing what you love to do. I think if your mom could talk to you right now, she'd tell you that she's happy you talked to Brooke, and she'd tell you she's proud of you. And if she can't be here to tell you that herself, I'm sure she would want other people to tell you that, including Brooke."

I ran my hand over the top of Sebastian's head a few times. "It's okay to like hearing it. It's okay to want hugs from Brooke. It's okay to like hanging out with her. You're not betraying Mommy. You're not hurting her feelings. I know that because I felt that way for a long time too, and I had to learn that just because I love someone else doesn't mean I love her less. Does that make sense?"

"Yeah. Makes sense." He nibbled on his lower lip. "I like Brooke."

I smiled, cuffing him lightly on the side of the head. "Me too."

"Do you love her?"

"Yeah, buddy, I do. I love Brooke. I love her like you love Mackenzie Dooling."

He pushed my hand away. "I do not!"

I sat back in my chair, satisfied we'd made it over that hump relatively painlessly. "If you say so."

He scratched at a divot in the table with his index finger. "I was thinking that maybe we should go see her."

"You want to go see Mackenzie?" When he shot me a glare, I held my hands up in innocence. "You want to see Brooke?"

"She told me she wants to play Go Fish with all of us, me, you, Lulu, and her."

I crossed my arms, assessing him. He seemed clear-eyed and, even more, clearheaded. "You ready for that?"

He nodded, his knee bouncing. "Yeah. I think…" He shrugged. "I think it could be fun. I mean, Go Fish is stupid, but whatever. Amelia likes it."

"Amelia does like it," I said and swiped my palm over my mouth and beard. "And you'd be okay doing this more than once? Us hanging out all together?"

He shrugged. "Yeah, or, like, if you wanted to go out on a date or whatever."

"Oh." I waved my hand with a flourish, bowing my head. "Thank you for the permission. I'll remember this when you want to, like, go out on a date or whatever."

He pursed his lips, holding back a smile. I let mine loose, a weight lifted off my chest. "I love you."

"I love you too," he said and stood up from his hair. I didn't go for the hug because he was a cool fifth grader now. I went for the high five instead.

"What do you say we go pay her a visit tonight?"

"Yeah. That'd be cool."

I had my phone in hand immediately. "Tell your sister to put her shoes on."

He pivoted away, yelling, "Amelia! Put your shoes on!"

I texted Brooke.

Where are you?

BROOKE

The farm.

We're coming over, and we're bringing Go Fish.

Half an hour later, I parked in my usual spot, the sun already set but the lights of the tiny house on. Brooke was waiting at the door, holding it open for us. Amelia bounced up, flapping the deck. "Hi! Hi! Hi! We're here to play Go Fish. You want to play with us?"

"Yes," she answered, laughing. The sweetest sound in the whole goddamn world.

Next, Sebastian stepped up with the pan of brownies I'd made earlier this morning. He offered her his cool guy head nod. Brooke gave him one back with a wink.

And then it was finally my turn.

"Honeybee." I hooked my arm around her waist and buried my face in her hair. She'd worn it down today, and she smelled of lavender and honey. My favorite. I inhaled deeply, releasing a contented sigh.

I felt her smile against my throat. "You're here. You're all here."

"We are."

She draped her arms around my neck as she pulled back, her eyes crinkling in the corners and glassy. "For good?"

"Forever."

I pulled her to me, kissing her, for the past six weeks, for the last few months, for the years we'd been friends. She tasted sweet like sugar and salty like the tears streaming down her cheeks, caught between our lips. I tunneled my fingers into her hair, angled her head back, and found her tongue with mine.

"Ugh. Gross."

We broke apart, turning to find Sebastian and Amelia

standing in the doorway between the kitchen and her office. Him cringing, her clapping. Brooke and I laughed.

I felt high.

Higher than I'd ever been.

I had my kids and Brooke, our future laid out in front of us. Sure, it would be slow going, making sure nobody got left behind, but this was the first step.

"Come on," I said, taking that step with Brooke at my side and the kids in front of me. "Let's play some Go Fish."

We sat on the floor, which seemed much easier for Brooke. "All the yoga," she said. "You should come with me."

I rolled my eyes. Always trying to get me to be healthy.

Sebastian dealt the cards as Amelia curled into Brooke's side, and we played as many rounds as we could, joking and giggling, until my daughter yawned more than she talked.

"I think we've had enough fun for one night," I murmured, gathering her in my arms.

Brooke agreed and piled up our dishes to take to the sink while Seb packed away the cards. We all walked out to my car, where I buckled Amelia into her seat. Brooke leaned in, kissing her temple. "Sweet dreams."

"Night night, Brooookie."

Brooke smiled and brushed her palm over Amelia's curls then looked to Sebastian. "Thanks for coming over tonight. I had fun."

"Me too."

"Want to do it again?"

The shadows couldn't hide his smile as he opened the car door. "Yeah."

With the kids in the back seat, I laced my fingers with Brooke's, tugging her toward me. Or maybe I floated toward her. Couldn't quite be sure with how my feet didn't touch the ground.

"I didn't think I'd get another shot at being happy," I told her, and she smoothed her hands up my chest to curl around the nape of my neck. "You are literally a dream come true. I hope you know that."

"I hope you know you're never getting rid of me. I'm supergluing myself to you."

"Stuck like a barnacle," I suggested, earning a quiet giggle.

She nodded, happy with herself. "Never leaving."

"Like a bad rash."

That got me a huge guffaw, and I bent to kiss her throat when she tossed her head back, laughing.

"You and me, friend," she said once her amusement subsided. "Best friends for infinity."

I held up our linked hands between us. "Double infinity."

I started to kiss her again, but Sebastian stuck his head out of the window. "Can we go now?"

Brooke snorted a laugh and pushed me away, telling my kid, "Yeah, you can go now."

I dropped down behind the wheel, turned the ignition over, and rolled down the window. "I love you."

"I know." She smiled and waved. "I love you too."

"I know."

EPILOGUE
JUDE

They had decorated Imagination, a mixture of trees and lights, streamers and garlands, all celebrating Christmas, Hanukkah, and Kwanzaa. I brought along homemade peppermint bark. The kids had helped Brooke and me make it last night, although Amelia said it was too "spicy" to eat.

She'd warned all the kids off it when I offered some. Tucker was the only one to accept a piece. That kid would eat anything.

"What's everybody up to next week?" I asked, nibbling on a bit myself.

With only a few more days until Christmas, the guys and I thought we'd get one last playdate in for the year.

"We're doing Christmas in Boston again," Liam said, surveying his third of the place, where Finn and Tucker played.

I poked Dylan in the side with my elbow. "What about you?"

"Me and Gen are going over to see the kids open presents at Paige's on the twenty-fifth, but then we're getting them for the week because we're taking them to Arizona."

"Nice."

Dylan lowered his voice, resting his elbows on his knees, holding his to-go cup of coffee between his hands. "But I don't how much longer Scarlett will keep going with the whole...S-A..."

He slowed, his dyslexia obvious, but Liam and I got the idea.

"Seb stopped believing in second grade," I said, double-checking he still lounged in the corner, playing on his Switch. "Caught me wrapping the gifts."

Dylan grunted next to me. "I still haven't bought anything for Gen yet."

Liam peered around me. "Clock's ticking."

"I know, but I don't know what to get her. She keeps saying nothing, but I'm not giving her nothing." He toyed with the brim of his baseball cap. "What'd you two get your girls?"

"Day at the spa and..." Liam pulled his cell phone from his back pocket to show us something on the screen, a picture of a picture. "I found this woman on Instagram. You send her a photo, and she draws it."

The picture was an illustration of Finn in Kennedy's lap at a table, both of them grinning in front of what appeared to be a mug of hot chocolate and a can of whipped cream. Kennedy held her finger in the air with some cream on it, probably after she'd wiped it off Finn's face since he still had remnants around his mouth.

"Aw, man," I crooned. "I love that."

On the other side of me, Dylan agreed. "Maybe I should give Genevieve something like that. How much was it?"

"Couple hundred."

Dylan huffed. "Or maybe I'll frame a picture of my dick."

I shook my head in amusement. "I got Brooke this thing that clips to her e-reader and a remote, so she doesn't have to hold it. Evie likes to read, right?"

"Yeah, but mostly audio. We listen together."

"You still doing that?" Liam asked, and Dylan nodded.

"Not often, but sometimes it's better than watching TV."

"Brooke and I read books together." I stopped myself. "I mean, she sends me books to read."

Liam grinned like the Cheshire cat. "Got your own book club, huh?"

"Bet you're into some kinky shit." Dylan smirked. "It's always the ones you wouldn't think who are."

"I plead the Fifth," I said, and then, "Why don't you ask Nate what to get his sister?"

Dylan lost his shit-eating grin real quick. "That guy's on my last nerve."

"What happened now?"

"He's trying to convince me to make him my best man."

Dylan had proposed to Genevieve this past June, and they'd set the date for this coming June after her dance recital since she ran a studio and wanted to wait until the season was over.

"Why not?" I shrugged. "He was mine. Makes a good best man."

"I told him we weren't doing that. You know it's gonna be small. Tucker and Scarlett are going to stand up with us."

"That's nice," I said, and Liam nodded.

"Yeah, but now he's giving me shit about doing a bachelor party and all that." He waved his hand as if batting away a fly. "I don't want it."

I bit back a smile. That was the thing about Nate. When he wanted something, he could be really persistent. Annoyingly persistent. He'd also go to the ends of the earth for the people he loved. "Eh, he's a good guy."

Dylan grumbled his agreement.

"What are you doing for Christmas?" Liam asked me. "You never answered. Hey! Boys!"

Finn and Tucker turned to him in plastic firefighter

helmets, stopped midstride, on their way to running into each other headfirst. Tucker jumped up into the little fake fire truck, while Finn changed direction and ran headfirst into the wall. Liam heaved a sigh. "For Christ's sake." He stood up, gesturing at his son to chill. "Remember when you got staples in your head? You want more?"

Finn shook his head, tossed the helmet down then zipped over to the opposite end of the room, now in Dylan's zone.

Once Liam relaxed again, I said, "Brooke's going to come over Christmas Eve to exchange a few presents with the kids. We haven't done any more sleepovers yet, so she's not going to be there in the morning, even though I invited her. She thought it was too much, too soon for them, so I'm gonna pick her up to have dinner at my parents'."

Dylan spread his legs out wider, slouching more. "It's going good?"

"Yeah. It's going really great. If it were up to me, she'd move in tomorrow, but we know that's a while off. She's going to come to a few counseling sessions because we want to build a house on her land, and we figured between moving out of our house and selling the kids on the idea of a new one, it'll be a lot. I mean, realistically, until everything is all said and done, that wouldn't be for at least two years."

Liam helped himself to a little piece of the peppermint bark. "You thinking you're gonna get married?"

"Yeah, actually, we are. Not for a while, but we want to make sure the kids are good, and when we do, we'll involve them."

"You've got it all settled. I can't believe you were sitting here a few months ago, saying you wanted to hook up with somebody."

"I know." I couldn't believe it myself. "I guess I needed something to make me see what was right in front of me."

"A kick in the ass," Dylan said around his coffee cup. "We all need it every once in a while."

Liam aimed a meaningful brow at him. "Or a punch in the face."

"Bro, don't start."

Liam smiled and patted my back. "I'm happy for you."

"Thanks."

"Gen really likes her," Dylan told me and then pointed to the right, past Liam, at where Finn had his head stuck in the mailbox. "Hey."

Liam covered his face with his hand, his Boston accent thick. "I swear to god, I'm gonna lose it."

I bit back a laugh and got to my feet. "I'll get him. We dads gotta stick together, right?"

Dylan and Liam both raised their coffees to me in salute.

I snapped my fingers as I crossed to Finn. "That's what I'm getting you two for Christmas. Matching T-shirts."

"But none of us are single anymore," Liam noted as I pulled Finn free. He scurried away, heading for Amelia and Scarlett in the grocery store.

"Married Dads Association," Dylan tossed out, and it sounded damn good to me, although that left out one person.

"What do we do with Nate?"

Dylan shook his head. "Can't be initiated."

Liam agreed. "No kids and not about to be married."

"Sucks for him," I said. A person to love and kids running around didn't make a life, but they did certainly make it brighter. Wilder.

I sat back down, my gaze coasting around this veritable jungle of children, my two accounted for, with plans for Brooke to come over later with dinner. My life had been a roller coaster, with the lowest of lows and the highest of highs, and if I'd learned anything, it was to appreciate those highs. Ride them until the end.

Life wasn't perfect, but it was pretty damn good.

WHAT'S NEXT?

If you want more Jude and Brooke content, use the QR code to have it delivered straight to your inbox!

Loved The Dating Pact? You'll definitely want to check out The Bartender's Baby, the next novel in the Single Dads' Club series!

ACKNOWLEDGMENTS

Indie publishing is a wild ride. Thank you, reader, for coming along with me.

Thank you to Hiba for making sure my Arabic was correct and huge shout out to Echo Grayce for the amazing cover, and to Libby and Lisa for editing my brain vomit into an actual book. I'd especially like to thank my street team for helping me spread the word about my books. I'm forever grateful.

If you'd like more information about me, you can find it at https://sophieandrewsauthor.com/

ABOUT THE AUTHOR

Sophie Andrews is a contemporary romance author who writes steamy books that will leave you smiling. As a millennial, she's obsessed with boybands, late 90s rom-coms, and will always be team Pacey. When she's not writing, she's most likely trying to wrangle her children or drinking red wine. Or both at the same time.

ALSO BY SOPHIE ANDREWS

Tangled Series

Tangled Up

Tangled Want

Tangled Hearts

Tangled Beginning

Tangled Expectations

Tangled Chances

Tangled Ambition

Single Dads' Club

The Rehearsal Fling

The Nanny Tenure

The Dating Pact

The Bartender's Baby

Stand-Alones

How to Ruin a Wedding

Love at a Funeral and Other Awkward Conversations